Praise for the Giulia Driscoll

"Giulia is a sympathetic, well-drawn character who has built a full life for herself after she leaving the convent, but appealing touches of the former nun remain."

– Booklist

"Driscoll's second solo turn as a sleuth (after *Nun Too Soon*) offers a fun and fast read with a lot of appeal."

– Library Journal

"Former nun and current private eye Giulia Driscoll tackles ghosts with the same wit and wisdom she uses to tackle crooks. Great fun."

– Terrie Farley Moran,
Agatha Award-Winning Author of the Read 'Em and Eat Mysteries

"Loweecey's characters are colorful without being caricatures, and once again we're lucky that Giulia Driscoll left the convent behind. She solves the crime with a happy mix of online savvy, humor and intelligence."

– Sheila Connolly,
New York Times Bestselling Author of An Early Wake

"How can you not love an author who quotes from the movies *Airplane* and *Young Frankenstein*? Giulia's recent marriage adds a delightful dash of romance, but the real appeal of this series is her genuine likability and fiery independent streak that could never be hidden behind a veil."

– Kings River Life Magazine

"Loweecey has once again crafted a delightful, sassy, smart tale that will send the hair on the back of your head skyward and keep your eyes glued to the page. I loved it!"

– Jessie Chandler,
Author of the Award-Winning Shay O'Hanlon Caper Series

"Exciting and suspenseful."

— *Publishers Weekly*

"For those who have not yet read these incredible mysteries written by an actual ex-nun, you're missing out...Brilliant, funny, a great whodunit; this is one writer who readers should definitely make a 'habit' of."

— *Suspense Magazine*

"With tight procedural plotting, more flavoured coffee than you could shake a pastry at, and an ensemble cast who'll steal your heart away, *Nun Too Soon* is a winner. I'm delighted that Giulia—and Alice!—left the convent for a life of crime."

— Catriona McPherson,
Agatha Award-Winning Author of the Dandy Gilver Mystery Series

"You'll love Giulia Driscoll! She's one of a kind—quirky, unpredictable and appealing. With an entertaining cast of characters, a clever premise and Loweecey's unique perspective—this compelling not-quite-cozy is a winner."

— Hank Phillippi Ryan,
Mary Higgins Clark Award-Winning Author of *Truth Be Told*

"Grab your rosary beads and hang on for a fun ride with charming characters, amusing banter, and a heat-packing former nun."

— Barb Goffman,
Macavity Award-Winning Author

"Loweecy pulls off an incredible balancing act, whipping up the perfect blend of humor, suspense, and poignancy. I lost track of how many times this book made me laugh out loud, even as I rooted for Giulia and double-checked to make sure my doors were locked."

— Jess Lourey,
Lefty-Nominated Author of the Murder by Month Mysteries

The Clock Strikes Nun

**The Giulia Driscoll Mystery Series
by Alice Loweecey**

The Clock Strikes Nun

A GIULIA DRISCOLL MYSTERY

Alice Loweecey

HENERY PRESS

THE CLOCK STRIKES NUN
A Giulia Driscoll Mystery
Part of the Henery Press Mystery Collection

First Edition | May 2017

Henery Press
www.henerypress.com

Trade Paperback ISBN-13: 978-1-63511-215-3
Digital epub ISBN-13: 978-1-63511-216-0
Kindle ISBN-13: 978-1-63511-217-7
Hardcover ISBN-13: 978-1-63511-218-4

Printed in the United States of America

For Pat,
the best friend anyone could ever have.

ACKNOWLEDGMENTS

Without the help of friends and experts, this book would not be complete. Thanks to fellow Hens Annette Dashofy and Wendy Tyson for answering my panicked questions about Pennsylvania highways and vehicle rules. To Natalie J. Case for the crash course and ongoing advice on Tarot reading. To Joe Nickell, Senior Research Fellow of the Committee for Skeptical Inquiry: for sharing his years of expertise in finding the truth behind hundreds of so-called "hauntings." (Plus a secret thank you to my friends who graciously allowed me to give them cameo roles.)

One

Giulia Driscoll, formerly Sister Mary Regina Coelis, fell to her knees before her admin.

"Zane, please tell me one of your friends works in cloning."

Zane Hall, Summa Cum Laude at MIT, survivor of telemarketing hell, and Driscoll Investigations' unofficial bouncer, gaped at his boss.

"Ms. D., please get up."

"I planned to prostrate myself at your feet, but this one would object." She laid a hand on her barely there baby bump.

Zane's ghostlike complexion tried to pale even further. "You're still kneeling."

Giulia stood. "I spent ten years on my knees and have the calluses to prove it. Ninety seconds is a vacation."

Sidney Martin, DI's all-natural earth mother assistant and master unveiler of prenuptial secrets, peered over the top of her monitor.

"Why the interest in cloning? Although our farm would save a boatload on breeding fees if we could make test tube alpacas."

Giulia raised her voice over the early morning traffic noises coming through the open window. "Because it would take three of me and two of both of you to handle every potential new client in my inbox."

"Why are we the flavor of the month?" Sidney waved the words away the moment she said them. "Who cares? Now we can start Jessamine's college fund way before her first birthday. Olivier's already hinting at making her a brother or sister."

Giulia groaned. "Please don't have another baby until I'm back from maternity leave with this one."

Zane's Humphrey Bogart baritone tagged onto Giulia's plea. "I'm sorry, Ms. D, but nobody in my circle was into cloning tech."

"This might be the first time you've disappointed me." Giulia pressed one hand into the small of her back. "I don't know whether to send Stone's Throw a thank you note or see if one of our prospective clients will let us borrow their ghost."

"Their what?" Sidney said.

After a few mouse clicks, Zane turned his screen to face the room. The home page for Stone's Throw Lighthouse Bed and Breakfast proclaimed:

Have a Haunted Holiday!
Thanks to Driscoll Investigations, the Stone's Throw Ghost
has been Tamed!
Can YOU sleep in the Haunted Room?
Now Taking Reservations for Halloween Weekend
and Beyond!

Luminous ghosts in old-fashioned costumes flitted across the screen. When Zane turned up the volume, a female voice moaned in time with the flying ghosts.

Giulia sagged into Sidney's client chair. "Every single email asking us to de-haunt a house is connected to Stone's Throw."

"But you proved there wasn't a ghost in the lighthouse."

Giulia rested her forehead on her arms. "Why let facts get in the way of a good advertising scheme?"

The phone rang. "Good morning, Driscoll Investigations," Zane said and listened. "One moment, please." He put the call on hold.

"Do we perform exorcisms?"

Without lifting her head, Giulia said, "We do not."

Zane gave the answer to the caller, listened a moment, repeated the answer, and hung up.

Sidney said, "Exactly how many emails this morning?"

Now Giulia raised her head. "Eight. Two poltergeists, four Ouija Board requests, and two asking for Tarot readings."

"But we don't do any of that," Sidney said.

"Thanks to Stone's Throw, the entire state of Pennsylvania thinks we do." She raised her head. "My floor is covered with failed attempts at drawing up schedules to accommodate our regular caseload plus the possible paranormal branch of the business."

Sidney held up a much written on spreadsheet. "I know I don't need to refresh you on our current caseload."

"You do not. But the wise business doesn't dismiss a whole queue of new customers beating on its door. In a manner of speaking." From her private office, her incoming email Godzilla roar punctuated her sentence. "I couldn't be more popular with the ghost-hunting crowd if I added purple streaks to my head and went to work for Lady Rowan across the street."

"You'd match the décor," Zane said.

"I'd almost be willing if I could reverse it when I need to work on regular jobs."

"I can change the phone greeting," Zane said. "For Tarot readings, press two. For Ouija Board sessions, press three. For exorcisms, dial 1-800-NEEDAPRIEST."

Giulia smiled for the first time that morning. "I will not dare you to follow through on the idea." She turned her head toward the door. "Did you hear that?"

The barest shadow of a human being faded from the frosted glass as everyone looked.

Sidney cupped her hands around her mouth. "It's the Driscoll Investigations ghooooost."

Giulia buried her face in her hands. Sidney scurried out of her way and opened the door.

The woman in the hallway plastered herself against the opposite wall. Over Sidney's shoulder, Giulia saw golden blonde hair, blue eyes, and pale skin.

Only the woman's dress stood out: white with a subtle jacquard pattern, it shimmered in the cool dim hall. Giulia estimated its price equaled a month of her own salary.

Sidney glanced back at Giulia before facing the hall again with a warm, welcoming smile on her face.

A single vertebra in the scared-rabbit woman's spine relaxed. "I'm, that is, I want to talk to, I mean, is this the Driscoll Investigations on the websites for Stone's Throw and Lady Solana?"

Giulia counted to five in Irish, a skill learned from her husband's grandmother. Then she walked into the hall holding out her hand. "I'm Giulia Driscoll. How may I help you?"

Two

Giulia plugged in her electric kettle. "Would you like some tea?"

The woman perched on the edge of the client chair in the temporary shelter of Giulia's private office. Her thin hands gripped the arms of the chair like Giulia's former Novice Mistress used to grip the arms of her seat in an airplane. Of her mental list of reasons clients this fearful knocked on her door, Giulia chose spousal abuse or a guilty conscience worthy of a tell-all biography.

"Oh—that's Cissy's favorite tea." The woman pointed to the "Constant Comment" picture on the box of Bigelow's assorted tea.

Giulia took her Godzilla head mug from the shelf under her small tea table. The woman flinched. The mug vanished under the tabletop and Giulia opened her door.

"Sidney, would you bring me two Styrofoam cups from the supply cabinet, please?"

Three minutes later, Giulia poured hot water over the orange spice tea bags in both non-threatening cups. Constant Comment was the only tea three-months-pregnant Giulia didn't actively hate.

A few more of the woman's vertebrae loosened at the first sip of "Cissy's favorite tea," but that was all. Her eyes twitched to the desk, the painting on the wall, the curtains, the filing cabinet, and back to the tea table. She didn't come anywhere close to meeting Giulia's gaze. Her hands clutched the flimsy cup, and Giulia, watching, could barely detect her chest rising and falling as she breathed. This woman could've been hired as one of those human statues she'd once seen in New Orleans.

Since her first afternoon appointment wasn't until two thirty, Giulia accepted the challenge of drawing out the potential client.

"Would you like sugar for your tea?"

The woman started but avoided a "Caution—Hot Tea Is Hot" accident. She sipped.

"No. No. It's fine."

The statue returned. An evil imp on Giulia's shoulder tempted her to check for a talking doll pull string in the woman's back. Giulia dispatched that particular imp with a mental fly swatter. Instead, she let the silence lengthen. Despite the woman's makeup, an ashy tinge marred her flawless skin and circles the size of dessert plates ringed her eyes. Close up, the shadow-patterned dress—real silk—and the unusual diamond and silver wedding ring confirmed Giulia's initial impression of serious money.

When Giulia had suffered through as much of the tea as humanly possible, she said, "Have you stayed at Stone's Throw?"

Another full-body jerk. "Oh, no." A police siren screamed along the street and her head snapped toward the window and away again.

Giulia set down her cup.

The woman blurted, "You get rid of ghosts," and slugged her tea like it was whisky.

Behind her polite smile, Giulia gave a point to one of the old clichés: prying information out of a clam would be easier. "Is there a ghost in your house?"

The big blue eyes finally latched onto Giulia's. "I'm so happy you believe me. Yes, there is, or maybe there are. We're not sure how many. The ghosts are trying to drive me out of my mind or out of my house or maybe both, and Pip is wonderful, Pip is my husband, and he's made my life exactly like a fairy tale. The ghosts are tormenting him as well as me. They won't let him sleep. They won't let me sleep unless I play my nursery rhyme recordings. You don't think I'm silly for listening to nursery rhymes even though I'm an adult, do you?"

"Of course n—"

"The ghosts must have been there all the time, even all those years ago when Mama and Daddy renovated the castle from top to bottom. We call the house a castle because Daddy always called me his little princess even though it's only a plain old house. Do you think ghosts hide when certain people are around? I do. I think they were scared of Mama and maybe of Aunt Caroline too. When Pip and I were married and he came to live in the castle with me I think maybe they were waiting to see if Pip would scare them too." A fleeting yet stellar smile. "You'd love Pip too if you met him. Pip is wonderful and he's not scary at all, but now the ghosts are making our lives a living hell."

"In what way are—"

"Harriet showed me her Tarot cards when I was small, but Mama sent her away. Mama wouldn't let me have any Tarot cards, but now that the ghosts are ruining our fairy tale, I bought my own set. I'm still learning how to read them. You know Ouija and Tarot and have all kinds of occult knowledge. I read the Stone's Throw website over and over. You banished the ghosts from that bed and breakfast. Will you do a Tarot reading for me and Pip and see what the ghosts are planning for us? Then we can form our own plan of attack—you, me, and Pip—to kick out the nasty ghosts and make the castle all our own again." She drained the last of her tea.

Giulia's own breathing had speeded up to match this breathless monologue.

Voices from the main office penetrated the closed door. The intercom buzzed.

"Ms. Driscoll, your client's husband would like to join the meeting." Zane never called Giulia "Ms. D." when a client could hear.

This time the woman started so violently her empty cup went flying. Giulia snatched it in midair and slam-dunked it in the trash can. With her other index finger, she pressed the reply button. "Please send him in."

If Paul Newman had smiled instead of smoldered in *Cat on a Hot Tin Roof*, Giulia would've sworn young, handsome, chiseled Paul Newman now strode into her office and gathered the brittle woman in his arms.

Giulia kept her *Oh, my* reaction to herself.

The woman launched into another monologue: "Don't be angry, please, Pip. I couldn't take it anymore, and when I saw the wonderful reviews of this agency I thought I'd found the one person able to help us banish the ghosts."

Giulia resolved to police her language for the word "wonderful."

Paul Newman/Pip radiated soothing, adoring protector. "Honey, I was worried about you. I called home to see how you were and Cissy told me you'd gone out. She heard you give the address to the taxi driver, and I came right over."

Giulia also noticed the way he said "you'd gone out."

Pip said to the trembling lips upturned to his face, "You're my brave princess. You know that, don't you?"

Giulia worked hard not to gag as they murmured endearments to each other.

Pip detached one hand and shook Giulia's. "Ms. Driscoll, isn't it? Thank you for consulting with Elaine, but I'm sure we'll be able to deal with our unfriendly ghosts by ourselves."

"But, Pip—"

With another gleaming smile, Pip said, "You need to trust me on this, sweetheart. I'm working on a few of my own ghost-busting plans."

With the aid of a completely relaxed spinal column, Elaine draped herself like a mink stole onto his broad chest. "You know I trust you for everything, darling."

Pip repositioned Elaine over to his left hip. "Ms. Driscoll, what's the charge for today?"

Giulia put up her hands. "Initial consultations are free of charge."

He nodded. "Always a good business practice. I run a marketing firm. You'd be surprised how many small businesses lose customers because their thinking is too short-term."

Elaine's brief farewell touch of Giulia's hand couldn't remotely be called a handshake. Giulia didn't feel condescended to though. It was more like the woman had little to no face-to-face interaction with strangers.

Pip led Elaine into the main office. She squealed and unpeeled herself from his side.

"Pip, look!" Her thin finger pointed out the window. "A Tarot reader."

Giulia said, "Lady Rowan is the Tarot reader for the owner of Stone's Throw Bed and Breakfast."

Another squeal. "Pip, it's serendipity. Do you have time to go with me now, right now, please?"

The gleaming smile reappeared. "If you're sure this outing hasn't been too much for you, darling."

"Not a bit. I've been preparing myself since last Thursday when I found the websites. I know I can handle a Tarot reading." She reenacted her mink stole impression on his broad chest.

"Then I can't think of a better way to spend my lunch hour."

They left after another round of thanks. Sidney watched their progress from the window. "I hope she didn't drive here."

"She came by taxi," Giulia said. "Why?"

"She's glued to the curb. He's encouraging her to cross the street. The light's changed twice already. Third time green...and there they go to land safe on the opposite sidewalk. She's pointing to the merchandise in Rowan's window. Okay; they made it inside." She faced the room. "Cinderella and Prince Charming?"

"Definitely," Giulia said. "I'm trying hard not to lust after her clothes."

Sidney shook her head with vehemence, her long brown braid swishing back and forth. "Fancy clothes all have to be dry cleaned. Did I ever tell you that perchloroethylene causes cancer in humans and animals and can harm your central nervous system, your kidneys, and liver?"

"But does it contribute to the honeybee die-off?" Zane said.

Sidney glared at him. "One day I will wash out your mouth with organic soap."

Desperate not to laugh, Giulia bit the inside of her cheek until her eyes watered. When Sidney became a mother a whole new side of her appeared at the same time: Organic Mama Bear.

Zane cleared his throat. "Do we have a new client?"

"Not this time. They're making a husband and wife project out of it."

"You know," Zane continued in a thoughtful voice, "if you could create a bogus haunting in her house and then sign on to banish the evil spirit, she'd swallow it whole."

"Fortunately, I possess an active and healthy conscience."

"I'm just thinking of those months when money is tight." Zane's charming smile rivaled Pip's.

Sidney returned to her desk. "If we turn into Cottonwood's Spooks 'R' Us, I will quit to raise the alpacas full-time, no matter how much spinning their wool gives me a backache."

Three

At eleven o'clock the next morning, three pairs of hands on computer keyboards made most of the sound in both offices. Zane muttered at his screen as he worked on the complex research Giulia had assigned him.

Sidney's head turned left and straight, left and straight as she typed up case report notes. On cue, at least once for every case, she muttered, "I should never have cheated in typing class."

"You can still teach yourself to touch type," Zane would reply, and Sidney would shake her head. "No time," and return to her head-pivoting exercises.

Inured to this eternal exchange, Giulia typed a paragraph in her lengthy email to the Diocese of Pittsburgh. She read it over and deleted it. Another paragraph. Another deletion. She had a strong desire to lay a curse on an institution overburdened with wealth that nevertheless tried to cheap out on every business transaction. She had friends who could teach her how to lay such a curse too.

As always, she thought better of the karma hit and tried a third paragraph.

Liszt's "Hungarian Rhapsodies" played at low volume from Zane's phone. Giulia pictured Bugs Bunny and Daffy Duck descending on the Archbishop's office. The imagined chaos significantly improved her morning.

The outer door opened. All sound except Liszt ceased for three...four...five seconds. Giulia stuck her head around her monitor. Sidney's face could've posed for a surprised emoji.

As the music climaxed with crashing cymbals and crescendoing brass, Zane shut it off.

In a thinner baritone than normal, he said, "Welcome to Driscoll Investigations. May I help you?"

A feminine voice in the alto range said, "I do apologize for barging in here without an appointment, but would it be possible to see Ms. Driscoll for a mere fifteen minutes?"

Even though Giulia's door was open, Zane buzzed her. His vocal cords under control again, he said, "Ms. Driscoll, are you available?"

Of course Giulia had to know who'd reduced her staff to speechlessness. "Please send the visitor in."

A throwback to the late eighteen hundreds swept into Giulia's office, ruffled parasol and all. The visitor wore white leather button boots, a black and white striped tea-length bustle, copper underskirt, and ivory corset with matching striped underblouse, all crowned with a miniature top hat fascinator balanced on jet-black curly hair.

Because Giulia had the advantage of Zane and Sidney's reactions, she stood and held out her hand without missing a beat. She figured the woman was either a major crackpot or here to raise money for charity using steampunk cosplay to grab her victim's attention.

If the parasol concealed a rapier, Giulia was prepared to sacrifice her keyboard as a shield and call on Zane's muscle. He gave her a short nod as he closed the door on them.

The woman hung the parasol on the back of Giulia's client chair but didn't distress the bustle by sitting. "It's very kind of you to see me without an appointment. I'm Muriel Lockwood. I'm here because of my cousin Elaine."

All Giulia's spidey-senses went on alert.

The brisk voice continued, "Do you know who she is?"

"She visited us yesterday," Giulia said, not wanting to reveal the first name was all she knew.

"She's Dahlia." In a voice which implied Dahlia was recognized the world over.

Giulia's mind scrolled through possibilities. Dahlia as in an actress? A singer? An international spy? No way was the scared rabbit a real-life James Bond. She responded only with interested silence. Her visitor stalked to Giulia's side of the desk.

"Have you been living in a cave? Everyone knows Dahlia." She pointed a long copper fingernail at Giulia's monitor. "Google it."

Giulia indulged the imperious woman. The search brought up a fashion website. Giulia clicked through.

"That page, there." The fingernail pointed again. "Elaine designed that dress. Nordstrom's stocks it. The purple one too. Dahlia is *the* place for unique designs, and Elaine's owned it since her twenty-first birthday."

Giulia blinked at the prices and said to Muriel, "Ms. Lockwood, how can Driscoll Investigations help you?"

"Do you really not know anything about Dahlia?"

"Shall we pretend I don't?"

Muriel's curls jiggled as she flipped up her striped bustle and settled into the client chair, but the fascinator never budged. "How anyone over the age of fifteen can claim ignorance of Dahlia...All right. In the days of young Madonna and her bullet bras, Elaine's grandparents expanded their quirky dress boutique into a chain of exclusive clothing stores across the country and into Canada. Then the recession in the early 2000s hit them and they decided to retire. Left the business to Elaine's parents and promptly died when their Cessna crashed into Lake Superior." Her thin lips curled into a ghoulish smile. "I heard they only found three pieces of the fuselage and her grandfather's false teeth." A shudder wiggled the curls. "Wish I'd been alive to see it. Nothing beats a good murder."

Giulia stopped taking notes on her legal pad. "Did the police think they were murdered?"

Muriel's hand flipped back and forth. "No, no, no. All perfectly straightforward and boring. He had a heart attack, and by the time his wife got her act together and radioed for help," her hand stiffened and performed a nose-dive, "*neeeeooow,* splash, boom."

A wink accented the smile. "If they'd been more famous, the story would've been optioned for a made-for-TV movie on the fashion channel. Anyway, Elaine's mom and dad were already going all slash and burn on grandmama and granddaddy's business. They closed three-quarters of the stores and concentrated on the web presence. You'd think they'd be drowning in bad press from that, right? Wrong. In three years, Dahlia was *the* hot website and a textbook example of 'lean and mean.'" The smile turned hard and the lips became a straight copper line. "Elaine's parents bought and renovated the castle and everybody, absolutely everybody in the fashion and financial magazine crowd tripped all over themselves to feature them."

Giulia kept writing. "I'm not sure I see how this relates to your interest in our services."

With the smoothness of instinct—or of an accomplished actress— Muriel seized the knobby end of the parasol and thumped it on the wood floor. "How else do you think Elaine got enough money to be a princess in her castle?"

Honks, bus airbrakes, and unintelligible loud conversation drifted through the window, as did the aroma of barbecue sauce and pineapple for Hawaiian pizza: the restaurant across the street's Tuesday special.

Muriel sniffed. "Ugh, pineapple. Unless it's in a piña colada, I'm not interested." She gave the side-eye to Giulia's tea table. "Let me guess: Elaine saw the Constant Comment and her Xanax-fueled brain rolled over and wagged its tail."

Giulia smiled. "She mentioned it was the favorite tea of someone named Cissy."

"Her housekeeper. Been with the house since Elaine's seventh birthday. Real mama bear, which Elaine needed since her actual mama stopped just short of going all *Mommie Dearest* on her little princess." Muriel leaned forward on the parasol, looking more like a crotchety old woman than a vibrant young one. "I'm airing the family's dirty laundry for a reason. Now listen: *House Beautiful* was one of the magazines that sucked up to Mama Dahlia and Daddy Dahlia. A few weeks after the issue hit the stores, three enterprising criminals invaded the castle, stole everything they could carry, and killed Elaine's parents."

Giulia looked up. Muriel nodded, her lips compressed with anger? Hate? Ghoulish delight? No, definitely hate.

"They didn't find Elaine because mama had locked her up in some closet or other as punishment. Mama liked doing that."

"That's appalling."

"You think? I hope the bitch is rotting in every circle of Dante's hell on a rotating basis. Sweet, innocent Elaine survived and inherited everything. But a nine-year-old can't run a company. Elaine's twenty-four now and still too sweet and innocent to see what's going on around her."

"Which is?"

"A bloodless coup."

This story was almost as entertaining as Muriel herself. "You're not exaggerating."

"I never exaggerate."

Giulia did not voice her opinion on that topic.

"The will left everything to Elaine—she's an only child—but in the meantime the company was to be run by the three major players: her mother's personal assistant, her father's personal assistant, and the Chief Financial Officer. The will named them the Board of Directors." Another wriggle of the curls. "What would you do if you'd run a fabulously successful company for twelve years and all of a sudden the heiress comes of age and Skypes herself into every board meeting? No more autonomous decisions. The owner checking over the books. Elaine has an MBA from Harvard, you know. It's amazing what you can accomplish online."

Giulia shook out a hand cramp.

"You can go ahead and type if you want," Muriel said.

"I'm fine, but thank you. Elaine has accomplished all this and yet she doesn't usually go out of her house?"

"Usually? Make that never. Yet here's the princess running the family company right out of college and doing a great job at it. Oh no, those three must be thinking, she won't need us anymore. And then along comes Prince Charming. You met him yesterday too."

Giulia nodded.

"Elaine worships him. He runs his own marketing company. If you were one of the big guns at Dahlia, what are you thinking now?"

Giulia played straight man. "I'd be waiting for the husband and wife team to force me out."

Muriel tapped the side of her nose with an index finger. "Egg-zactly. When I found out Elaine actually left the house to come to you yesterday, I had a talk with Cissy. She told me about how Elaine thinks the house is haunted and what it's doing to her. Haunted. Seriously."

Giulia surreptitiously checked her monitor clock. Still an hour to her next appointment.

"Does Elaine's housekeeper think the haunting is real?"

Muriel hesitated for the first time. "I asked her the same question. She didn't say no."

Giulia treated the idea as fact. "Has she seen any evidence of a haunting?"

"No, but Pip has. His formal handle is Perry Ignatius Patrick, born on Dickens' birthday and whose ancestors were some of the first settlers in the Massachusetts Bay colony. Frankly, if I'd been stuck with a ridiculous nickname like Pip I'd have my name legally changed to John Smith as soon as I turned eighteen. Where was I? Oh, right. The haunting. Pip's heard things and seen things, which is a huge relief, because if Elaine is starting to imagine ghosts, then those three at Dahlia will grab it and run an Olympic relay. Can you see the headlines?" She spread her hands like she was designing a theater marquee: "Crazy recluse heiress unfit to run Fortune 500 company. 'Loony Leader Dooms Dahlia.' Those three will hire a bunch of bottom-feeder lawyers to circle her like sharks. The shareholders will lose their minds, and the next thing you know Elaine will be under a shrink's care 'for her own good.'" Muriel shuddered. "Shrinks. Elaine's aunt and uncle—her parents named them in the will as her guardians—dragged her to monthly appointments with one of those leeches for a whole year after her parents were shot."

"That's to be expected after a traumatic event." The pineapple and barbecue sauce still wafting into the room was distracting Giulia. She blamed pregnancy.

Muriel thumped the parasol on the floor again. "If those three hand-pick a shrink to root around in Elaine's little gray cells, she'll end up with nothing to do in her own company except spend the money they'd be forced to deposit into her bank account. I'm not going to let that happen."

Since Muriel didn't think her cousin was the victim of an actual haunting…"Ms. Lockwood, what is it you want Driscoll Investigations to do for you?"

"Not for me, for Elaine. I want you to find out which one of those three is behind this haunting business. Maybe it's two of them. Maybe all three. Find out who's doing it and nail their greedy carcasses to the wall."

She appraised Giulia without seeming to judge Giulia's hair or makeup or clothes, bland as beige paint in comparison to her own. "I only came here because Elaine did, and I didn't have time to check up on you. Am I safe in presuming your agency has a positive track record?"

"We have several years of success stories and positive reviews on Yelp."

"Good. I like your no-frills office and your businesslike look. Besides, you didn't spook Elaine, which is one thousand points in your favor." Muriel opened her embroidered wrist bag. "What are your fees, and how much do you require for a retainer?"

Four

After Giulia showed Muriel out, she placed a small stack of fives and tens on Zane's desk. "We have a new client."

"Who pays with cash anymore?" Sidney said.

"Forget the cash." Zane said. "Is she a cosplayer? Her outfit would kill it at next month's Comic Con."

"She's eccentric because she appears to be wealthy," Giulia said. "The husband and wife from yesterday are her cousins. The whole extended family appears to have money."

"Which makes her eccentric and not a crackpot," Sidney said.

"Sidney, have you ever shopped at Dahlia?" Giulia said.

"Me? How long have we worked together?"

"I thought perhaps for a special occasion."

"No way. I'm into comfort. My older sisters bought from them when they could find an excuse to get a night away from the alpacas." She held up her combination diaper/messenger bag. "Jessamine is a teething machine now. My life is all about the drool. If drool ever touched a Dahlia dress, I bet a team of their personal ninjas would drop from the ceiling to slice the offender into artistic shreds."

"On that appetizing note, I'm running out for lunch before my one o'clock. I'll take orders if anyone's craving something specific."

"Pizza," they said in unison.

Zane inclined his head toward the open window. "We've been assaulted by barbecue sauce all morning."

Giulia returned with two slices of Hawaiian barbecue for Zane, one veggie for Sidney, and one plain cheese for herself. "The baby issued a firm warning against pepperoni or sausage. If he's messing with my taste buds at twelve weeks, what havoc is he going to wreak in the third trimester?"

Sidney said, "I'll tell you if you'll tell me the nickname you have for him."

Giulia drew herself up to her entire five feet five inches and said in her most dignified Sister Mary Regina Coelis voice, "I do not negotiate with blackmailers."

Sidney applauded. "That was brilliant. You channeled your nun self, right? Do it again."

Giulia's dignity collapsed. "You should be cowering. I've lost my touch."

She took her pizza into her office and spent forty minutes double-checking Dahlia's dirty laundry. Her one o'clock appointment resulted in another retainer and prenuptial research project, Sidney's specialty. For someone all about nature and alpacas and babies, she'd developed an incisive skill for personal and financial indiscretions guaranteed to ruin a marriage.

Speaking of incisive skills, Giulia hovered at Zane's desk until he finished the retainer paperwork.

"Yes, boss?"

"I require your dark magic."

Zane pushed all paperwork aside and cracked his knuckles in a bizarre toneless arpeggio. "Rub my magic lamp, and I'll grant your wish."

Sidney spewed water on her monitor. "Zane!" She wadded her napkins and caught the drips before they fell into her keyboard.

Giulia didn't watch realization turn Zane's face pale pink—the darkest his skin ever got—because she was bent double against the wall, clutching her stomach and trying to breathe through her semi-horrified laughter. When she dragged herself vertical, Zane had disappeared. Sidney pointed to the floor. Giulia spotted the toes of her admin's Converse hi-tops in the knee hole of his desk.

"Zane, come out."

"I can't, Ms. D."

Concern replaced amusement. "Did you hurt your back diving under there?"

"No. I'm too humiliated." His muffled voice sounded ten years younger.

"Zane, it's another learning experience. Come out and hack for me, please."

His muscular shoulders appeared first, then his ash-blond head, then the rest of him. Dust grayed the seat of his khakis. He stifled a sneeze.

"The cleaning service seems to be concentrating on only what our eyes can inspect." Giulia wrote a note on the fluorescent pink phone message pad and tore it off. "Zane, please find everything you can about the financial workings of Dahlia."

"Yes, Ms. D.," he said in the same too-young voice.

"At least it's not more ghosts," Sidney said.

Giulia capped the pen. "Sidney, what do you have against ghosts?"

Sidney turned big brown eyes to Giulia. "Olivier's little brothers have their own YouTube channel where fans send them challenges. Last fall someone dared them to create a haunting."

"That was a good episode," Zane said.

The eyes moved to Zane.

Without a shred of embarrassment, he said, "I subscribe to them."

"If I tell them, they'll try to pick your brain for their creations."

"Stop," Giulia said. "What does their YouTube channel have to do with your antipathy toward ghosts?"

"They film their show on our farm. Without telling me, they set up the haunting in our cottage. They had me convinced something terrible was in our house. When they made Jessamine cry, Olivier made them come clean." She bared her teeth. "They dismantled everything and as an apology showed me their gag reel of scaring students in their dorm's basement with phony hauntings." She crossed her arms. "They're all phony: the Amityville house, the house from that *Conjuring* movie, the house in California with a hundred rooms. Every single one."

Giulia's email roared again. "I haven't decided one way or the other." She held up a hand. "Yes, I'm including Stone's Throw. I was caught up in the physical danger then and never came to a conclusion about the ghost."

"You have an open mind," Zane said.

"Meaning I don't?"

Zane quailed before the Wrath of Sidney. "It, uh, appears you've reached a definite conclusion."

"Giulia?"

Giulia stood firm. "My mind is open."

The sound from Sidney's nose would've been labeled a snort if it hadn't finished with an ostentatious sigh. The real Sidney returned. "Is it okay to agree to disagree?"

Five

That night after supper, Frank Driscoll's ginger head bobbed up and down in their vegetable garden as he picked green beans. Giulia weeded the tomatoes at the opposite end. The garden threatened to take over the entire yard after weeks of hot July and August days. At least she had no trouble weeding in the first trimester.

"Sidney tried to blackmail me today into revealing the baby's nickname," Giulia said over the shouts and puck whacks of the block's never-ending street hockey game.

Frank's handful of beans fell into the metal colander with dull *plinks*. "Sidney the sweet? Sidney the Christmas Elf? That Sidney?"

"Yes. I fear the job is corrupting her."

"Next she'll bring processed cold cuts on white bread for lunch."

Giulia laughed. "Hell would freeze over first. I am not exaggerating."

"Agreed." More beans landed in the colander. "I could sneak into the office and leave clues. A soccer ball and a Manchester United jersey, maybe."

"You could set up a life-size cutout of the real Zlatan in the middle of the room and she would wonder which case it related to." With a final check of the weed-free tomatoes, Giulia attacked the encroaching invaders beneath the cucumber leaves.

"True. Also, jerseys are ruinously expensive." He slapped the back of his neck. "Stupid mosquitoes."

"They're better than wasps."

"I vote for neither." He squinted up at the gutters on the back of the house. "No new nests yet."

Giulia sat on her heels. "Did you hear that?"

"No."

"The doorbell." She got to her knees. "There it is again."

"If it's my grandmother with a cheesecake, she may enter. Everyone else gets threatened with a speeding ticket during tomorrow's rush hour."

She stood and stretched her back. "You haven't driven a patrol car in years."

"A few of the guys owe me a favor." He resumed the bean harvest.

Giulia walked through the house rather than around. If the person at their door wasn't a relative holding a cheesecake, she didn't want them following her into the backyard.

The doorbell rang a third time. Giulia used the archway between the kitchen and living room as cover. From this angle, the narrow vertical glass insets in the door doubled as peepholes to screen for unwanted guests.

A plump woman in khaki slacks and an orange blouse stood at the door. Her short, straight hair was an even mix of gray and blonde. A widow's hump made her appear older than she perhaps was. Giulia flipped a mental coin and chose "recruiting members for a new church." Maybe she hailed from the Church of Scientology. A Scientologist versus a former nun would make for a fun encounter. Giulia opened the door.

"Good evening, Ms. Driscoll. I apologize for interrupting you at home, but it's necessary." Her high, businesslike voice didn't convey "church lady."

"Good evening." Giulia kept the door ready to close and lock.

"I'm Cecilia Newton, Elaine Patrick's housekeeper. May I come in?"

Friends and relatives were certainly circling the wagons around Elaine. Giulia opened the door. "I can give you a few minutes."

She deposited the guest at the kitchen table and conveyed the nature of the visitor to her husband. Frank muttered comments Giulia knew she'd disapprove of if she could hear them clearly. She took the full colander and he nodded at the client before closing himself in the game room.

"I was shocked when I learned Elaine actually went to your office," Ms. Newton said when Giulia set iced tea before her.

"As opposed to asking me to go to her house?"

The older woman nodded. "Muriel told me she'd clued you in—her words—on Elaine's history. You're wondering how I survived the home invasion."

Giulia hadn't been, but now that she mentioned it...

"I was up in Montreal at my sister's wedding that weekend." She looked out the kitchen door at Giulia's vegetables. "The Japanese beetles are bad this year. A chameleon would do wonders for pest control in your garden." Without missing a beat, she returned to the main conversation. "I'd been managing the castle since Elaine was seven, and we got along well, but she was too young to come through such a trauma unscathed. I'm not a psychologist. I couldn't help her enough. I've always wondered if I'd had proper experience and training whether Elaine would've grown up differently." Her unpolished blunt-cut fingernails scraped at the moisture beading the glass.

Giulia's mental information list on this potential client—or suspect—filled as she talked: guilt, regret, nostalgia, greed (had the woman been mentioned in the dead parents' will?), possible acting skills. Because anyone could play the devoted companion with enough practice looking in a mirror and reading a pile of old-fashioned books.

Frank was going to rag on her for her shiny new cynical assessment of people. So much for the naïve optimism of Sister Mary Regina Coelis.

Newton continued, "Muriel is too hard-headed to believe us about the haunting, but I live in the castle and I'm hearing things too."

The neighbor's Jack Russell terriers began their nightly siege of the squirrel population. All conversation ceased for a few moments. When the chaos ramped down to huffs and whines, Giulia said, "Is it an old house?"

The polite woman indulged in a decidedly impolite look. "Certainly, but give me credit for knowing the difference between the attic floor settling and a pattern of knocks from one of the empty bedrooms."

Giulia inclined her head and the woman appeared to replay her last statement. She reached her hand across the table.

"I beg your pardon. Please blame the stress."

They shook hands. "Think nothing of it, Ms. Newton."

"Ms. Newton is too formal. I'm Cissy to everyone except the maids and the cook. Elaine's called me that since the day her mother hired me. It was practically her only act of defiance. Her mother always called me Ms. Newton and wanted Elaine to do the same." A smile brought out a forest of wrinkles around her mouth and eyes. "She and I used to play ghosts with the sheets covering the furniture in the attic when her parents needed the entire house to entertain." The smile died and the wrinkles smoothed away. "There were no actual ghosts in the castle then. At least we never encountered any. It would take a strong-willed person, dead or alive, to risk annoying Elaine's mother." She brought out a pen and a checkbook with a lizard-print cover.

"Ms. New—Cissy—Ms. Lockwood has already retained our services."

"I spoke to Muriel about this and she agreed." She handed Giulia a folded piece of paper from inside the checkbook.

Giulia opened the half sheet of gardenia scented paper and read a single sentence in bold handwriting written in purple ink with flourishes on all the serifs.

"Cissy is my partner in this enterprise now." It was signed with even more flourishes: "Muriel Lockwood."

Cissy said, "I'm easier to get in touch with than Muriel if you have questions. There is something other than trickery behind what's happening at the castle. There's no reason to scare Elaine into becoming even more of a recluse than she already is." She raised her glass to her lips.

"Therefore, someone is after control of Dahlia?"

Cissy set down the glass without drinking. "Muriel is trying to convince me Elaine's business partners are behind the noises and the things we've been seeing out of the corners of our eyes. She's won me halfway to her side, but the more it goes on, the more I'm becoming convinced it's all, well, not of this world." The dimples in her chin receded as she thrust it forward.

Giulia interlaced her fingers. "I'm neither going to tell you it's all in your head nor that ghosts do not exist."

The dimples reappeared. "You're justifying Muriel's report of you. 'Oozing common sense' is how she phrased it. What else do you need me to tell you about the workings of the castle?"

Giulia took the notepad from the refrigerator and started a bullet point list of the inhabitants of Elaine's house, the house itself, and more pieces of Elaine's *Oprah*-worthy life story.

Cissy finished, "Pip took Elaine to a Tarot reader yesterday after seeing you. Elaine is anxious to follow up on that aspect of the possible haunting, but it will be quite a while before she is strong enough to leave the castle again. I researched you and your success at Stone's Throw. Please consider my partnership in this as a request for Driscoll Investigations to provide Tarot readings, Ouija board sessions, and ghost detecting. Muriel and I need to either prove or disprove the haunting to Elaine and the rest of the household. Those services are in addition to your standard investigation of the company's chief officers."

She wrote a check equal to the cash Muriel had paid.

"I keep long hours. Feel free to call me anytime, but I promise I won't invade your privacy again. My worry about Elaine overrode my common sense."

When Cissy left, Giulia opened the game room door and waited for Frank to finish his session of Halo 3 and the required trash-talk with his brothers.

Her husband removed his headphones. "Well?"

"I may need you to run interference with your brother the priest."

"Dear God, don't tell me you're going undercover as a nun again?"

"A pregnant nun? It sounds like the plot of a bad horror movie." She fluttered the check in front of him. "Tomorrow I'll ask Rowan what it takes to create golems. We're going to need a lot of help."

Frank stared.

Six

"I always make the sitter cut the cards twice," Lady Rowan said. "The Rule of Three balances everything for me, plus they expect it, especially the ones who've watched a few movies and think they understand everything about Pagans."

Rowan Froelig teaching Giulia "the biz" at eight o'clock in the morning was a completely different person than Lady Rowan, Reader of Tarot and Certified Psychic Medium. Mentor Rowan, a dish towel tucked into her collar to protect her flowing scarves from powdered sugar, mainlined peppermint tea and had already demolished one of the raspberry-filled croissants Giulia had brought.

Over strawberry shortcake with Frank last night, Giulia had worked out a plan for Driscoll Investigations' new spinoff business. As the first step, she set up a lesson with the nearest expert.

Jasper Fortin, Rowan's war-hero clairvoyant nephew, poured more tea for his aunt and handed the cup to her with his prosthetic hand. An éclair occupied his other hand. "Vanilla cream belongs in my stomach, not on my metal joints."

Jasper waited until Giulia set down her French roast with cherries jubilee syrup before adding, "Your little guy says he's sorry you have to limit your coffee, but he likes grapefruit juice better."

Giulia swallowed. "Jasper, I'm not a customer."

"Correct," Rowan said. "You're our student. See how matter-of-fact he is? Certain customers prefer the blunt statement. Now pretend you're a divorced woman who is sure she'll never find the right man and in her heart wants to believe all this psychic stuff but has a hard shell because she's been an office grunt for ten years. She's looking for flaws in our presentation, but she also has a Kindle overflowing with paranormal romance novels."

Jasper set the unfinished éclair on a napkin and caressed the air around Giulia. He closed his eyes and tilted his head toward the ceiling. At the end of the air manipulation, his hands hovered over Giulia's head. His face took on a look of deep concentration.

"I see blue surrounding you. The deep blue of ocean waves as they rise to new heights. The waves enclose a soul whose depths mirror the ocean. It is filled with life yet constant as the tides. This soul...it is the soul of a man...he seeks a partner willing to plunge into his depths yet maintain her autonomy. One whose colors complement his. I see your auras touching, merging, dancing amidst the waves of life." He opened his eyes. "That's how the phonies do it. My readings never sound like bad romance novels. I prefer big-brother style camaraderie. People open up to a big brother." The rest of the éclair vanished into his mouth. "I love these things."

Giulia returned his smile. "I chose them without knowing your preferences."

"Are you sure you didn't know?" Jasper opened a fresh Dr. Pepper. "Maybe you're discovering talents you never knew you had. Ever think of dropping the detective business and working for us?"

"I think I'm okay with being the Missing Persons Whisperer. Someone has to do the legwork."

Rowan said, "Write this down." When Giulia's pen touched the legal pad she'd brought, Rowan dictated: "See how Jasper kept everything unspecific? Blue, the ocean, complementary colors, buzzwords like depths and dancing and auras. That kind of reading can be massaged to apply to anyone."

Jasper swallowed more Dr. Pepper and hiccupped. "Many of our clients come here knowing the answers to their questions but haven't admitted it to themselves. Take the office worker looking for romance. The reading I just gave would augment her inner confidence to attract the type of man she's looking for."

Rowan added, "About hauntings. Often something attaches to the person themselves, not the house or wherever they've been seeing things. Nonverbal cues are your best friends."

"You have lots of information about your new client," Jasper said.

"If you see an opening for a reading like the one I just gave this hypothetical divorcée, you'll find the right bits and pieces to make the reading seem authentic."

Giulia's voice filled with frustration. "It will all be a pack of lies."

"It will not, I'm not clairvoyant, but my readings sometimes give clients the impression I am. In your case, readings will be another method for you to extract necessary information. Or a way to give a client what they need without you revealing all your cards. No pun intended." Rowan gestured with the second filled croissant and dusted the Tarot cards with powdered sugar. "Banana peels."

Jasper picked up the top card on each stack and blew the sugar into the empty bakery bag.

Rowan said through a bite of pastry, "Jasper, I don't think her skills lie in clairvoyance."

He set down the bag and stared through Giulia. Rowan interrupted her monologue to do the same. Giulia refused to succumb to the urge to duck under the tablecloth.

"You're right," Jasper said.

"My name's on the door. I'd better be right. Giulia, did everyone treat you as their personal advice column back when you were a nun?"

She glanced from Rowan to Jasper. "All the time."

He grinned "I have skills. Here's your first homework assignment, which shouldn't be difficult since you're used to Catholic meditation: find a quiet space and practice opening your Sight."

Giulia's forehead wrinkled. "You said 'sight' with a capital *S*."

"I did. Let us know what happens."

Rowan took charge again. "It's time to finish today's lesson."

Rowan walked Giulia through the Celtic cross layout and the traditional order of reading the chosen cards.

"It's all about interpretation. You use your knowledge of each card plus the client's question or situation plus the rest of the cards. You read each card individually as you build a complete picture of the reading as a whole using all the cards." She peered at Giulia's notes. "It's a good thing you write fast."

"Years of practice." Giulia finished a sentence. "Speaking of said client, she owns a Ouija board. It may be my ingrained Catholic upbringing, but I have a bad feeling about using one."

"You should," Jasper said.

Rowan said. "I never touch them. Too many rules to follow. Miss one and the nasties are there to pounce."

"Nasties?"

When Rowan scowled, her face morphed into a walnut. "You're Catholic. Don't be dense."

"Always listen to those gut feelings," Jasper said, "whether you're using the cards or your mind to work with a client."

Rowan stabbed her index finger on Giulia's notebook. "Your client will respect you more if you don't cater to her every whim. Stand firm."

"What she said."

Giulia wrote a check for the session as Rowan showed her how to cleanse a deck. Then she handed her the used Rider-Waite set.

"These are yours now. Work with them until they feel comfortable in your hands."

Jasper wrote his phone number at the bottom of Giulia's notes. "This is my cell. We're here any time you need to consult us. You're not limited to business hours."

As they walked Giulia to the door, Rowan said, "One more thing: If the client chooses lots of major arcana cards, I tell them 'It's going to be a bumpy ride.' If they draw the death card, I tell them in three different ways how death means a new beginning. It doesn't mean the Grim Reaper will be waiting in their car."

Jasper tossed the empty cups and used napkins. "We got hired for a charity Halloween event a few years back and some moron dressed as Death really did that. Overheard Rowan's reading and hid in the guy's car."

Giulia made an apprehensive face. "Should I laugh?"

"Yeah, because it turned out all right. The guy had a license to carry and pulled his gun on Death. The prankster paid to have the guy's interior cleaned. Who knew Death had a loose sphincter?"

Seven

"Guys," Giulia said after everyone had dealt with the morning emails, "before you comment, I want you to listen all the way to the end."

Zane's voice lurched. "We're broke?"

Sidney said, "You're carrying triplets?"

Zane's eyes narrowed. "You agreed to hunt ghosts for the cash-only client."

"As if," from Sidney.

"Yes," Giulia said.

Traffic noise filled the moment of silence.

"Sidney, your head is not going to explode," Giulia said.

Sidney pounded her forehead on her desk. "Yes, it is. What is this business coming to?"

"You said it: it's a business. Elaine's housekeeper visited me last night."

"Circling the wagons?"

Giulia stared at her Christmas Elf assistant. "Since when do you watch ESPN?"

"Jessamine loves sports. The crowd noise puts her to sleep almost as quickly as a lullaby. Besides, everybody knows Chris Berman's signature phrase about the Buffalo Bills." She cocked her head at Giulia. "Did you forget my NCAA swimming career? Baby Brain really has taken hold."

Giulia attempted dignity. "I had not, thank you, but the exact same phrase popped into my head when Cissy Newton arrived. Elaine inspires fierce loyalty."

"I don't see it," Zane said.

"The protective instinct," Giulia said.

"Come on. Helpless females went out of style with corsets and high-button shoes." He caught Giulia's pointed expression. "Oh. Right. Ms. Steampunk."

"Also known as our client. Besides, Elaine has a dreadful history." Giulia gave them the high points of the double murder and its aftermath.

"Why on earth did her guardians stop the psychiatrist visits?" Sidney said.

"Not sure. Something Muriel said made me wonder if Elaine acted like the perfect little girl to fool the psychiatrist into thinking she was all better."

Sidney's long hair whipped around her face as she shook her head. "Incompetence. Olivier would never be fooled by an acting job of mental health."

"Your husband is a treasure to us, the police department, and most of all to you and Jess."

"But not the alpacas." Sidney opened her phone. "He doesn't know I took this one." In the picture, a green glob of regurgitated alpaca stomach goo dripped down the side of his face.

"I've never seen him look angry before."

"Worse, Jessamine thought it was funny and he had to pretend to laugh with her. I would've videoed it if I wasn't occupied with leading him away from the silly beasts."

"Mongo punch horse." Zane did a decent Alex Karras impression.

Giulia picked up a pen from Sidney's desk. "Once again we're off track. I may establish a group lunch fund jar. Every time we get sidetracked from a work topic whoever initiated the derail has to donate a dollar." She wrote the idea on a sticky note. "All right. We've established Elaine's relatives and long-standing employees protect her like she's a rare china figurine. Cissy Newton requires we indulge Elaine's ghost obsession. Since I've accepted her as a joint client with Muriel, my morning has been spent at the feet of Rowan and Jasper."

Sidney's voice came out quite small. "Learning to do what?"

"Tarot reading and clairvoyance." She paused but no further comments emanated from Sidney's desk. "Part of today will be spent practicing with my new Tarot deck. Tonight I'll read for Frank, and tomorrow I'll try readings for both of you." She didn't mention her homework assignment from Jasper.

Zane turned his phone toward Giulia. "Ms. D., you're going to need these."

Giulia and Zane bent their heads over his screen.

"Zane, if I believed in psychics, I'd think you read my mind." She opened her own phone and downloaded two apps. "Sidney, those ghost hunters on TV use EMF meters and EVP detectors, right?"

"I curse the day I told you Olivier likes to watch those shows."

Without looking up, Giulia said, "You help even when you don't think you're helping. What a team player."

"The old Giulia was never sarcastic."

The Ghost Radar Legacy app opened as Giulia laughed. "My career is corrupting me."

"Me," said a robotic voice from Giulia's phone. Everyone jumped.

"The Electronic Voice Phenomenon recorder works at close range. Let's try distance." Giulia pointed her phone at Sidney. "Say something."

"There are no such things as ghosts."

"Ghosts," said the mechanical voice.

Zane downloaded the app. "I'm going to freak out the guys this weekend during our Madden multi-sports gaming tournament."

Bouncy video game music blared from Giulia's phone.

"Commercials; ugh." She found the "Remove ads" screen and paid for the full versions of both apps. "Pop-up ads in the middle of a ghost hunt are not professional. I know what else I need. A night vision camera." She searched. "This one looks good." She escaped into her office and closed the door, reopening it a minute later. "Very nice. A green glow makes everything look eerie."

Sidney maintained an unusual—for her—silence.

"Let's check the Electromagnetic Field detector." Giulia adjusted levels and walked the perimeter of the office. "Spikes at both computers. Also at the light switch. If I'm going to make this new gig believable, I'll have to find someplace in the castle without obvious electric hookups."

"Castle?" Sidney said.

"Elaine, Muriel, and Cissy all called the house a castle. I confess I'm looking forward to seeing it."

Zane stopped configuring his Ghost Legacy app. "Call me cynical, but I don't see that princess running a Fortune 500 company."

Giulia tucked her phone into her skirt pocket. "What else have you found out about Dahlia's finances?"

"Still working on it. Their IT guy graduated seven years ahead of me at MIT. I'm treating this as a personal challenge."

Sidney straightened as though she wore an invisible corset. "Giulia, seriously. If we're going to become Sleuths to the Spirits for this case, please tell me it's not a permanent shift."

Giulia sat in Sidney's client chair, arms on a pile of folders. "Seriously here too. Will this be a problem?"

The door crashed open and a petite woman ran into the room. At eleven o'clock on a Wednesday morning she wore silver flip-flops, black leggings, a white lace broomstick skirt, a tank top covered in black glitter, and miniature white carnations braided into her short black hair.

"Giulia, my friend, my personal Dear Abby, the only one who holds my hand when I get a new piercing, you have to save my tattooed soul."

Eight

Sidney unfroze first. "Mingmei? What's all the glitter for?"

"Tell me I look gorgeous."

"You do. You look awesome."

The morning barista at the coffee shop below DI ran to Sidney and kissed her. "You're the sweetest person I know." She took Giulia by the shoulders. "Well?"

"You're beautiful." After Mingmei kissed her as well, Giulia said, "Why do I have to save your soul? Have you sold it to the gods of glitter?"

"Because I'm getting married in forty minutes."

Giulia was seldom unable to formulate a correct response, but her friend's announcement achieved it.

Sidney said, "He stopped waffling after five years?"

"Five years, four months, and six days, not that I was counting." The bride opened her black glitter clutch and produced an opened condom wrapper. "I have to take a break from the Pill because of my blood pressure, and I told him we should also take a break from sex. Did he listen? No. He bought these and I bought those suppository things." She turned her face to the other desk. "Sorry, Zane."

He waved away her apology. "The stories I've heard in this office have inured me to anything."

"Good. We tried it with double insurance last Wednesday." She flapped the condom wrapper. "Except the seams of this fine product decided to unseam themselves."

All three of them grimaced.

"Don't make those faces." Mingmei wiggled her fingers and the diamond on her ring sparkled. "The next day when I opened the fridge to start making supper there was a Garden of Delights bakery box on the top shelf. I opened it because anything from the Garden is worth spoiling supper for. Inside was a cheesecake with this on the top. He popped out from behind the fridge and said it was time for him to man up."

Giulia inspected the ring. "Are you pregnant?"

"Don't know yet. That's the fun of it. He gave me the ring on Thursday. On Friday we shopped for wedding clothes and his ring, lined up my friend Maureen to marry us, and got the license." She clutched Giulia's hands. "Maureen says her grotto's ghost is acting up. I told her you could calm it down."

"I don't—"

"You do too. We're splurging on a wedding night in the haunted room at Stone's Throw Bed and Breakfast. The owner has to be your biggest fan." She affected embarrassment. "When I told her I've known you forever and we used to work at the same coffee shop, she gave me a discount. Then Maureen told me her pet ghost has been making all kinds of trouble ever since she upgraded her video equipment. I told her about your new skills. She says your reputation in the spirit world plus your extra Catholic mojo will scare the bejesus out of her ghost." She pulled Giulia out of the chair. "Please please please, darling Giulia, make my wedding a success."

Sidney poked Giulia. "Get out of here."

Giulia had no time to wonder if Sidney was indulging Mingmei or had accepted DI's new enterprise. She followed Mingmei downstairs to a lime green VW Beetle. Thanks to Mingmei driving at a steady twenty miles over the speed limit, they arrived at Reverend Maureen's Grotto in nine minutes instead of the legal fifteen.

A near-perfect replica of an Irish cottage nestled amid maples and chestnuts a hundred feet back from the suburban street. Rosebushes surrounded one story of ivy-covered stone walls, slate roof, green door, and matching shutters.

The front door opened as they walked up the cobblestone path. A fluffy calico cat sauntered past them without acknowledging their existence. The statuesque silver-haired woman at the threshold made up for the cat's indifference.

"Darling!" She swept Mingmei into her arms. "Stephan is pacing the grotto and checking his watch at every other step." She dropped the bride and held out a hand. "You must be Giulia. I'm pleased to meet you. Are you ready to administer some good old-fashioned Catholic discipline to my ghost?"

Mingmei ran around the house, the iconic noise of her flip-flops echoing off the stone walls. "Stephan! I've saved the day!"

Maureen and Giulia trailed in her wake. "I call it my ghost, but it was here when I bought the land. It likes to make my wind chimes drown out the ceremonies when it's in a snit. I've wondered if it's a jilted bride or failed musician."

The lawn behind the house dipped into a bowl protected by trees with an open grotto of natural stone at the far side. To the right, a pond with a wooden bridge arching over it led to the center of the grotto where white flower lights twinkled. To the left, a knee-high waterfall cascaded over stones accented by flowering stonecrop and sedum. A breeze touched three sets of wind chimes—high and tinkling, sweet notes in the middle range, and deep pipes resembling a church organ.

Giulia took in the layout, the lights, the water, the wind. A spur-of-the-moment wedding wasn't the place she would've chosen for the test run of Driscoll Investigations: Ghost Tamers. But like her first day of teaching in a Catholic high school with only six weeks of Methods classes under her veil, she alone held the power to flop or triumph.

She channeled Sister Mary Regina Coelis, who had indeed triumphed all those years ago, and said to Maureen, "You're on a tight schedule?"

Mingmei's friend adjusted her posture. "Yes, Sis—Giulia." She cleared her throat. "Mingmei and Stephan's wedding at noon, another wedding at one thirty, and a midsummer ritual at dusk. The ritual requires a complete change of decoration plus a cleansing."

Giulia made a note to have Rowan check her aura for lingering elements of the veil and habit. To her own surprise, the mental note didn't cause her to laugh at herself.

She gave Maureen a short, sharp nod. "All right. Please take Mingmei and Stephan into the house."

"Yes, ma'am." Maureen clapped twice. "Lovebirds, we need to give Giulia space. Come inside and share a pre-ceremony tea ritual."

New, cynical Giulia didn't believe her for a Pittsburgh minute. Maureen might brew three cups of tea, but Giulia would bet one of her own two daily allowed cups of coffee that the "ceremony" involved standing at the windows watching the Ghost Tamer do her work.

She kept her back to the house. Where to start to create an atmosphere of authenticity? This morning Jasper's hands kneaded the aura of the fictional divorcée looking for love. She could imitate him.

Giulia walked the curved back wall of the grotto, feeling the air and the undressed stones with precise, slow arm movements. At the halfway mark the breeze struck music from the pipe organ wind chimes. Giulia snapped her head in its direction. The breeze died. She stepped toward it with a show of purpose.

An unexpected benefit from all the years in the Cottonwood Community Theater orchestra pit: basic acting skills. She'd never labeled herself an actor, but what else could she call undercover work?

With her head tilted up toward the chimes, she manipulated the air around them before adopting her "scolding teacher" stance: feet slightly apart, left hand on hip, right finger pointing.

The wind rattled the other two sets of chimes. Giulia wagged her finger at them but kept her gaze on the most impressive set.

The topmost leaves in the grove of forty-foot cottonwoods fluttered, then stopped. Excellent timing.

Giulia coordinated her next series of gestures with the wind. First, extravagant hand-waving at the chimes. Second, wait for the treetop wind to make its way down to the grotto.

The pipes flung themselves back and forth. She brought her gestures in tighter and tighter until she appeared to create a bubble around the chimes. The wind slackened, then picked up.

Now what?

She paged through the last few musicals on which she'd worked the Pit.

Musicals.

The entire Driscoll clan had gathered for the birthday of one of the nieces this past weekend. The *Frozen*-themed party included a showing of the movie.

Giulia channeled her inner Elsa from the climactic thawing scene and flung the bubble up and away at the same moment the wind died.

All the chimes stilled. The lights flickered once.

Something tickled the back of her neck. Rather than slap the bug, she let it feast on her so she could maintain her potent ghost chaser image.

Another tickle, almost like a breath fluttering the hair at the nape of her neck. In other terms, instant karma in the form of a wasp sting as a reward for her fabricated performance. She waited a few heartbeats for the burning pain, but her skin remained inviolate. It must have flown away. Thank you, Saint Francis.

As though one of the Saints would get involved in this enterprise.

Giulia lowered her arms and held her breath. The wind did not return. She nodded at the pipe chimes, a final oversized gesture.

Flip-flops slapped the stone path behind her. Mingmei crashed into Giulia.

"Oh my god, oh my god, Giulia did you see it? Maureen saw it better than us, but as soon as she pointed it out we both saw it as clear as we saw you." She hugged Giulia hard enough to crack a rib.

Giulia had forgotten Mingmei possessed a black belt in karate. "Do not squash the pregnant woman's internal organs, please." Her voice was thinner than usual. Her lungs were not happy.

Mingmei leaped back. "I totally forgot. I'm such a moron."

Giulia took a deep breath—ahh—and smiled. "No, you're getting married in—"

"Seven and a half minutes," Maureen said. "Giulia, I admit I had my doubts, but you silenced them. You have the gift. Even I've never seen my ghost after all these years, yet one good rebuke from you and he comes like my Corgi when I shake the Beggin' Strips bag."

"He wore a morning coat," Mingmei said. "Like a butler or a groom or somebody from *A Christmas Carol.*"

Maureen beckoned them all under the lights. "He's certainly a flirt. Did he say anything when he touched your neck? His lips appeared to move."

Giulia crushed a wave of goosebumps with resolution. "No."

"He should know enough to keep his wandering ghost lips away from the neck of a married woman," Mingmei said.

Stephan spoke for the first time. "His face looked like you were his mom and you caught him stealing cookies." His *Beavis and Butthead* laugh was at odds with his Mixed Martial Arts physique. "Giulia, if our dojo in Kansas City turns out to be haunted, we're hiring you."

"What?" Giulia looked to Mingmei for an explanation.

Maureen took charge. "Wedding now. News later. Obey your Justice of the Peace. Where's the best man?"

A clone of Stephan in an identical suit appeared. Stephan produced incense and a small statue of Buddha. Mingmei latched onto Giulia's arm. "Did I mention you're my matron of honor?"

The brief ceremony combined the standard civil wedding plus traditional Buddhist vows with the lighting of candles and placing flowers before the Buddha.

A teenage boy with a brave attempt at facial hair took pictures. Completing the assistant manifestations, another teenage boy offered champagne flutes of Perrier from a scalloped tray.

Mingmei explained after the toast. "You heard right. We have our very own dojo at last." She kissed her new husband. "It's part of an initiative to work with at-risk kids. We applied a few months ago and they asked us if we'd be willing to relocate. But you won't get rid of me, Saint Giulia Ghost Slayer. I have your Skype address."

Nine

"Jasper, they all said they saw a male ghost in a Charles Dickens type of outfit."

Giulia sat at the table in the Tarot Shoppe's smaller reading room clutching a bottle of Sobe Mango Melon with a little too much force. Her right foot tapped the purple carpet in triple time.

"I felt something touch my neck, like a wasp or a mosquito. I was into the performance, so I didn't swat it away. They all said his—its— lips moved."

Jasper leaned against the wall, his voice as serene as always. "Rowan will be thrilled and annoyed she isn't hearing this in person." He touched the back of her hand. "Goosebumps aren't an unusual reaction the first time."

The bottle shook a little despite all her efforts.

"Can you find your center? I'd like to try for an impression of what connected with you."

"You think something really happened?"

"Certainly, and you do also." His eyebrows reached up to his hairline. "You didn't think we were a scam outfit, did you?"

Giulia controlled the urge to blush. "I'm forced to admit I've wondered about some things you've said. But in this case it's not you, it's me."

His laugh didn't disturb his serenity. "Isn't that a bad breakup line?"

She replayed it and managed a smile. "Clichés are not a service we usually offer."

"What you mean is you doubt your own skills, correct?"

She shook her head. "I've gone undercover enough. I know my acting limits."

"I'm not referring to stagecraft." Jasper hooked one foot around the leg of the other chair and pulled it next to Giulia. He sat with both hands on his knees and breathed in a slow, regular rhythm. Within a minute, Giulia's foot stopped twitching and she relaxed her death grip on the Sobe.

Her lips twisted. "I see what you did there."

"My bubble of personal space is as large as yours."

"And you seem to be aware of the defenses I've constructed around the bubble."

His slow smile appeared. "I have no desire to encounter them. Now here's my professional opinion: relax."

"Isn't that the favorite word of NFL quarterbacks when the fans are panicking?"

The smile turned into a laugh. "True. It's good advice. You're discovering a new dimension to an old skill. Give yourself time to get used to it, the way you break in a new pair of jeans."

Giulia put a hand on her belly. "By the time we return to jeans weather, this one will require me to buy the maternity kind."

Ten

The afternoon threatened to be a letdown after an impromptu wedding and ghost hunt. Wrong. Research into Dahlia's Board of Directors rivaled the plot lines of *As the World Turns*, not that Giulia ever watched soap operas.

Dahlia's newsworthy financial turnaround two decades ago began three rabbit trails which didn't end in three neat points. Financial side branches, gossip, and too little attention to the internet advice "think twice before pressing Send" afflicted the Board of Directors.

Giulia rubbed her hands à la Zane's "Simon bar Sinister" imitation and dialed the CFO's direct line.

Half an hour later she'd secured two appointments for today and one for tomorrow morning. With a stuffed veggie pita from Common Grounds in one hand, she drove to Dahlia's offices.

Only an October day with leaves at kaleidoscopic heights could increase the attractiveness of the office park Dahlia had chosen. Three different types of maples, plus sweet gums, oaks, and birches camouflaged one-story brick buildings and overhung narrow unlined roads. Multitudinous birds crowded the branches. Picnic tables, a bicycle path, and even a short Frisbee golf course filled the spaces between the trees.

Much like longing after Elaine Patrick's fabulous silk dress, Giulia was quite certain DI could not afford to relocate here. Office space in the suburbs was a whole 'nother world from town office space, even in a middling town like Cottonwood.

She parked in the twelve-space lot in front of the Dahlia side of its cozy building. A discreet sign on the other side advertised a chiropractor's holistic healing offices.

The lobby's gray carpet coordinated with the tasteful grouping of chrome art deco chairs and oval coffee table. A vase of real red and white dahlias graced the receptionist's chrome and glass desk.

"Welcome to Dahlia, the leader in elegant fashion. May I help you?"

The red and white pattern in her silk blouse coordinated with the flowers. Giulia gave it a seventy-five percent chance the effect was intentional.

"Good afternoon. I'm Giulia Driscoll with Driscoll Investigations. I have a two fifteen appointment with Mark Pedersen."

The young woman's eyes narrowed, but Giulia saw calculation in them rather than suspicion. She picked up her phone.

"Dona, Mr. Pedersen's two fifteen is here." A moment later she hung up and pointed down the hall to her left. "First door on the right."

Dona's closet-sized office barred the uninvited from the Chief Financial Officer's sanctum by virtue of her desk acting as drawbridge and moat to a cherrywood door. Dona did not rise when Giulia entered her doorless vestibule. Her silver hair coordinated with her blue and gray checkered dress. Giulia resisted the cumulative Dahlia effect's attempts to dismiss her as "bargain store knockoff." It didn't matter whether or not the label was correct. Intimidation and Giulia were familiar adversaries, and she had emerged victorious in ninety-nine percent of these battles.

"Mr. Pedersen asks that you give him a few minutes." She did not offer the lone chair to Giulia.

"Of course."

The vestibule lacked a bookshelf for her to study. Giulia checked out the walls. Surprise: The frames showcased magazine covers of movie stars in Dahlia creations. All except two: a small photograph of a smiling, plump older couple standing by a two-seater Cessna and a studio portrait of a severe, columnar woman next to a chinless man with a handlebar mustache. A young blonde girl stood between them.

Pedersen's guard must have known how to touch type, since her dark eyes followed Giulia's progress around the moat while her fingers kept moving over her keyboard.

The phone buzzed. "Mr. Pedersen is ready for you now." When she stood, Giulia was not surprised to see her high heels matched her dress.

Without further conversation, she opened the door behind her desk and closed it as soon as Giulia passed through. Perhaps Pedersen secretly longed for a butler.

A tall man of medium build sat at a huge mahogany desk with an inset leather surface. A glassed-in bookcase faced a wall of framed dress designs and more magazine covers. Giulia sensed a pattern.

He half-rose and held out a hand crisscrossed with tiny scars. "Ms. Driscoll, I'm Mark Pedersen. What can I do for you?"

If Pedersen did want his own butler, he needed to up his study of the British aristocracy. A member of that class definitely should not have moist palms. Or wear a camouflage baseball cap and a polo shirt with an embroidered smallmouth bass caught on a hook.

Fishing could be the sole reason he ate regularly, what with alimony payments to his two ex-wives and child support to three children in Catholic high school.

"Mr. Pedersen—"

"Mark, please." His mechanical smile conveyed the opposite of geniality.

"Mark. Driscoll Investigations has been retained to inquire into Dahlia's infrastructure."

The smile twitched. "May I see some identification, please?"

She placed her license in his outstretched hand. He inspected it like a bar bouncer checking for fake IDs. When he returned it, damp on the underside, his smile projected even less cordiality.

"I don't see why someone wants us to open our books to a private dick." He glared as though daring her to call him on his choice of words. "Who's the troublemaker?"

Giulia could produce a mechanical smile too. "Our clients are confidential."

"Don't bother with that old dodge. Blonde bitches number one and number two called me at two in the morning last Saturday hammered out of their greedy minds. Tiffany texted me a picture of her with her Justin Bieber clone of a boy toy while they talked. They're blonder than they know if they think they can squeeze even more alimony out of me. I don't care what the last stockholders' report said."

Keeping the insincere smile on her lips, Giulia brought out a pen and a miniature legal pad from her messenger bag. "I'm not at liberty to reveal our clients' names. Now according to my information, Dahlia is run jointly by you, Ms. Konani Hyde, and Ms. Sandra Sechrest."

"Darn right we run it, and have been for the past fifteen years. Elaine is a figurehead."

"Elaine?"

Smug looked much more natural on Pedersen's face. "The bottom-feeder lawyers are out of touch. Did Tiffany and Christie tell you Elaine started showing up here at the office to actually earn the huge salary she's entitled to?"

Giulia took meticulous notes on everything Pedersen was not saying, just like Rowan taught her this morning.

"That's the girl, get it all in writing. I'd like to have half a chance the next court date doesn't go all in their favor." He paused long enough for Giulia to look up.

"Your daddy give you our job too? At least you don't cower in the house and spend your allowance online."

Giulia experienced a strong desire to go drinking with Tiffany and Christie. Her pen hovered over the next empty line. "Elaine is not a regular contributor to the business?"

A shrug. "She is, but on her terms. She designs for us sometimes, but everything has to be conducted via Skype and email." He pointed with his thumb at a framed award on the wall behind him. "Her new line won second place in this year's CFDA Fashion Awards. But my ex-blondes should know better than to think an award translates to instant cash. You've got material to purchase, stock to produce, marketing and promotion, plus all the labor involved. We don't outsource to countries paying seven-year-old kids twenty-five cents a day to sew dresses in sweatshops."

"A decision one doesn't often hear about these days."

"It's good business, as well as the right thing to do."

Pedersen as *The Picture of Dorian Gray* appeared before Giulia, his touch of pomposity overlaying the suppressed anger on his face.

"Making our clothing in America puts our stock up, figuratively and literally, with the buying public. Our actual stockholders don't gripe because our clothes get into more upscale boutiques. The more boutiques we're in, the fatter their dividend checks get."

Zane would be able to corroborate or refute these facts soon. Giulia gave Pedersen a wide-eyed interested look. He bit.

"Konani, Sandra, and I consistently took Dahlia to new heights in the nine years we ran it ourselves. Even with Elaine as titular head, our P&L sheets are positive overall. Have you checked our stock numbers?"

"Yes." With a straight face, even though she hadn't.

"At least you didn't take the blondes' word for everything. It's refreshing to see a woman know enough to do the research before making a decision."

Non-violent Giulia checked an impulse to chuck his half-full coffee cup in his face. It must've been baby hormones.

"Yet two women are equal partners with you in Dahlia."

"It's a women's clothing business. Elaine's mother was a smart cookie who thought like a man. She knew we'd have to have females at the top to take the pulse of women's fashion trends."

Pitching the coffee was looking more desirable every second.

Pedersen placed both hands flat on the desk and leaned across the leather inset. "I'm now four minutes late for a three o'clock meeting. You tell the vampires they'll get zilch from their latest ploy. They'll have to support their boy toys on what they're already sucking out of me."

Giulia returned her pen and pad to her messenger bag and luxuriated in thoughts of the dirty laundry Zane would unearth about Pedersen. She would never use it unless they had a direct correlation to the suspected hostile takeover, but she didn't pretend to be above devouring them like Pedersen was in the crosshairs of *The Scoop*.

Picturing the local TMZ wannabe siccing their fangs into the CFO's ankle, she stood and held out her hand. "As one professional to another, thank you for sharing your information."

If Pedersen caught the sarcasm, his face didn't show it. But the heightened moisture level in his brief handshake left condensation on her palm.

Eleven

Pedersen buzzed his intercom, and Dona opened the door for Giulia.

"I'll be unavailable until after my three o'clock finishes," Pedersen said.

Dona nodded and with an equally expressionless face indicated the way back to the main lobby.

"May I help you?" the receptionist said. "Oh. Is your appointment finished? Thank you for visiting Dahlia."

Giulia was relieved to bring up a genuine smile. "My first one is, but I have another one with Konani Hyde at three fifteen."

The manicured eyebrows rose a fraction. "Let me see if she's available."

After a second discreet phone call, the receptionist pointed to the right-hand hallway. "Down this way. It's the last door on the right, just past the kitchen."

The closed doors of the first three offices on either side of the hall revealed nothing through their inset glass. Noise from an open office on her left spilled out into the hall long before she reached it.

Slowing her pace, she allowed herself a lengthy glance into an open workspace the size of three offices grouped together. Four computers and two wide format printers ringed the perimeter, but two long Formica-topped tables hogged most of the space. Bolts of cloth and paper dress patterns covered them. Mannequins and old-school dress forms huddled at one end next to four sewing machines. A radio balanced on a windowsill. Country-western hits competed with the printers, the sewing machines, and five people talking with or cussing at scissors, material, or screens.

A voice hailed her as she reached the kitchen archway.

"Are you Ms. Driscoll? Come on in. I'm Konani Hyde. The air conditioning in my office is on the fritz, so I'm camped in here for the duration. Don't you miss offices where windows actually opened? God, I could kill for fresh air, especially when the lilacs out there bloom in the spring and the leaves turn in the fall. Fall's my favorite season, especially since those are my best colors. Want some iced coffee?"

"Thank you, yes."

"Old school manners. Nobody says that phrase properly anymore. I bet you had a drill-sergeant grandmother like I did. Decaf? Me too. Pick a flavor."

Konani moved as rapidly as she talked. As the Keurig prepared two cups of Irish Crème decaf, she filled plastic cups with ice from the full-sized refrigerator/freezer and set out a carton of half and half.

"Stevia okay for you? I love the stuff, plus it's Fair Trade. All our supplies are Fair Trade, including our materials." She plucked at her shirred floral top. "This was made in Hawaii by my very own distant relatives." She filled Giulia's cup with coffee and cold water and passed it over.

They sat at a turned wood bistro table. Konani's ample rear overflowed the chair, which had apparently been chosen for its charm rather than its fitness for adult butts.

"I'm detoxing, but I can't give up my coffee." She pointed to said butt. "You don't want to know how long it took me to convince the stick women who design our clothes to create a line for women with real figures." She sipped through the ice. "I miss sugar, but my kids ruined my body. At least I blame them for it, especially when they're giving me the preteen Eyeroll of Death. How's your coffee?"

Giulia sipped and said it was fine. She used the moment to bring out her pad and pen and ask the same leading question.

"Our infrastructure? Really? Everything we're required to make available to the public is out there."

Dona came into the kitchen and went straight to the Keurig. When she started the brew cycle, she said over her shoulder, "Did she make the joke?"

"No. Can you believe it?"

Giulia put on Polite Smile Number Two. "The joke?"

"Jekyll and Hyde. I've only heard that line about ten thousand times." She turned her face toward Dona. "I'm not surprised she didn't because she's like Miss Manners in person. I wish I could convince her to take my brats for a week and beat politeness into them."

Lest Konani could read upside down, Giulia did not write out her annoyance at being discussed as though she wasn't in the same room with these women. She settled for joining the conversation. "Hyde is an unusual name these days."

"See? Is that the epitome of courteous conversation or what?"

Dona added milk and real sugar to two coffees. "You should've listened to your mother."

"I know, I know, but I was really full of myself when I snagged my hot babe." To Giulia again: "Elaine's mom had just cherry-picked me out of the secretarial gulag to be her personal assistant. This nobody army brat with no roots was important for the first time in my life. I refused to take my husband's nice, ordinary last name."

The middle finger of the hand holding her coffee cup raised itself toward Dona's exiting back. Her voice dropped. "She talks like she's far above the rest of us because she's Pedersen's guard dog." She leaned across the tiny table and lowered her voice further. "It kills her that she's not even the power behind Pedersen's throne. She's number four here behind Pedersen, Sandra, and me."

"I thought Elaine Patrick—"

"Yeah, yeah, that's what I meant. Elaine on top of the pyramid standing on our shoulders." A sigh. "Speaking of stick women, if only I had her figure."

What Giulia wrote now had more to do with Konani's patently false bonhomie than with Dahlia's internal structure. She tilted the legal pad a fraction closer to herself as she finished her current note with, *I wonder why I used to think the convent was the only morass of power plays and petty backbiting.*

"Belinda—Elaine's mom—was super to me. We worked together for three years. I never pushed her buttons because Mama Hyde didn't raise dummies."

"Elaine's mother was a shrewd business owner?"

"Her picture should be in the dictionary next to the word. Since someone sent you here to dig for dirt, you should know all about her slash and burn resurrection of Grandma and Grandpa's little dress shops."

Giulia drank more of the too-thin, too-sweet iced coffee. "I understood she and her husband owned the business jointly."

Konani crunched an ice cube. "You don't look the type to watch horror movies, but there's one from the eighties called *Basket Case*. This guy carries his surgically separated twin around in a basket. It's a hoot. The twin in the basket couldn't do much unless the full-sized twin let him. That's how important the Chinless Wonder was to Belinda's business plan. He golfed with dealers and drank with suppliers. Belinda brought the money and the balls."

"I see."

Another ice cube disintegrated under her teeth. "Seriously, can I pay you to come out to my place and teach my kids? You've got this conversation stuff down cold." She pointed a sky-blue fingernail at Giulia. "Joke. Nobody tells my kids what to do but me. And my hot babe, of course." Her head came closer to Giulia and her voice dropped again. "This will sound callous, but I'm glad the thieving masked killers got to Belinda before I had my own kids."

"Why?" Giulia stifled the need to push back from the table. Konani's bubble of personal space wasn't anywhere near big enough for Giulia.

"Because I'm not raising my daughter to be a fantasy-prone little princess. Elaine's going to end up like Howard Hughes: locked in her castle, peeing in bottles, and saving her toenail clippings." She circled a finger in the air next to her temple.

A young woman and younger man from the atelier entered the kitchen, arguing in an authoritative manner about rolled hems versus fused. Giulia and Konani finished their decaf while the designers popped open cans of Diet Pepsi and returned to the studio, debating and drinking.

Konani made a face at her coffee. "These hipster sugar substitutes may be good for the hips, but they don't have the heft of the real stuff."

"The small perks here at Dahlia appear to represent a management that wants to keep its employees happy," Giulia said.

"Yeah, we're all creative types except our number one number cruncher. We live on caffeine and junk food when we're on deadline."

She pushed her empty cup as far across the miniature surface as possible. "I'll say one thing for Elaine, she doesn't nickel and dime us while she lives in luxury. Have you seen her house? All it needs is the Knights of the Round Table." She patted her butt. "I live in a big old three-story monstrosity halfway to Mt. Lebanon. Keeps me active, otherwise I'd be able to carry groceries home on these cheeks. Are you one of those people who can eat anything and stay thin? No, don't tell me. I'd get jealous. Elaine's aunt is like that. Then again, her aunt probably keeps skinny worrying about how much of their allowance her husband loses on the horses every month."

"Allowances to relatives and a well-stocked refrigerator are all right for the bottom line?"

"If she wants to blow her money on useless relatives, that's her business. Dahlia has always given its designers bonuses when one of their dresses makes it to a magazine cover. Well-fed artists and healthy competition make for healthier profits."

"Then Dahlia is generating a profit?"

"You bet. Your client got hold of some outdated figures if they think we're easy pickings for a hostile takeover. We don't even need a white knight, if you know the term?"

Giulia donned her best imitation of a sparrow's bright interest in a tasty looking grass seed. "Outdated?"

"It's the aunt and uncle, isn't it? You can tell me. We've known they were social climbing parasites since the first Christmas after the murders." She checked the screen on her phone. "It's my turn to pick up the kids from soccer camp. Walk out to my car with me."

The hall easily accommodated two people side by side. Konani told Giulia about her twelve-year-old son's skills as a goalkeeper and her ten-year-old daughter's ability to nutmeg defenders at will.

"Her nickname on the pitch is Meg. The boys hate it. I made her a charm bracelet with it. I have my own jewelry storefront on Etsy, but I'm sure you know that. You look like a rose gold with lapis lazuli. My daughter wants a 'Meg' tattoo. Over my dead body, I told her."

As they crossed the parking lot, she slipped her arm through Giulia's. "Look, I know you can't tell me who hired you because of client privilege and all that." She waved at Dona and another woman smoking at one of the picnic tables. "We'll both pretend you're not mining us for a buyout by some super-rich player to be named later. Elaine can buy out pretty much any company if she wants to and not have to live on ramen for a single meal. Your clients are wasting their money."

"Thank you for the coffee."

Konani's laugh echoed across two parking lots. "I'm serious. You should open up a finishing school, like they used to have in the fifties and sixties." She released Giulia's arm and looked her up and down, tapping a finger against her pointed chin. "Definitely stick to etiquette advice and not how to dress, because you really aren't qualified for it." The wide smile reappeared. "I've subbed my own designs to that department's Powers That Be. I really hope they get accepted, because college isn't cheap. Have a nice day."

She bounced into her Mazda crossover and drove away. Giulia stared after her, wondering if she wore her hair high and puffy to hide the demon horns.

Twelve

"Psst. Ms. Driscoll. Over here."

Dona beckoned Giulia to the table where she and another woman were sitting.

"She got you with one of her zingers, didn't she? She taps that claw against her chin every time."

The other woman blew a smoke ring. "I'm head of design. One day I wore a lime green sundress and Konani told me it made me look like I was about to hurl." Another drag; another ring. "I'd love to deep-six her designs out of spite, but she's good. We'll sell a few thousand of each, and we'll all get Christmas bonuses. Cigs cost too much nowadays."

Dona said, "When my hair went all silver, she told me in that sugary voice how nice it was to see a woman not afraid to show her true age." The cigarette got stubbed out with extra vehemence. "I recommended she try Boudreau's Butt Paste for her neck pimples."

The head of design snorted. "I'm Shandeen, by the way. You set up a meeting with my boss tomorrow morning. Like my hair?" She ran her hands through her waist-length cherry red waves.

"It's lovely. Is it your own color pattern?" Giulia remained standing as neither woman had yet invited her to sit with them.

"See, Dona? That's a sincere compliment. Yes, I pick the main color and choose highlights to either blend or contrast. This time I wanted a summer evening, and I streaked it with violet and sapphire."

"It took Konani a whole day to come up with a sweet passive-aggressive insult." Dona checked her phone. "Cancer break over."

Shandeen took a last, long drag and extinguished her cigarette. "What did she say to you?"

Giulia repeated the judgmental clothing advice. Both women said, "Ouch."

"Let it roll off your back," Dona said. "Being targeted by Konani is a rite of passage at Dahlia."

They walked with Giulia to the Nunmobile. Shandeen ostentatiously pointed out a row of peonies in full bloom for Giulia to admire.

"Don't believe a thing either of them said about Elaine." With equally large gestures, Dona invited Giulia to smell a bush covered with small, old-fashioned pink roses. "Elaine is too sweet and their guts curdle every time they visit her."

"When Elaine got married three years ago, she inaugurated a Dickens Christmas party every year at her house. The difference between Elaine and the other three is Elaine treats us like we're all of equal importance to the company. How many super-rich business owners do that?" Shandeen gave Giulia an elaborate wink. "Admire the flowers a little more, okay?"

Dona said, "The other three thought for sure she had one foot in a padded room ever since her parents died. Pedersen convinced her aunt and uncle to funnel him the shrink reports when she was nine."

"Sechrest, my boss, used to offer the aunt first pick of new designs so she could get all the dirt on the heiress." Shandeen lit another cigarette. "She'd deliver them to the castle in person, stay two or three hours, then call in Pedersen and Konani for a conference."

"We'd gather at Shandeen's desk and listen in on her intercom. The other admins rigged it. You think Dona and I are snarky? We're amateurs compared to the Big Three." She held out her hand to Dona. "Rescue me, please."

Dona passed her the cigarette. "I've sat in on all Elaine's Skype conferences. You should've seen the faces on those three when Elaine pulled up a gigantic spreadsheet covering the past five years of the business and gave orders for a handful of operating changes."

The cigarette changed hands again. "Open your car door and start getting in. It'll give us another minute. Everything Elaine had us change improved the business. Those three bitched about it for weeks, but the next stockholder meeting was a smash hit."

Dona leaned through Giulia's window. "Elaine knows her stuff.

The big three are good, but they got too comfortable with being in charge. You know about Pedersen's two ex-wives, right? He's so broke he bummed lunch money off me twice last week. You'd think a CFO could manage his personal finances better."

Shandeen crushed the cigarette beneath one strappy pink sandal. "Konani's a greedy little beast. She plays at going back to a simpler era in her antique house—bought in imitation of Elaine's, you know—but she's like that old Mr. Magoo Christmas movie, where he plays Scrooge. She'd like nothing better than to roll around in piles of money."

Dona took Shandeen's place. "They both spend a little too much time at the casinos. Pedersen more than Konani. If he'd stop chasing gold-diggers, he might not have to beg his long-suffering admin for the price of a Big Mac."

Giulia stopped hiding her suspicions. "I appreciate this revealing gossip, but why do you trust me? Aren't you afraid you'll lose your jobs?"

Shandeen mimed patting Giulia on the head. "Every computer in this place pulled up your website a millisecond after you made the appointments."

"Pedersen called his divorce lawyer," Dona said, "then Konani stomped past me like I wasn't there and cut him off mid-call. Sechrest made it a threesome. When they split up, Konani's seasick-green tinge didn't blend with her orange dress at all."

They grinned in tandem.

"Start your car, okay?" Shandeen said. "We're not afraid to talk to you because we're two of the four employees who've been here since Elaine's parents took over. Elaine's grandparents were old school: they gave a crap about their employees. Elaine's parents were the opposite. No one was safe. My head was on the block once, but I worked up a spreadsheet showing the profit I generated was triple my salary and the length of the learning curve for the cheap college grad they wanted to dump me for."

Dona leaned into the window. "My longevity is simpler: I know too much about my boss. Plus I'm awesome at my job."

Shandeen leaned next to her. "Everyone, including us, thinks you're here to cut dead weight. Don't try to convince us otherwise. The

Holy Trinity has already knifed each other in the back. You can thank Belinda and Arthur Davenport for making your job easier."

Giulia returned the head pats. "Or perhaps making it harder."

The light dawned in tandem.

Dona slapped the door. "That's why you make the big bucks."

Shandeen stepped away from the window. "If you want to avoid the construction during rush hour, take the West End bridge."

Thirteen

The Nunmobile crept forward another car length. Three blocks in twenty minutes. Little Zlatan was suggesting she should've visited the bathroom before leaving Dahlia.

She risked taking her eyes off the road to search for an alternate route on Apple Maps. The phone's voice said, "In two hundred feet, turn right on Steuben Street."

"Thank you, Siri."

A motorcycle passed her on the shoulder. The light changed. Everyone moved forward another car length, including the Jeep with the shuddering bass on her left and the dueling panel vans behind her and the Jeep. A block ahead, a city bus cut off a taxi, crushing an orange traffic cone beneath its wheels.

Her closed windows and air conditioning spared her most of the car horn and pneumatic drill cacophony. Siri nagged her to turn right in one hundred feet.

"I will when I can move, thank you."

Another half-block. Relative freedom beckoned. Only one car in five chose the bridge route. More creeping. The thumping bass stopped for a blessed moment, then restarted with a new song.

A quarter-block. An eighth.

The Nunmobile took advantage of an opening too small for most of the other vehicles around her and made Siri happy.

"In one mile, take ramp on right to West End Bridge."

"Yes, ma'am."

One of the vans squeezed itself through the same opening, but the thudding Jeep did not. Traffic clogged the entrance ramp, but at least she could accelerate onto the bridge itself.

CRACK.

The steering wheel jerked out of her hands.

WHAM.

SCREECH.

The passenger side of the Nunmobile scraped along the guard rail at forty miles per hour.

POW.

A tire blew and the right front bumper twisted and smashed into the rail. The airbags deployed with the force of a prizefighter's punch to her chest. She slammed the brakes. The back end of the car lifted a hair, sending Giulia's stomach into outer space. She wrenched the wheel around. The right front tire spun in mid-air.

A van sped away.

Giulia stared out at the Ohio River, thinking irrationally, "At least I'm wearing clean underwear."

Her next thought: "Zlatan."

A bright red Dodge Caravan pulled over to the rail in front of her. The second the vehicle stopped, three small faces appeared in the back window. Another second later, two doors opened and six kids in soccer uniforms spilled out.

Giulia's ears rang. When she blinked, the deflating airbag pulsed before her eyes like a lava lamp. A sharp knock on her widow penetrated the temporary tinnitus.

"Miss? Are you all right?"

Giulia turned her head in a comical imitation of slow motion. Six young faces clustered around a woman wearing a backwards baseball cap and a t-shirt with a soccer club logo on the pocket.

The woman handed a phone to the tallest child. "Call 911."

"Cool!" The teenager dialed.

The woman knocked again. "Miss, can you hear me? Are you hurt?"

Giulia's hands, still clutching the steering wheel around the sagging air bag, refused to move. She scowled at her left hand. One by one, her fingers unclenched. She pressed the window switch. Cars roared past her faster than her eyes could process. She blinked several times.

"I don't think so. Hurt, I mean."

Relief filled the woman's face.

"This is just like *CSI*," said a young girl with a Captain America headband.

"Wait 'til I tell the guys at camp," said the smallest boy.

"Mom, we have to help her," said a boy with a mop of red hair.

"Avengers assemble!" said another boy with big brown eyes.

The soccer mom tapped the heads of the four smaller children. "Go stand by the back of the car."

"Mo—om."

"Now." Wind from the passing traffic snatched at her baseball cap and she stuffed it into her back pocket. "Crazy traffic. Move."

With much pouting and shuffling of feet in turf shoes, they obeyed. A double semi thundering by at that moment may have convinced them of the wisdom of getting out of the way.

The tall teenager returned the phone to her mother. "The 911 operator said maybe ten minutes because of the construction."

The mother pointed to the oldest boy. "Look under the front of the lady's car to see if anything's leaking."

"On it, Ma." He dropped flat on the pavement. A moment later his brown eyes reappeared above the crumpled hood. "I smell brake fluid and antifreeze, but no gas. No smoke either."

"Good." She leaned into the window. "Miss, I'm going to open your door. You should get out of the car just to be safe."

The adrenaline rush hit Giulia. Both hands started to shake.

A siren undercut the continual undercurrent of cars and motorcycles and trucks whizzing past.

"Miss, is anything broken?"

Giulia clenched her fists until the slight pain from her short nails digging into her skin pierced the reaction fog and quakes. She touched her legs, knees, elbows, and belly. "Everything appears to be intact."

"Good. My son is going to help you out of the car. Unbuckle your seat belt."

A strong, skinny arm came around Giulia's shoulders. "I've got you, ma'am."

Giulia allowed him to ease her up and out. She took a long, shuddering breath, another, then smiled at her efficient angels of mercy.

"Thank you. I'm a little wobbly."

"No surprise there."

Giulia turned her head. "Ow. Could you turn off the ignition?"

The boy grinned. "You bet." He stroked the key before handing the keyring to Giulia. "How does it handle? Can it drift around corners?"

His mother held up a warning finger. "This is not an episode of *The Grand Tour*." She transferred the finger to her other teenager. "I see the police and ambulance are about to reach us if enough people obey the law and let them through. Please herd those four back into the car."

Howls of protest from the players in question.

"Misfortune of being the youngest. You can watch through the back window. You two take their spot by the back of the car, please. Everyone stay out of the way of the emergency medical technicians and the police officers. Now."

All the soccer players obeyed as the ambulance and a black-and-white arrived simultaneously. Giulia's head threatened to burst from the combined lights and sirens. Fortunately the sirens quit when the vehicles stopped. To avoid the lights, she inspected the front end of her car. What she saw made her sit down hard on the lip of the guard rail.

The ambulance set out flares and one of the uniformed officers directed traffic out of the right-hand lane. The other approached the Nunmobile.

Soccer Mom took over. "Officer, this is all the fault of a dirty white panel van, one of those anonymous ones we always warn our kids about in Stranger Danger classes. It cut us off and deliberately *slammed* into this young woman's car. It didn't drive away after the first slam either. It pushed her car against the guard rail and it was going at least ten miles over the speed limit."

"Just like NASCAR, Ma."

"Hush up. Then, officer, it *rammed* the front of her car into the guard rail." She pointed out the obvious. "I'm quite sure the maniac wanted to push her right into the river."

"The back wheels got airborne, Ma. Tell him that."

"Just like Paul Walker in *The Fast and the Furious*, Ma."

"Both of you hush this instant. Don't distract the policeman."

While this triangle of information bombarded the police officer, the EMT put Giulia through concussion protocol.

"I didn't hit my head." She blinked after the flashlight stopped blinding each eye. "The seat belt kept me in place."

"You would've pitched through the window and into the river without it," he said.

Giulia swallowed.

"Sorry. I was trying to compliment you on your foresight."

She clutched his wrist. "I'm three months pregnant."

He fired questions at her: First pregnancy? Any complications? Any pain in your abdominal region? Then he had her lay supine on the asphalt and listened for the baby's heartbeat.

"Good and steady, from what I can hear with this crazy traffic." He helped her sit up. "Pregnancy hormones made my wife cry all the time too." He handed her a piece of gauze. "Closest thing I've got to a tissue."

Giulia pressed the thin white material to her eyes while he worked on her shoulder. "Ouch."

"You've pulled a few muscles here. Rotator cuff seems intact. Doesn't require a sling unless you'd like extra sympathy from the husband." He winked.

That brought out a real smile. "I'm good."

He finished with the rest of the points of contact between her body and the insides of the car. "So are your neck and knees. I think you avoided whiplash too."

"They came at me from the side."

"Right. You're not in your third trimester, so take ibuprofen for the aches you'll have tomorrow morning. See your GP for the shoulder, and I recommend a sonogram for the baby as a precaution."

"I'll make the call as soon as I get home."

Both older soccer players hovered at the elbows of the police officer now.

"It really was like watching *Rizzoli and Isles*."

"The van went after the little car like Godzilla stomping Tokyo."

"I only wish I'd seen the license plate," their mother said. "Just a second." She signaled the four inside to come out. "Did any of you see the white van's license plate?"

Eagerness drained from their faces.

"No, Ma."

"It looked dirty."

"Yeah, like it was covered up on purpose."

Enthusiasm returned.

"Maybe it's a bank robbery gone bad!"

"Or Homeland Security chasing a terrorist!"

"Cool!"

The officer turned away from the kids to hide a smile. "Ma'am, can you give me your version of what happened?"

Giulia thrust calculations of the repair bill and concomitant insurance increase out of her head. Speaking at a pace to allow him to write without strain, she described the traffic jam, the jeep and two vans, the turn off, the single van, and the attack.

"It was deliberate. I'm sorry I didn't get a look at the license plate. I should've thought as well as acted."

"Ma'am, your instincts prevented a much worse outcome. Did you notice anything unusual about the vehicle?"

Giulia squeezed her eyes shut and blocked out the traffic, the lights, and the chattering soccer family. "No." She opened them and made a frustrated face. "It was a plain white panel van with no markings I could see. Like *The Scoop*'s van."

She heard her own words. Why would *The Scoop* try to run her off the bridge?

The officer said, "The who?"

Giulia's grin stretched her entire face. "You just made my afternoon."

A flatbed tow truck pulled inside the perimeter created by the flares. Giulia finished giving the officer her information and handed her AAA card to the truck driver. As they discussed collision shops, the soccer family piled back into their Caravan.

With the Nunmobile's triage destination agreed upon, Giulia retrieved her messenger bag. The driver winched the car onto the flatbed.

Giulia walked over to the soccer family. "Thank you for all your help."

"Are you okay?" said three of the six.

"Would you like us to follow you?" said their mother. "Everybody buckle yourselves in, please. We're going to get McDonald's for supper."

Cheers from the passengers.

"Tonight was supposed to be mystery leftover packets on the grill. You're their hero, Ms.—I never got your name."

Giulia handed her a business card. "Your kids might be interested to know what I do for a living."

The mother held the card at arms' length. "My reading glasses are in my purse...holy cow. They're going to mob you." She steered Giulia by the elbow to the Caravan's middle window. "Guys, we've been helping a real-life private eye." She held up the card.

Six voices answered at once.

"No way!"

"Cool!"

"Lemme see—" A hand snatched the card.

"Can we see your gun?"

"Can we take your picture?"

"Mom, please take our picture with the private eye."

"Please?" Five voices echoed the request.

The tow truck driver yelled, "Ready to go."

Giulia put her back against the side of the Caravan, and six mouths breathed down her neck and into her ears.

Their mother said, "One-two-three—everybody say 'Sherlock.'"

Fourteen

"I'll get black-and-whites to stop them for speeding every time they get on a highway. I'll get their drivers' licenses suspended. No. I'll get them revoked."

Frank paced the kitchen of their Cape Cod, gesturing at the windows, the walls, the ceiling. Giulia sat at the table drinking sweetened iced tea to wash down the ibuprofen.

"Honey, I don't know for certain it was their creeper van. *The Scoop* doesn't own the only unmarked white panel truck in town."

"If you'd seen the license plate I could go after them with a clear conscience." He opened the refrigerator, unscrewed the cap of a Black and Tan, and drank.

"As I told the uniformed officer at the scene, I was occupied with keeping my poor car out of the river."

Her husband stopped pacing to embrace her. "Screw the car. You kept yourself out of the river." He placed both hands over her stomach. "Zlatan, what do you think of your mother's driving skills? Can she perform under pressure or what?"

Giulia said in all seriousness, "I'm worried he'll be born an adrenaline junkie."

"Why is that bad? I'll strap him to my back and take him motorcycle riding for his first birthday."

"Only if you agree we are naming him Patrick or James or something else Irish and normal."

"Anything for my kickass wife."

The doorbell rang. Frank left the room and returned with two thick, wrapped sandwiches.

"No cooking after traumatic experiences. Your dinner, madame."

Giulia unwrapped hers. "Bánh mì?" She pulled Frank's face down to hers and kissed him. "Zlatan and his mother approve." She didn't speak again until she'd swallowed the first bite. "Please tell me this was hideously expensive so I'll be compelled to learn how to make it at home."

"This is why all my brothers are jealous." He opened another beer and refilled Giulia's iced tea.

She took her time chewing her next bite. "Another reason the van might not belong to *The Scoop*." She told him about Shandeen and Dona and their "helpful" directions to avoid the road construction.

"What is this company? Real Housewives of—" He directed a helpless look at her.

"Dahlia."

"Yeah, the flower." He opened a search window on his phone. "Dresses. More dresses." A whistle. "They have to be making money hand over fist with these prices."

"I was informed today they use all fair trade labor and materials." She finished her sandwich. "This is definitely going to be added to my copycat takeout recipes."

"The husband approves." He gathered the wrappers and tossed them in the trash.

Giulia opened her phone. "Hold on to something." She dialed *The Scoop* and put it on speaker.

"You've reached *The Scoop*. We want to know all the details! Leave us a message with your story and our investigative team will turn over every rock."

"This is Giulia Driscoll. An unmarked white panel truck tried to shove my car into the Ohio River a few hours ago. Convince me it wasn't yours."

Fifteen

Ken Kanning, the face of *The Scoop*, picked up before Giulia completed her final sentence.

"Ms. Driscoll, what? Where? Today? Did any traffic cameras catch it?" If he was anxious or guilty, his mellifluous voice betrayed nothing.

"I am not aware of any traffic cameras on the West End Bridge."

Frank mouthed *On the ramps* as the sounds of keystrokes came through the speaker.

Kanning confirmed it. "Only on the entrance and exit ramps, dammit. Where's excessive government oversight when I need it?" More typing. "What time?"

To her chagrin, Giulia spoke reasonably fluent Kanning. "Approximately quarter to five."

New, faint clicks replaced the keyboard taps coming from Giulia's speaker. *Mouse clicks* Giulia and Frank mouthed at each other, then grinned.

"There it is. Maybe. These traffic cameras are pieces of crap." His voice changed. "Note to Bull: we need to do an in-depth on the tax dollars wasted by Cottonwood's bloated political machine."

Frank smothered a laugh. Giulia made a face at him and said into the phone, "You haven't answered my question."

The typing stopped. "You had a question?"

In precise syllables, Giulia repeated her reason for dialing him.

"Ms. Driscoll—Giulia—I'm stunned you'd consider *The Scoop* your antagonist for even an instant of time."

Frank dashed into the garden and smothered his laughter in a zucchini leaf the size of a dinner plate.

Giulia put her back to the garden to avoid the laughter contagion.

"Mr. Kanning, please don't waste my time or your acting skills. We have always been antagonists. Our temporary truce over the Doomsday Prepper camp was exactly that: temporary." She cut off a splutter. "You stop at nothing for a story, and I do everything I can to protect my clients. You have one chance to tell me which of your developing stories you think I'm sabotaging before I involve the police."

A melodramatic sigh. "Ms. Driscoll, I solemnly swear we would never resort to thuggery." More keystrokes. "I'm sending you today's itinerary. Pit Bull can verify it."

"Your cameraman is hardly an impartial source."

"Jesus, did you break your minuscule funny bone in your accident?"

Silence from Giulia caused muttering from Kanning.

"Okay, okay. I apologize. From eight to eleven thirty we were in the studio making final edits to today's episode. At eleven thirty we ordered in dim sum. I have the timed and dated receipt. We drove to the Cottonwood Central School District offices at quarter to one to set up our exposé of the county-wide high school football underground gambling ring."

Giulia followed his recital on the itinerary she'd opened on her phone screen.

"We left at 3:10 when two power-grabbing underlings threatened to have us arrested for trespassing and endangering the welfare of a child. In July, when the youngest person on the grounds was the twenty-something lawn maintenance guy. We drove from there to the Mobil Station on Maple and French. You know it?"

"Yes. It's the one with the Model T mounted on the roof."

"Okay. We gassed up and Bull saw our left rear tire was low. Took the pit jockey almost an hour to squeeze us in and repair the leak. After that we drove back to the station to work on the gambling footage."

With the exception of the time spent on the flat tire, Kanning's recitation matched the day's planned timeline.

"Well, Ms. Driscoll? Are we exonerated?"

She allowed herself an inaudible sigh. "Yes."

"Don't we get an apology?" A pout crept into his glib voice.

She did not allow herself to gag. "You'll admit your track record lends itself to suspicion."

Self-righteousness eclipsed the pout. *"The Scoop* is dedicated to exposing corruption, to giving our viewers a story they don't dare miss, and of course to non-violence." When Giulia didn't reply, he continued: "Think about it, Ms. Driscoll. You're on our side now. *The Scoop* protects its benefactors."

Frank whispered in her ear, "I bet now you regret calling them in to help bust up the Doomsday Prepper sex and drug cult."

Giulia jumped. She hadn't seen him return to the kitchen. He backed away from her Unruly Student Glare, but the grin on his face said it all.

Kanning's voice: "Ms. Driscoll? You still there?"

"Yes. Thank you for your infor—"

"Don't hang up. You must be on a hell of a trail to have someone gunning for you."

"Our clients are confi—"

"Hold it. I just realized something. Your car crasher drove a white van like ours. They must be trying to frame *The Scoop.* Son of a—" He hung up.

Giulia's forehead came to rest on the cool glass top of the kitchen table.

Frank came to the back of her chair and massaged her shoulders. "Maybe his narcissistic conspiracy theory will keep him out of your hair."

"I will never be that lucky."

Sixteen

At six the next morning, Giulia's muscles discovered a correlation between overdoing it at the gym and surviving a car accident.

Despite the seventy-four-degree temperature at that hour of the morning, she ditched her plans for a cool shower and instead soaked in a tub loaded with Epsom salts. A fresh dose of ibuprofen and liberal slathers of Biofreeze followed. The pungent scent preceded her into the bedroom. Frank rolled to the other side of the bed between one snore and another.

By seven thirty she was armed with strong, caffeinated, homemade coffee, had left a full travel mug on the counter for Frank, and had worked through most of the stiffness.

Bracing herself, she opened the garage door.

A school-bus yellow Chevy Aveo hatchback squatted in the Nunmobile's place. She'd expected a troupe of circus clowns to tumble out of its five doors the moment she saw it. It had been the only sub-compact available in the Enterprise lot attached to the collision shop.

She hated it, but she was also a Cradle Catholic and the proper response had been ingrained in her since grade school. She settled herself in the Clown Car, turned the ignition, rolled down the manual window, and offered it up.

Frank had limited his comments to a spate of laughter and a photo sent to his partner, his boss, and all four of his brothers. The replies had been as expected.

"Give it some HGH."

"Is it still using a pacifier?"

"Where's its clown nose?"

She settled into the driver's seat. "All right, Clown Car, let's make the best of our temporary partnership."

Forty minutes later, she pulled into the same Dahlia parking spot as yesterday. A black Nissan Sentra took a spot up against the landscaping a few minutes later.

Giulia chomped an Altoid and got out first, leaving her empty travel mug in the single cup holder. She'd forced herself not to dress up for this last Dahlia interview. When Sandra Sechrest stepped onto the blacktop, Giulia knew her decision had been correct. Nothing in her closet was worthy of Sandra's black and white spectator pumps, white linen sheath dress with black edging, and onyx earrings and pendant.

"Ms. Driscoll?" Sandra's voice was as cool and cultivated as her ensemble.

Giulia held out her hand. "Good morning, Ms. Sechrest."

"Please call me Sandra. Thank you for being prompt. I'll let us into the building."

She unlocked the main door and entered a code on the security system keypad. A red light changed to green and a repetitive beep-beep-beep fell silent.

"May I offer you a cup of coffee?"

"Thank you, no."

Sandra nodded and sipped a green concoction from a double-walled tumbler. "I haven't touched coffee in years. Probiotic smoothies with matcha tea are essential for the modern hectic lifestyle. They have detox benefits as well. Have you tried them?"

"Not yet." Giulia wondered if Sidney had discovered the joys of drinking what looked like toxic miso gazpacho.

The third member of the Dahlia trinity expounded on the gastrointestinal and complexion benefits of her drink. "People insist I look much younger than my actual age." With a hand on the doorknob of the office opposite Mark Pedersen's, she rounded on Giulia. "How old do you think I am?"

Giulia earned her reputation for diplomacy once again by answering "Thirty-three" when the honest answer was "Mid-forties with a face lift and possibly a lift of other parts."

Sandra opened her office door with a satisfied smile on her frosted rose lips. She cranked the air conditioning and turned on a desk lamp. The burnt orange and gray décor complemented her skin tone and clothes. Even the required Dahlia magazine covers were framed in burnt orange and gray.

"Please have a seat. I suppose it's useless to ask who hired you?"

Sandra's desk was positioned so her back was to the west-facing window. Even without the afternoon sun, the light imparted a soft-focus halo to her face.

At least Giulia didn't have to squint to see her at this hour. "Our clients are confidential."

Another nod. "I expected as much. What do you want to know?"

"How has Dahlia progressed now that Elaine Patrick has been its official head for three years?"

"I see." Sandra swirled her cup of green ooze. "Our financial statements are always available to our stockholders, but to prove to your client we have nothing to hide, here is the secure web address and the password." She wrote on a white sticky note watermarked with a pink dahlia flower. "Our finances are robust. Our clientele is loyal. Our employee turnover is one of the lowest in the industry." Another camouflage movement, this time a green probiotic sip. "No offense to you. You're only doing your job, but I can't stand the practice of poking and prying for a business' weak spots. Mark, Konani, and I have maintained a successful company under circumstances that would have collapsed a weaker infrastructure. Konani and I may have held subordinate job titles nine years ago, but we were indispensable to Belinda and Arthur, Elaine's parents. I don't fault Elaine for wanting to take an active role in her family's business. It's what anyone would do. But the minute she turned twenty-one, she dug her pastel pink fingernails into the guts of our hard work. Word got out—how could it not?—and the survivor of the Masked Massacre became news again."

As much as Giulia typed faster than she wrote, she stuck to her legal pad. Sandra didn't recoil when Giulia flipped to a new page, confirming her assessment of the Dahlia Triumvirate's aura. Technology = Spies. Unplugged note taking = Safe. She'd encountered otherwise sensible business people like Sandra before, who embraced most technology but continued to believe that if they somehow didn't type a fact into a computer themselves, their company's information was hidden from the Zanes of the world.

Giulia's Dahlia Suspicions Bullet List expanded.

- Double books?
- Snogging the boss?
- Snogging bosses, plural?
- Skimming the profits?
- Padding the expense accounts for Fair Trade buying junkets?

She'd have to tell Rowan and Jasper about how she tuned into the Dahlia aura, but first she interrupted Sandra's flow. "Masked Massacre?"

Dyed platinum eyebrows rose toward a matching platinum widow's peak. It hit Giulia that even the green of the smoothie complemented Sandra's color scheme.

"It's good to discover not everything is public knowledge."

Giulia didn't crack. "May I ask for the relevant details?"

Sandra leaned forward, the corners of her mouth crimping. "You'll think I'm a scandal monger."

Seventeen

"Not at all," Giulia said, and it was true. Dahlia wasn't staffed by scandal mongers. That label implied amateurishness. Dahlia was a Jerry Springer show waiting to happen.

Sandra fiddled with her telephone cord. Giulia catalogued this first edgy movement from her.

"Are you familiar with sugar skulls?"

Talk about a question out of a clear blue sky. "I've seen them on the news for *Día de los Muertos* celebrations."

"Never up close?" A shiver. "They're worse than those antique china dolls, the kind with eyes that follow you."

If Giulia were to practice Tarot reading on Sandra, would she include skeletons or dolls in the interpretation to spook her into revealing more, or would she craft a soothing, positive reading to encourage further shared confidences? She'd have to check how Rowan would handle it.

"Were Elaine's parents in Mexico when they were killed?" She didn't have to flip to her notes on Muriel's version of Elaine's history. The details were at the front of her brain.

"No. Nothing like that. They were in their own house. Multiple murders in the sanctity of the American Dream generated more splashy headlines and paparazzi fodder." She pushed the remains of her smoothie to one side. "Belinda and Arthur slashed and burned Dahlia to make it profitable again. Practically every business magazine wrote a feature piece on them."

"Isn't that a good thing?"

"It was, until one magazine published a photographic tour of their house. You know Elaine calls it a castle? I refuse. At the time the police were dealing with a series of unsolved home invasions. Security systems were disabled and only drugs and money were taken. Each time, the police found the homeowners tied to chairs and shot through the head."

"I see."

"One Monday morning Belinda and Arthur didn't show up for scheduled meetings. Trust me when I say this was unlike both of them. Arthur was more easygoing than his wife, but he knew how to run a business as well as she did. Konani called Belinda's cell. I called Arthur's. Then Elaine's private school called. She hadn't shown up either. When we called the house and got no answer there, we drove over. The front door was locked and we went around to the back door." Another shiver. "A sugar skull mask stared up at us from the threshold."

"The home invaders liked to brag?"

A nod. "It was their trademark. We called the police and Mark Pedersen. Everybody showed up at once."

"What did you find?"

"A stench I never want to experience again as long as I live, that's what we found first. The medical examiner concluded they'd been killed on the Friday before. Belinda and Arthur had been tied to kitchen chairs and shot through the forehead. The maid, the cook, and the butler were in the kitchen, also dead. All of them wore sugar skull masks. Their open, cloudy eyes stared out at us through the eyeholes." She groped for the rest of the smoothie and finished it. It appeared to steady her. "I'm better now. I don't tell this story too often."

Her lips crimped again. Giulia decided it was Sandra's way of expressing Muriel's ghoulish interest.

"They'd opened the safe and ransacked the medicine cabinets. Belinda liked Xanax, and Arthur had a stash of Oxycontin from his back surgery. They'd also found the wine cellar and the Glenmorangie. Have you ever had a taste? It transports you to another world. However, the reporters showed up while only the one patrol car was there. They took pictures through the windows and then Mark ran out the door to lose his breakfast on the back porch. They fell on us like rabid weasels. Konani, that airhead, talked to them. The ambulance and coroner and a dozen more police finally arrived and herded them off the property."

"What about Elaine?"

The air conditioning turned off, and Giulia's ears throbbed with the silence. Sandra's voice came out too loud.

"We forgot about her at first." She lowered her voice to match the quiet room. "Nobody liked her back then. She was a prissy little goody two-shoes. We avoided her as much as possible. But when we didn't find her body, we scattered throughout the house. The police were furious."

"Because you might have been destroying evidence."

"We didn't care. Just because we didn't like the little princess didn't mean we wanted her dead. We ran into all the rooms like those panicky idiots from the movie *Clue*. We finally heard this creepy muffled crying and moaning on the second floor." Her crimped edges turned wry. "The three of us thought it was a ghost. In a perfectly normal house."

"A perfectly normal house where multiple murders had just taken place." Giulia used her own body language to convey a conspiratorial "I'll never tell of your lapse in adulting."

Sandra straightened her spine. "We found Elaine in a closet. She was starving and dehydrated. The most she remembered afterward was Belinda locking her in there as punishment."

"Did the reporters take that part of the story and run with it?"

"Good God, no. The police and the ambulance techs made themselves into a wall and got her away to the hospital with those jackals thinking it was one of the dead bodies." A sneer distorted her frosted lips. "All reporters should get genital herpes. But that wasn't the scandal. The Sugar Skull murderers weren't used to Glenmorangie. Two of them got drunk enough to leave DNA on the lips of the bottles."

"Criminals always seem to make one crucial mistake."

"I've heard that before. It certainly proved true in this case. A week later, the police caught up with two of them as they tried to sell the Oxy and Xanax. Talk about headlines. There were five in the gang, and they'd been living in non-chain hotels using fake IDs where they could pay cash." An elaborate wink. "They were living together. All five of them. They liked to videotape, if you get what I mean. They still had some of the Glenmorangie, and two of the women were wearing Belinda's diamonds. You should look it up. There was talk of making their crime spree into a movie, but it fizzled out."

Giulia finished a sentence on her legal pad. "I gather the story resurfaced when Elaine turned twenty-one."

The grey eyes conveyed disgust. "Perry Ignatius proposed to her on her birthday. The society pages lapped it up. 'Heiress to Dahlia More Than a Pretty Face.' You get the idea. But she refused to give them interviews and Perry Ignatius called in some favors. Voilà. The jackals slunk back to their holes, and Elaine was free to rearrange Dahlia to her liking."

"Not to yours?"

A single eyebrow raised itself. "Elaine may have achieved an MBA faster than most mortals, but she'd do well to ask the advice of the three people who kept her business solvent while she was hiding in her bed listening to her nanny read soothing pabulum."

Sandra tilted her head as she scrutinized Giulia. "You should wear red. Claret and crimson are your colors." She typed and spun her monitor to face Giulia. "These are from our new fall line."

Giulia complimented the dresses. The colors glowed and the linen and silk appeared fine enough to flow like water through her hands. The prices reflected her assessment.

"You're pregnant, aren't you?"

Caught off guard, Giulia admitted the fact.

"I graduated from nursing school a few months before Arthur hired me. I never looked back, but some skills stick with you." She spun her monitor back around. "I've been telling Mark we need a maternity line. It's a huge untapped market. I'm sending him another email while it's fresh in my mind." As she typed, she continued, "Your boss isn't happy, right? Male supervisors always see pregnancies as a personal inconvenience."

How fascinating. A woman in power assumed the woman in front of her must be in a position of subservience. Giulia wrote in the margin of her current sheet: borrow *Remington Steele* DVDs from the library.

While Sandra typed Giulia said, "You mentioned that Elaine's noises from the closet sounded ghostlike. Did you have any reason to think the house might be haunted?"

Sandra hit the Enter key with force. "Ridiculous. Ghosts are nothing more than a device used to frighten children into obedience."

"I see."

"We only thought of ghosts because we'd just discovered five dead bodies one floor below us."

"I see."

She stood. "I have three more appointments this morning. If you want to know who put ideas into Elaine's head about how we kept Dahlia afloat, talk to her tutors. I'll spell their names. Veronika Cameron and Clark Wagner. Veronika was the first nanny. When Elaine got old enough, her aunt and uncle replaced her with Clark." The rose lips pressed together. "Never trust an MIT grad. Every one I've encountered thought only of how to take advantage of anyone not in their exclusive geek club."

Giulia tallied the collateral damage as Sechrest buzzed her out.

- Sechrest suspects Elaine's tutors control her mind after all these years and they've convinced her to make a clean sweep of Dahlia.
- Hyde fingers Elaine's aunt and uncle because they have a history of mistrust.
- Pedersen defaults to his ex-wives.
- Dona and Shandeen give even odds to the Board of Directors secretly initiating the investigation.
- Everyone is willing to trample everyone else to be the last one standing when diabolical DI turns in its report.

If life imitated the movies, the Dahlia building would ooze fear and mistrust like the grocery store in *The Mist*.

Eighteen

Giulia checked Dahlia's parking lot for white panel vans. Giulia checked the streets for white panel vans. Giulia checked her rearview mirror every block for white panel vans.

At least the radiology clinic's parking lot was large enough to give her a three-hundred-sixty-degree view of all cars in all rows.

An hour later, she called Frank. "Zlatan is one hundred percent fine. Growth rate normal, development on track, and his mother suffers only from bruises and the lack of her Nunmobile."

Twenty minutes later, Giulia entered DI's building through the back door, paused to inhale Common Grounds' Thursday special—Crème Brulée—and promised herself a large with half and half as her second allowed Real Coffee of the day.

Her legs protested the steep stairs. Another reason to seek and destroy the creeper van. How many more after effects would surface? She didn't have time for this.

Zane held out muscular arms to her as soon as she walked in the door. Half a dozen pink phone message slips fluttered from one hand.

"Thank the gods you're here. Ken Kanning called at seven and left a message. At seven thirty and left another message. At eight he demanded to know where you were. At eight thirty, ditto. At nine he got huffy. At nine thirty he accused me of blocking his access to you. What got his panties in a bunch?"

Giulia tried without success to keep a straight face. Zane's answering look would've wrung pity even from Giulia's former Superior General.

"I was nearly run off the West End bridge and into the river yesterday by a white van. I called Kanning last night and made him prove he wasn't responsible."

"What?" Both Sidney's soprano and Zane's Bogart baritone leapt into higher registers.

Giulia held up both hands. "I'm fine. Just some sore muscles. The baby is fine too. The Nunmobile is in the shop, but is expected to make a complete recovery."

The normally unobtrusive Zane rivaled Sidney for babble after that. Giulia told them the entire story, emphasizing the Soccer Mom with her van full of players and her own delight at the officer's complete ignorance of *The Scoop*.

The phone rang. Zane picked it up, held it away from his ear, and put the caller on hold. "Talk of the devil."

"I'll take it. Go downstairs and take a look at the abomination I'll be driving for the next several days."

Giulia sat at her desk before she took her personal cross to bear off hold. "Giulia Driscoll speaking."

"Finally. You have to tell me the name of your client."

"Mr. Kanning, our clients are confidential."

"Only to the public and the press. Not between colleagues. Come on, Ms. Driscoll. You have to admit we're allies now. *The Scoop* is mixed up in this adventure. Our necks are on the line with yours."

"I'm sorry, Mr. Kanning, but no."

She got the impression he was gathering his forces. When he spoke again, Ken Kanning the silken-voiced replaced Kanning the ambulance chaser.

"Ms. Driscoll—Giulia—you know when we work together we bring the culprit to justice faster. Remember what a great team we make. You did watch our two-part special on the Doomsday Cult exposé, didn't you?"

Only because Frank DVR'd it and brought his entire family over for a viewing party. Four Driscoll brothers plus wives, Father Pat, Giulia's in-laws, and grand in-laws all clustered around the TV in their Cape Cod's not nearly big enough living room. Frank and Pat *MST3K*'d the entire hour.

"That's not the issue, Mr. Kanning. You've established your alibi for yesterday's accident. Any connection with our current case is ended. Goodbye."

Sidney poked her head around the doorframe. "You look like curdled milk."

"A standard effect of a conversation with Kanning. He may leave us alone for a day or two."

Zane's head appeared on the opposite side of the doorway. "Ms. D., you've been cheated. That's not a car in the parking lot. It wants to be a car when it grows up."

"I think it's cute," Sidney said. "How's the gas mileage?"

"Very good, but it's no substitute for the Nunmobile. We have bonded like a rescue dog and its owner." She winked at Zane. "Now if a gaggle of ghost clowns come piling out of the yellow nightmare at midnight, I'll be able to use them as practice for our new client's requirements."

Sidney huffed and returned to her desk. Giulia followed, beckoning to Zane.

"Guys, the suspects in this one are multiplying like coat hangers in an empty closet. Can I hijack you?"

Zane held up his thumb and index finger a millimeter apart. "I'm this close to getting into Dahlia's financials."

"You're excused. Sidney, what about you?"

"I have to meet a suspicious future father-in-law at eleven."

Giulia glanced at the clock over the main door. "A little less than an hour. We can start."

Sidney sat in Giulia's client chair with her preferred note-taking vehicle, a single subject college ruled notebook. "What were the major players like?"

Giulia shook her head. "We'd use up all our time. A multi-platform presentation is required to do justice to the Holy Trinity of Dahlia."

Sidney, snorted, coughed, and scowled at Giulia. "You'd better confess that to Father Carlos or I'll tell your brother-in-law on you."

Giulia pretended to pout. "You never used to be evil."

"Catholicism has irrevocably altered me." But Sidney couldn't hold her serious face and ruined the drama with giggles.

"Pat will have a great deal to answer for one day."

Sidney opened the notebook. Giulia spelled out the names of the aunt and uncle, both tutors, and the two smoking admins and described their relationship to Elaine. Sidney tugged her left earlobe, a habit she'd admitted to acquiring from singing lullabies to Jessamine.

"All these plus the original three? Money corrupts."

"It does. Speaking of such corruption, it's a good thing Cissy Newton joined up with Muriel, because costs are increasing exponentially."

"Now that I'm a homeowner with a family, I love the sound of client invoices multiplying." Sidney stood. "I'll start at the top with the aunt and uncle."

"I'll take the admins at the bottom."

Giulia finished with Dona in short order. She participated in every activity sponsored by the Polish Falcons and engaged in multiple pierogi and Krupnik discussion groups. Her worst fault appeared to be addiction to high-profile causes. Giulia's favorite was a front-page newspaper photo of Dona and four other women chained to the porch of a Planned Parenthood office as six perplexed uniformed officers attempted to arrest them. Giulia wondered how she found time to sleep.

Shandeen's hobbies were equally innocuous: artistic hair dye, homegrown tobacco, intricate tattoos. And *The Scoop*.

"Zane, Sidney, you have to see this."

They came running. Giulia pointed to Shandeen's blog up on her screen.

"She photobombed Ken Kanning?" Sidney, laughing.

"Multiple times?" Zane, incredulous.

"Watch." Giulia double-clicked on one video clip after another. Through luck or persistence or both, Dahlia's chief designer managed to be within Pit Bull's viewfinder in Dahlia clothing a dozen times. Here, leaning against a wall somewhere in Pittsburgh. There, loading groceries into a car outside the Cottonwood Giant Eagle. In the park. Next to the police station, with the added entertainment of two officers politely asking Kanning to leave, now. Which he did, in a manner the unkind might describe as "scurrying."

"It's wrong of me to enjoy Kanning beating an ignominious retreat." Giulia replayed the last clip. "But I do."

"Everyone has a vice." Zane retreated to his desk. "I'm a breath away from breaking through."

The phone rang. Sidney picked it up at Giulia's desk. "Good morning, Driscoll Investigations...One moment, please."

She put the call on hold. "It's Ms. Newton, and she sounds as desperate as Ken Kanning."

Giulia suppressed a sigh. "A calm morning in the office would be a welcome change."

"I'll close the door."

"Thanks." She pulled her legal pad toward her and pressed the hold button. "Giulia Driscoll speaking."

"Ms. Driscoll, this is Cissy Newton. The situation here has escalated. Our cook and the upstairs maid have threatened to quit."

"I sympathize with your employment difficulties, Cissy, but in what way is this situation related to your belief that Elaine's business partners are working against her?"

"*Tch.* There is more to this than greed. The maid insists she has evidence a demon has infested the library."

Giulia opened her mouth to soothe and refute.

And closed it again.

Since Elaine didn't leave the house, someone from the outside might be working with—who?—to unsettle the fragile heiress and the rest of her household.

Cissy interrupted her lightbulb moment. "We require an exorcism."

Giulia stared at the sunny garden watercolor on the wall facing her desk. Curse Rod Serling and his *Night Gallery* TV show for not giving step-by-step instructions on how to disappear into a painting.

"I'll call you back."

Nineteen

Father Patrick Driscoll, O.F.M., M. Div., Th.D., stared at his sister-in-law and uttered the distinctly un-priestlike, "Are you kidding me?"

Giulia passed a Sonic limeade and two of the restaurant's Chicago dogs across his small kitchen table. "I am not."

Frank's second oldest brother shared the looks and build of all the Driscoll men: ginger hair, green eyes, rugby player muscles, and that disarming grin. The grin was nowhere in sight as he took out one-third of his first hot dog in a single bite.

Giulia added two orders of tater tots to the hot dogs. For herself she unpacked tots, a pretzel dog, and a cherry limeade.

"My current clients think their employer's and cousin's business partners are trying to force her out. The alleged victim is an agoraphobic who thinks her house is haunted. There's a possibility the business partners are working with someone in the house to get her declared incompetent."

Pat's eyes never left her face as the rest of the hot dog disappeared unerringly into his mouth.

"Hear me out. I'm now trained in Tarot reading and clairvoyance. My client called today because members of the staff claim to have seen signs of demonic activity. I need a crash course in exorcism." She popped the plastic lid off the Styrofoam cup and drank much too fast. When the brain freeze passed, she said, "Will you help me?"

Tater tots vanished into Pat's mouth like he was a human assembly line. When the first sleeve emptied, he said, "What's Carlos' opinion?"

Giulia breathed. "He says I'm pushing the envelope with Tarot and clairvoyance."

A short laugh. "A bit."

"He also says it falls within my SOP." She explained the pre-confession system she and Carlos had worked out back when she first began working for Frank. "Carlos mentioned he wasn't trained in exorcism and you were."

"Great. Can no one be trusted anymore?"

Giulia nibbled her hot dog. Her phone call with Father Carlos, her parish priest, had been enough to give her heartburn. Carlos was the kindest priest she'd ever known, which was saying quite a lot, but he was still a member of the clergy operating within the strictures of the Roman Catholic Church.

Patrick taught at Carnegie Mellon. He substituted at several churches as needed but didn't have his own parish. Perhaps because of his daily interactions with college students, he skewed on the strict side of current church teachings. And as the temperature in Giulia's office dropped ten degrees when she explained her exorcism needs to Carlos, she'd expected a minimum thirty-degree plunge here at Pat's.

The longer Pat stared at his second hot dog without eating it, the air became less frigid. It could be because she was Frank's wife, or because he knew she treated religious matters seriously, or because she used to be a nun.

At last he moved a hand toward his limeade. Giulia drank more of hers—slowly this time—while she debated on instituting the ten percent "grief" upcharge on Muriel and Cissy's invoices. She, Sidney, and Zane had all nominated clients for the inaugural padded bill, but so far they'd talked themselves out of it.

Pat punched in a number on his cell phone. "Wait until our weekly poker game, you tight-ass Jesuit."

Father Carlos' deep laugh carried across the table to Giulia. "Franciscan slacker. Tell Giulia she should name the baby Carlos."

"Not on your life. It'll be Owen or Finn."

"Remember, I'm her confessor."

"No pulling rank."

"Franciscans are a blot on humanity."

"And the Jesuits still have to atone for the Inquisition."

"Oh sure. Throw that in my face. Prepare to lose big at Texas Hold 'Em Monday night."

"In your dreams." He hung up and said to Giulia's concerned face, "What?"

"Pat, you're both barely squeaking by."

"Oh, the gambling? You're too literal. Last week I lost and had to wash his rustbucket Ford Taurus. If he loses on Monday, I'm going to make him fix the leak in my toilet. My water bill's creeping up each quarter." He wolfed down the second hot dog. "How's your Latin?"

Twenty

"No," Pat said after an hour of Latin recitation. "Don't chew the scenery. People expect priests—in this case, you—to diffuse authority and power. Be firm and maintain control. When you say '*Et potestas Christi urget vos*' your clients will figure it out because everybody and their grandmother has seen *The Exorcist* or that TV show with the codependent brothers fighting demons and angels."

"*Supernatural.*"

"That's the title. Every female in my comparative religion classes is addicted to it." He flagged another page in a well-read copy of *Manuale Exorcismorum.* "Emphasize the mystery of it, the otherworldliness, because I'm not convinced there's a demon in the house or that one of the inmates is possessed."

Giulia took the small leather-bound book. "I'm bringing my admin to watch everyone's reactions to the ritual. He looks like Paul Bettany's character in *The Da Vinci Code.* He'll take mental notes for me."

Pat nodded as he set a sheet of heavyweight writing paper on his desk. "The only tangible result of the two actual exorcisms I've performed has been to calm and comfort the 'victim' and their family, after which all supposed demonic activity ceased." He wrote a few lines, dragged over a huge reference book, wrote a sentence, looked up something else, wrote another sentence, and signed with a flourish worthy of John Hancock. "Grab the matches over the refrigerator, would you?"

Giulia returned with the box of safety matches. Pat lit a stick of crimson sealing wax and pressed the seal on his ring into a puddle of hot wax next to his signature. He blew on it a few times and passed it to her.

She read the Latin out loud for practice. "As an ordained representative of the International Association of Exorcists, Father Patrick Driscoll, O.F.M., M. Div., Th.D. bestows upon Giulia Maria Falcone Driscoll the title of Extraordinary Handmaid of Exorcisms. May the Holy Trinity, Father, Son, and Holy Spirit bless your endeavors on their behalf." She looked up at the Driscoll grin on his face. "It sounds quite official in Latin."

"It always does. Here." He handed her a somewhat scuffed hip flask. "Don't give me that look. It's holy water. Use it to bless the house for real. It doesn't matter that you've been released from vows. Chosen is chosen."

She tucked the flask into her messenger bag. "When I was little and all the neighborhood kids played Mass with Necco wafers, I always demanded to be the priest. It made my little brother furious, but I was born the stronger person. Or the pushier one."

"Depends on whether or not you're feeling charitable?" He became serious. "How's the situation with him?"

Giulia stuffed empty food wrappers in the takeout bag. "I'd like to stuff his head in here and shake it until it rattles."

"What happened with his marriage counseling? Carlos said he was making progress."

"Oh, he has. He stopped pretending his wife doesn't exist. Last week they met with a family counselor and all three kids ran at their mother so fast they knocked her down." Giulia's smile flashed steel. "Her oldest refused to stop hugging her as he told the family counselor if he was married to Salvatore he would've run away too."

"Jesus, Mary, and Joseph."

"Indeed. Now that their mother has her old job back and is in a small apartment, the kids will be able to see her and Salvatore can't stop them." The smile faded. "Carlos is a miracle worker."

Pat folded the letter into an envelope and handed it to her. "Does your brother still pretend you don't exist?"

Giulia laughed without a speck of humor. "That would be too good for me. He got my cell number off his phone records from when his daughter was calling me. Now he spews ultra-religious invective into my voicemail at least once a week."

"I don't need to quote you the relevant chapter and verse regarding his behavior."

"You do not." Giulia dropped the bag into the trash. "His kids are going to end up teenage parents or in juvie. Also probably atheists. I'm working with Carlos to see about having their visitation with their mother at our house." She shook herself. "He raises my blood pressure simply by thinking about him."

"Which is bad for little Zlatan."

Giulia groaned. "Is nothing secret among the Driscoll clan?"

"Not much." He rose and opened the door. "Blot your brother from your mind and think about your upcoming ritual. A good exorcist is immune to distractions."

"If this massive house really does have a pet demon, I might put you on retainer."

Twenty-One

Giulia hung up the phone from a terse conversation with Cissy Newton, waited until all sounds from the main office ceased, and posed dramatically in her doorway.

"Guys, I am descending into the depths of hell. I require assistance."

As though joined at the hip, Sidney and Zane laughed, caught themselves, coughed, and turned startled eyes on Giulia.

"Someday I'll remember to video your reactions." Giulia abandoned the doorway. "Half of our client team demands an exorcism because the staff wants to quit. Ignoring the simple fact that demons don't infest houses, they possess people, I have shiny new credentials to impress said client."

"Hold it." Sidney hit Ctrl-S on her keyboard. "You're an exorcist now?"

Zane stood and pointed toward the printer. "The power of Driscoll Investigations compels you!"

Sidney choked.

"What? It's been jamming." But when he looked over his shoulder at Giulia, his pink-tipped ears belied his attempt at comedy.

Giulia grinned. "Clever. If this type of client keeps up, we should add it to our business cards." She pretended not to see the narrow line of flop sweat trickle down Zane's cheek as she handed her official letter to Sidney. "This is how I'm an exorcist."

Sidney squinted at it and then at Giulia. "Who reads Latin anymore?"

"Latin? Let me look." Zane scrutinized the paper but handed it back after two stumbling attempts. "I admit defeat."

Giulia translated her letter of authority. "You see, I'm official."

Sidney spoke with deliberation. "I want to make it clear that I'm not refusing to do my job. But first ghost hunting and now demon evictions? We sound like a lead story for *The Scoop*."

"Perish the thought. What we are is evolving. Organisms which adapt, survive. Basic biology and basic marketing."

Sidney's disappointment appeared for an instant before she masked it with as neutral an expression as Giulia had ever seen her assume. She commandeered Sidney's client chair.

"What's the real problem?"

Sidney's hands clenched together. "No laughing, okay?"

"Never."

"One winter when I was little we lived with my grandmother in one of those big old houses meant for about fifteen people."

Zane got up and closed the window. Giulia nodded at him. The traffic was overpowering Sidney's voice.

"My older sisters shared one bedroom, but I wanted my own room. The house was full of steam radiators and the floors creaked and cracked all night." Her hands tightened. "Every Saturday night I'd wake up after midnight. It felt like someone was watching me. I was too scared to tell mom or dad, but I asked my sisters if they saw anything weird in their room."

"Did they?" Giulia's voice was as subdued as Sidney's.

"They said no, and of course the very next night they both hid under my bed to scare me. If they hadn't giggled, it would've worked too. I went to the bathroom and filled two cups with freezing cold water, and when they tried to rise up like ghosts I drenched them." A small smile. "They'd put on white face paint and the water made it drip all down their nightgowns. Mom was ticked."

Zane, also quiet: "But that wasn't all?"

Sidney appeared to come to grips. "No, eleven more times that winter I woke up positive someone was in the room with me. We moved to the farm over spring break and never went back to grandma's house. When I was a senior in high school I helped take care of Grandma before she passed, and I asked her about the house's history.

She said she could never get one of her cocker spaniels to go in my room, but she never saw anything."

While Giulia tried to find the right words to ask her next question, Zane stuck his foot in it.

"You're scared of ghosts."

Sidney flipped him off. "Sorry, Giulia."

All the times Sidney had insisted "There's no such things as ghosts" fast-forwarded through Giulia's head.

"I never dreamed I'd want us to take divorce cases again, but I do. A whole parade of cheating wives and scumbag husbands would make me happy."

"Divorce cases?" Giulia raised one eyebrow. "You wouldn't really."

Sidney sighed. "You're right. I wouldn't really. But I'm going to need more time to adapt than the genius at the other desk."

Giulia squeezed her hands. "Take all the time you need. Zane, are you up for some undercover?"

Zane rubbed his hands in the universal mad scientist gesture. "Ms. D., my girlfriend is going to look at me like I'm Superman."

"I'm pleased to add spice to your relationship. We're off to Elaine's castle tomorrow morning for an eleven a.m. exorcism."

Zane checked his desk calendar. "If only tomorrow was Friday the thirteenth."

After supper, Giulia rooted around in the spare room closet where they kept the winter clothes and emerged with a plain purple scarf. She seldom wore it since the plum tones of the scarf clashed with her beloved violet wool coat.

Frank followed her into the kitchen. Giulia brought the trash can out from underneath the sink and attacked the scarf's fringe with the scissors from her sewing basket.

"Honey, what are you doing?" Frank's voice conveyed trepidation.

Giulia looked up and grinned. "Worried about crazed Sicilian woman with potential murder weapon? I'll keep this in mind." She started on the other end of the scarf. "I need a reasonable facsimile of a priestly stole for tomorrow."

In the same tone of voice, Frank said, "Why?"

The scissors paused. "Does my church-avoiding husband think I'm going over to one of the sects that allow women priests? You forget I'm married and pregnant."

"Well, Pope Joan..."

Giulia laughed and resumed de-fringing. "Drag yourself into the twenty-first century, dear husband."

"All right then, why are you creating a fake stole?"

"Because I'm going to perform an exorcism on my client's house tomorrow." She put the scissors aside and began to slice the remnants of fringe with an X-Acto knife.

"I thought you were giving Tarot readings and going all clairvoyant for this client?"

"They upped the ante. I upped ours."

Frank turned on his bare heel and snatched his phone from the coffee table. "Come on, come on. Don't be teaching a night class...Pat? Frank. How did my ex-nun wife wrap my dogmatic priest brother around her little finger?"

"Don't blame him," Giulia said from the kitchen.

"Of course I blame him. Driscoll men were raised to be immovable as the Richmond Tower."

"As the what?"

"Famous Dublin landmark." He put the call on speaker. "Well?"

The sound of tapping came over the phone. "Have you forgotten the tower was dismantled and relocated in the mid-eighteen hundreds?"

"Damn. Yes." Frank recovered. "Then you're malleable as long as the right circumstances arise. Who's your confessor?"

"Frank, dear, stop harassing your brother. Who better than he and I to know when to adapt to the needs of the afflicted?"

"And you're sure afflicted now," Frank said. "What if *The Scoop* tails you?"

"I'll fling holy water on their creeper van and watch it burst into flames. Do we still have s'mores fixings?"

Both Driscoll brothers laughed.

"Giulia," Pat said over the speaker, "what are you wearing?"

"Oi. That's my wife you're talking to."

"Frank." From his wife and brother.

"At the second used clothing store of the day," Giulia said, "I found a plain floor-length black dress. It makes me look like one of Jane Eyre's bridesmaids."

Silence.

"I weep at your dearth of classic literature knowledge." She sheared a few stubborn fringe remnants. "Think of an extremely plain choir dress which flatters no one."

"She's shaving the fringe off a purple scarf," Frank added. "It's like our kitchen has been transformed into a vestry for my wife the priest. It's unnatural."

"Excellent touch, Giulia," Pat said. "Frank, be a man."

"Jump up my butt, older brother."

In a pious voice Pat said, "Allow me to recommend several ejaculatory prayers, the repetition of which will decrease your extensive time in Purgatory."

"Only if I get to make adolescent jokes about ejaculation."

"Good night, baby brother. Giulia, if you forget a line, slip in a Paternoster."

"What do you think?"

Up in their bedroom, Giulia modeled her black dress with the long ends of the altered scarf hanging down to her waist.

Frank gave an exaggerated shudder. "It's almost as bad as the time you went undercover in your old convent a few years ago."

"Good." She slipped into her black flats and studied the complete impression in the wall mirror. "If it affects you, then it should impress the client."

"Take it off, okay?"

Giulia looked at his reflection. "I hate it, but I have reason to. After ten years of wearing nothing but black from veil to sensible shoes, the color gives me flashbacks. But why does it bother you? You can be my research subject since I don't know how the client will react to it."

He closed the distance between them. "Because it makes you look like the church is dragging you back into its maw. You're not a Bride of Christ anymore, you're my wife and Zlatan's mother."

"Of course I am."

"Damn right." His arms circled her waist and he turned her around.

"Please stop blasphem—" His lips on hers cut off the rest of the word. She steered him toward the bed.

And stopped when his legs bumped into the mattress. "Wait."

He kept moving. "What?"

"I don't want to have to iron this."

"Works for me." He ran his hands along her ribs, over her hips, and down her legs until he reached the bottom of the dress. Grasping the hem with a light touch, he pulled it up and off, hanging it from the footboard's corner post.

"You're the perfect husband."

"Of course I am."

Twenty-Two

The next morning, Zane drove to Elaine's house in his silver Cruze because the school-bus yellow Clown Car clashed with their exorcist image. Zane wore all black as well: a button-down shirt and plain trousers.

"I should've tricked out my speakers." Zane gestured as they waited at a red light. "We could've broadcast 'Tubular Bells' as we drove."

"Copyright infringement." Giulia opened up a Google search on her iPad. "A classic hymn instead...'Solid Rock' or 'Blessed Assurance,' but the usual arrangements are dirges." She played a sample of each.

Zane stuck a finger halfway into his mouth to an accompanying gagging noise. "No offense, Ms. D., but Catholic music is a cheap alternative to Ambien."

Giulia laughed. "You're preaching to the choir. Now these arrangements—" She played the opening bars to the Denver and the Mile High Orchestra arrangements of the same hymns.

"Yeah." Zane drummed on the steering wheel. "When did the Catholics get into Big Band style music? Love that beat."

"They didn't. These guys aren't Catholic. Their arrangements are also copyrighted." She closed the tablet. "Besides, if we're going to be the Mr. Softee of ghostbusting, we should've taken my too-bright rental car."

"I've got it. We can design one of those car wraparounds with our phone number and our new slogan: The Power of DI Compels You. I can doctor a photo of you when you were a nun to make laser beams shoot out of your eyes. People would take pictures and post them online. We'd go viral in a week. What do you think?"

"I think I'd get excommunicated."

"We'd be swamped with business. We'd have to move into a bigger office and hire more people." He glanced over at her. "All the financial gurus say you should start saving for your kids' college education from the moment of conception."

"You are shrewd."

"I'm practical. You don't want to know how much a year at MIT cost when I graduated. It'll be astronomical in eighteen years."

The sound out of Giulia's mouth combined a sigh and a chuckle. "Get thee behind me, Satan."

The car swerved. "What?"

"Look it up later. We are not going to remake ourselves into *The Scoop*."

"My hopeful spirit is crushed underfoot." Siri's voice from his phone told him to turn left in half a mile.

"Why do I doubt that?" Giulia said. "Did I mention you look completely unlike yourself in that outfit?"

"Back at you, Ms. D. My girlfriend says I look like a community theater ghost. I reminded her of my smashing success as multiple ghosts on the MIT stage."

Giulia reopened her iPad.

"Come on, Ms. D. Don't disappoint me."

"All right." She closed it and ran through her knowledge of Gilbert and Sullivan's repertoire without benefit of checking the online archive. "It begins with R...No. It's not coming. I surrender."

"*Ruddigore.*"

"Drat."

Zane laughed. "I was the ghost of Sir Roderic Murgatroyd. The director said my hair and skin color made me the natural choice. I only needed to add dark makeup under my eyes and white on my lips. Good thing I'm a baritone."

Siri informed them their destination was two hundred feet ahead on their right.

Giulia slid her iPad into her messenger bag. "I'll get everyone together and let them talk. Please key it all in for me. Afterward I'll put the electronics away. Today your otherworldly looks should make our clients give you enough personal space to let you take mental notes unimpeded."

Zane pulled into the driveway. "Holy One Percenters, Batman. No wonder she calls it a castle."

The three-story stone house did indeed have a huge tower on one side. And a front balcony with a smaller tower. And a wraparound water feature long enough to be a moat with a miniature waterfall at each end. The stone colors shaded from fawn to buff to tan, the shapes ranging from huge square blocks to narrow vertical and horizontal strips and smaller squares of several sizes. Two arches spanned the first floor porch with a smaller arch at the top of the wide entrance stairs. Long ivory curtains softened the stone arches.

A wrought iron fence enclosed it all, naturally. A short one, allowing the peasantry a glimpse of heights unattainable even in their dreams. Artistic arrangements of roses and dahlias around the moat reflected the graceful iron flowers atop the enclosing pickets.

Four-petal openwork designs in the stone bordered the porch and balcony. Two chimneys, one on the right, and a narrow one rising from the tower continued the shaded browns theme. The roof was the only part of the castle with a connection to the average house. With dark brown shingles interspersed with random squares of tan, it made up for its ordinariness with dahlia-shaped finials at every corner and a copper bouquet of dahlias on the weathervane.

"It has its own parking lot," Zane said. "I am officially intimidated."

"Choose a parking space like we own it. Pretend it's the Middle Ages when the Church had more authority than any king."

"Don't say 'Middle Ages' to a Pagan. We get collective memory flashbacks of the Inquisition."

"Don't look at me. I was a Franciscan."

He parked in the first space in the four-car parking lot. "I knew there was an underlying reason I like working for you."

"Time for a last-minute rehearsal. Who are you?"

"I'm your assistant. I'm the strong, silent type. No conversation with anyone after introductions and handshakes."

"Correct. We will wrap ourselves in a remote and confident aura.

Today we aren't smiling, helpful Driscoll Investigations making a house call. We are Driscoll Investigations, Spiritual Roto-Rooters." She giggled, slapped her hand over her mouth, and held her breath until the urge passed.

"I didn't hear that," Zane said. "I am Zane, possessor of mystery and power. Maybe you should teach me some Latin."

Giulia shook her head. "My official letter mentions only me. Ready?"

"We are a united front. I'll take all my cues from you."

"I'll tell your girlfriend to dress you as a Minion for Halloween."

He turned pale eyes on her. "Please don't give her ideas."

"Far be it from me to jeopardize the mental serenity of my employees." She returned the letter to her messenger bag—one of the few black accessories she'd bought on purpose. The sparkly violet bag she really wanted to buy would not have inspired confidence in potential clients.

Zane adjusted his collar and slid a pencil and a folded piece of paper into his pocket. "I'll scribble blind during the ceremony if I think something is too essential to risk forgetting."

Giulia touched everything in the bag: flask of holy water, ornate ebony and silver crucifix, and a Bible sized to fit comfortably in one hand. She'd bought an Estonian translation because Zane wanted to see it and because she didn't know a word of Estonian. With this open in her hand, she wouldn't be distracted from her memorized Latin.

They exited the car as a team. Zane said, "Curtains at a side window just twitched closed."

"Here we go." Giulia kept one pace ahead of Zane as they opened the gate and walked sedately up the front steps.

Overstuffed ivory jacquard cushions topped the brown wicker sofas and chairs on the porch. At the arms of each sofa and chair were small pebbled glass tables. Ivy on trellises anchored in matching wicker baskets flanked the furniture groupings. Suspended from the ceiling, long octagonal church lamps. Giulia had spent thousands of hours in pews beneath the light shining through the same buttery glass insets.

She led Zane down the short stone-lined path on the left side of the porch and rang the doorbell. The door combined the church lamp glass with the wrought iron fence flowers.

A maid in a black knee-length dress with white collar, cuffs, and apron opened the door. Giulia applauded the choice of black nursing-style shoes for support but cringed inwardly at her stockings. She cherished an eternal hate for those uncomfortable, impractical, rip or run at the touch of a butterfly wing torture devices. Which is probably why the maid needed only a veil to resemble Giulia in her early convent years.

"Good morning." Giulia did not smile. "We are here to see Ms. Newton."

The maid paled beneath her olive skin. "Yes, ma'am. Please come in, ma'am."

Driscoll Investigations, Spiritual Spring Cleaners, entered the Dahlia castle as though their very presence would make malign influences tremble in their ectoplasmic boots.

No wonder Muriel mentioned interior design magazines beating down the castle doors for a chance to feature it. The foyer begged to be the setting for bridal photoshoots. Polished oak flooring led the eye to a graceful sweep of carpeted stairs with a curved oak railing. The newel was dahlia-shaped. Of course it was.

The main hallway ended at a small screened-in back porch with a stairwell next to it. Directly to the left, an archway led into the parlor seen from the front porch. Around the stairs, another archway gave a glimpse of a dining room table.

No church lights in here. Two skylights flooded the foyer with natural light and the oak gleamed in response. A hanging group of glass-and-gold lamps waited for nightfall.

The maid pressed a discreet intercom next to the light switch. "Ms. Newton, they're here."

Giulia did not think of Carol Ann in *Poltergeist*. Absolutely not.

Cissy Newton bustled into the foyer from the dining room. With her khaki trousers and white blouse, she blended in with the maid. Then again, Giulia's and Zane's choice of clothing blended in as well, making the entire bunch of them look like various ranks of servants.

Cissy's open arms dropped to her sides before she hugged Giulia. Her sneakers squeaked to a halt on the oak, and she grasped Giulia's free hand instead.

"Ms. Driscoll, we're extremely relieved you're here. It's been hel—

that is, dreadful." She tilted her head toward the maid. "Melina says we shouldn't mention certain words. I don't want to risk a horrible mistake through misplaced skepticism."

Giulia chose not to address the idea. "Before we start, please let Ms. Patrick know we're here."

When Giulia donned Sister Mary Regina Coelis' authority, Cissy responded like she'd been programmed. Catholic school in the old days without a doubt.

"Certainly." She went to the same wall intercom and pressed a second button. "Elaine?"

A light voice distorted only a smidge by the speaker replied. "Are they here? I'll be right down."

"Come on out, you two." Cissy beckoned toward the door behind the central stairs.

A rail-thin older woman with bright auburn hair and faded eyes reached the foyer first. She wore the same maid outfit. At her heels came a pudgy young man with small dark eyes, a small crooked nose, and a small plump mouth. Despite the decades between the two, he seemed the elder. The worry lines scored into his forehead, perhaps, versus the extreme vitality of the woman.

"Ms. Driscoll, this is the household staff. Melina you've met. She does most of the heavy work. Georgia is our whiz at light cleaning, and Mike is our treasure of a cook."

Handshakes all around. Melina bobbed a brief curtsy. "You are the holy one. Ms. Newton tells us of you. You will rid this place of the demon."

"That's why she's here." Elaine clattered down the central stairs in a daffodil-yellow skirt and leaf-green sleeveless blouse. The yellow and green beads on her sandals clacked against each other for a few seconds after her feet stopped moving. "Ms. Driscoll, I'm thrilled to discover you're more than the average bear." A breathy giggle. "Oh, dear. I stayed up late watching Yogi Bear cartoons. Do forgive me." She took Giulia by the shoulders and turned her right and left. "You look marvelous. I can't wait for you to evict the nasty old demon in my house." The shoulder grip became a weak hug. The thin fingers twitched on Giulia's spine.

Giulia allowed herself a light pat on Elaine's back and stepped away from the hug. Her first mental note: Elaine's mother took Xanax. Muriel had hinted Elaine followed suit. Check the med's side effects.

Elaine shrank into the cowed wallflower who'd knocked on DI's door a few days earlier. "I'm—I'm lucky to have so many wonderful people taking care of me. Cissy told me all about hiring you, and Pip says Cissy is the best manager ever." Her fingers twisted and untwisted.

Giulia said, "Is there a table large enough for all of us to sit at once?" She said it with a straight face too.

Elaine the princess of her castle appeared. "Oh, yes. Please come into the dining room. Mike, would you bring tea and scones, please?"

Giulia held up one hand. "Thank you, no. We are here on business."

Elaine saved Giulia from continuing the pompous speech. "Oh! Oh, of course, you must be fasting or something." She led the group toward the dining room. "I read all kinds of exorcism information on the internet last night." A shiver conveying delight rather than fear. "It's thrilling. What else are you able to do if we need it? Can you read Tarot cards? Can you cleanse a room with salt and sage? What about a Ouija board? I have a Ouija board. Oh—I suppose you'd want to use your own. Do you have a spirit guide? Is it from Ancient Egypt? Ancient Egypt fascinates me."

The twelve mahogany chairs at the dining room table were upholstered in ivory brocade. An oriental carpet in shades of crimson, ivory, and black covered two-thirds of the oak floor. A crystal vase filled with multicolored dahlias in the center mirrored one on the sideboard. The ivory wallpaper set off the crimson curtains. The floor and table glowed in the light of two chandeliers.

Giulia had to will herself to enter the room with confidence. Raised in a lower middle-class neighborhood and living on the edge of poverty in the convent, even now with a successful business she seldom spent money without three separate reasons. She'd never have thought the most difficult part of becoming Giulia Driscoll Ghost Breaker would be sublimating Giulia the perpetual drudge.

Elaine took the chair at the head of the table. Giulia sat in the chair to her right and slid her iPad across to Zane on her left. At a nod from Cissy, the other three took chairs as well.

Giulia didn't dare look at Zane lest they both break character. "I would like each of you to describe any anomalies you have seen, heard, or felt in the house. Mr. Hall will catalogue them in our database."

"You see?" Melina elbowed Mike. "They do not use only holy water and books. They are up to date. I told you."

Mike raised both hands in a gesture of surrender. "I concede. Chocolate soufflé for dessert tonight."

Cissy said, "Dessert is not why we're here. Georgia, please begin."

As one, the castle staff became serious.

"I'm going to be blunt." Georgia's voice was as deceptively youthful as her appearance. "I've never heard of a female exorcist before. What are your credentials?"

"Georgia," Melina hissed.

Giulia took Pat's letter out of her messenger bag. "I wouldn't expect you to believe everything I tell you without proof." She handed the letter to Cissy, who passed it down.

Georgia opened it and gave Giulia a "point to you" look. "The church seal looks genuine, but I don't read Latin."

Melina plucked it from her hands. "This is from a Franciscan. The Jesuits possess greater knowledge and history of the war against evil, but my great-grandmother would accept the word of a Franciscan."

Giulia bit the inside of her lower lip.

"Father, Son, and Holy Ghost..." Melina handed it back. "I only know words from the prayers my great-grandmother taught me."

Giulia translated the letter.

"You're related to this priest?" Georgia said.

"He's my brother-in-law."

"Good." Melina stuck a finger in Georgia's face. "I know what you are thinking, and you are wrong. No priest would risk censure from the Bishop and the wrath of the family at Thanksgiving dinner by falsifying these credentials."

Zane snorted and coughed together. Giulia held her breath until the same urge passed.

Georgia laughed out loud. "You're reasoning's cuckoo, but you have a point. I accept your authority, Ms. Driscoll. I haven't heard much out of the ordinary. Mostly odd footsteps in the upper floors when I knew I was the only one around."

"That could be the house settling," Cissy said.

"Not at noon. If I'd heard things early in the morning or at twilight, I'd give the house the benefit of the doubt." She sat back, arms crossed.

"Mike?" Cissy said.

Giulia may have drawn a parallel to her own teaching years calling on students in a classroom.

Mike tented his fingers. "I applied the Sherlock Holmes deductive rule to the problem. I ruled out rats and mice, because we don't have any, and I know by heart all the sounds Ms. Newton's chameleons make."

"Chameleons?"

Cissy said, "I breed chameleons. Not near the food preparation area, of course, but their sun porch opens off the kitchen hallway."

"We're all familiar with chameleon noises," Georgia said. "I stopped hearing them years ago."

"Like I said," Mike continued, "I eliminated critter noises and the house settling, same as Georgia. I also ruled out the usual stray radio signals my dental work picks up on cloudy days."

Georgia snorted. "You never told me that one."

"Because I knew you'd laugh, old biddy."

Cissy rapped her knuckles on the polished table.

The cook shifted his attention to his hands. The outer rims of his ears turned cinnamon. "When I eliminated the impossible, I knew that whatever remained, however improbable, had to be the truth." He met Giulia's eyes. "I fudged that quote a little, but you know what I mean." Back to his hands. "I keep hearing whispers. Not every day, and not at the same time or anything, but I'm alone in the kitchen a lot, and when I'm concentrating on a recipe I don't keep the radio on."

"Is it the same voice every time?" Giulia glanced across to confirm Zane's fingers were doing their job. She'd forgotten one of the iPad keyboard's selling points was its silence.

"Oh, God, do you mean there could be more than one?" Sherlock Holmes vanished. "Ms. Driscoll, can you do the kitchen first?"

Giulia didn't respond to the plea. "Please be specific about the voice or voices you have heard." Rowan was right. Certain clients responded better to the businesslike approach.

"First was the high, breathy one. I never understood what it said, and it only seemed to show up when I was using the mixer or some other loud appliance. It likes to play tag team with the giggler." He shivered. On Elaine, a shiver looked cute. On him, it looked like he needed his mother. "The giggler never says anything, it just laughs."

"When did the voices begin?"

Mike looked at Georgia, who looked at Melina.

"Six days ago."

"You forgot about the sunrise cackler."

"Was that my day off?"

"You are both neglecting the one who moans in the night."

"Tuesday, wasn't it?"

"Also Sunday and yesterday."

"The giggler is worse. It sounds like a demented circus clown. I hate clowns."

"Stop." Melina put out her hands to her co-workers like an old-fashioned traffic cop. "The evil has also touched Miss Elaine."

"Oh no, no, no, don't say 'touched.' Now I'll think a disembodied hand is lurking in the corners of every room." Elaine shuddered hard enough to rattle the flowers in the centerpiece.

Cissy's glare withered Melina.

"I apologize, Miss Elaine. What I should have said was that you too have experienced otherworldly phenomena."

Elaine smiled at Melina as friend to friend, not master to servant. "That's all right. We have to give our exorcist all the correct details or we're not helping her help us." To Giulia: "Pip heard things first. I tend to live in my own world, you know. People say it's because I'm an only child. Anyway, the first few times Pip heard things I was in the middle of designing a dress or reading a book. You could set a bomb off in the room sometimes and I wouldn't hear it."

"That's true," Cissy said. "Elaine's been like that since I first came here when she was seven."

Elaine's dazzling smile brightened every castle inmate's face. The room's gravity lightened. After a beat, Zane resumed typing. Giulia regretted not smuggling in Olivier as part of her entourage. She set herself to remember his name when she and Zane catalogued today's experience.

"Cissy always knows." Elaine included Giulia in her diffusion of sunshine. "After Pip twice heard sounds I missed, I put all my favorite books away and listened to my own house." She leaned forward a hair, well short of Giulia's personal space. "I heard the footsteps."

"Was that all?"

The blue eyes opened wide enough for the whites to circle them completely. "Oh, no. I heard the cackling too. And the books. Melina, tell them about the books."

"Three days ago, I found one of the family Bibles torn to pieces and scattered on the library floor." Melina crossed herself. "In Miss Elaine's bathroom we found a prayer book of her grandmother's in the sink. Such a beautiful book ruined."

"That particular faucet has a drip no one's ever been able to stop. I'd say it's the first sign of a haunting, but it's dripped ever since we bought the castle back when I was three. No ghost would dare haunt a house my mother lived in." Elaine's bright smile turned brittle. "If I didn't know better, I'd say my mother's haunting me because she doesn't approve of the way I decorated the house."

Despite the fascinating revelations everyone was gifting her, Giulia herded her clients back into line. "I want to be clear. Have you called us to exorcise a demonic presence, or do you believe nothing more than a ghost is disturbing the house?"

Silence. Surreptitious glances.

Melina: "It is a demon."

Georgia: "If it were only footsteps and whispers, I'd say ghost. If anything besides Bibles and prayer books had been destroyed, I'd go for poltergeist. But I have to agree with Melina."

Mike: "I guess I'm not sure. I mean, I'm not Catholic or anything. I'll defer to them."

Giulia gestured to Zane, who closed the tablet. Giulia pushed back her chair. "Ms. Patrick, please take us to the library."

They followed Elaine like ducks up the graceful central stairs: Giulia and Zane, Cissy, the staff.

Elaine played tour guide. "I was too young to remember, but the library started out as an actual chapel. The house's history is incomplete, but some order of nuns lived here once. I can't think of another reason for a house to have a chapel. Daddy attached a few pictures to the blueprints when he and mama renovated. There used to be a ten-foot privacy fence all around the property, and the front door had a little grille at eye level, like speakeasies during Prohibition."

She led them along a wide hall past piecrust tables, paintings that looked suspiciously like original works or art by some of the minor Impressionists, and a grandfather clock worthy of Uncle Drosselmeyer.

"Mama and Daddy had the chapel deconsecrated, of course. When they began renovations they discovered floor to ceiling bookcases hidden behind the drywall and incorporated them into the new layout. Mama was a top-notch designer."

They filed into a book lover's fantasy room. The library possessed the same dimensions as the dining room but with old gold velvet drapes and area rugs. Two groupings of deep, overstuffed armchairs and warm cherry tables waited to be lit by stained glass reading lamps.

Giulia's insides melted at the bookshelves. A connoisseur's assortment of colorful paperbacks and leather-bound matching sets, the latter's gravity dissipated by knickknacks tucked into every odd corner. Hummel figurines peeped between the Greek philosophers. Fu dogs guarded an inexpensive set of the Little House on the Prairie series. These patterns repeated on every shelf lining the walls and surrounding both the door and the fireplace.

All the Perrault fairy tale figures danced around the border of the hearthrug. Dahlias covered the mantelpiece: glass, ceramic, papier-mâché, wood, crystal.

The shelves themselves weren't lacking in character. On three walls they reached the ceiling in regimented rows, but a single glassed-in shelf rose above the fireplace. Starting at the middle glass front, the open shelves on either side slanted a gentle angle down toward the teak floor, up again, and down. Tiny framed portraits hung in the triangles created by the shifting angles.

"Isn't it—"

Giulia put up a hand and Elaine's voice cut off like Giulia pressed a mute button. In silence she walked the room, picking up a statuette on one shelf, pulling out a book from another. At the fireplace, she crouched to inspect the woven Perrault figures. When she reached the window seat, she turned and faced the room.

"You are correct."

Elaine covered her mouth. Melina gasped. Mike elbowed Georgia. Cissy reached up to rest one hand on Elaine's shoulder.

"The stench of evil permeates this room." Giulia pointed at Mike, wondering if dagger fingernails would've been dramatic or overkill. "Bring salt from the kitchen."

Mike skedaddled.

The rest of the castle's population huddled near the doorway, Cissy included. She might be a domestic despot every other day, but not in the face of a domestic demon.

Heavy footsteps on the stairs, then in the hall. A container of Morton's salt materialized four feet above the floor. Mike's face appeared above it. "It's iodized. We don't have any of the plain kind, and I used the last of the sea salt on the sweet potato fries yesterday." He angled the cylinder so the ceiling lights caught the offending word. "Will it still work?"

Twenty-Three

Forget the convent. Giulia knew now she'd missed her true calling: the stage.

"Certainly." She strode across the room and took the container. Channeling the always serious face of Castiel from *Supernatural*, she herded everyone except Zane into the corner by the fireplace.

"Mr. Hall and I are about to begin. Please do not step over this barrier." She hemmed them in with a wide ribbon of Morton's finest.

"But what about the Devil's Trap?" Georgia sketched a five-pointed star in the air with one hand and drew a circle around it with the other.

Clairvoyant Jasper must have been laughing with Rowan in her Tarot room right this minute as he described Giulia's apparent link with fellow *Supernatural* fans. If such a thing as clairvoyance existed.

Still on point, Giulia allowed the corners of her mouth to curl upward. "Real life is not television." She closed the spout. "I've seen a few episodes of *Supernatural* too."

Pink spots blossomed on Georgia's cheeks. "That Dean sure is easy on the eyes."

"Sam is better," Melina said.

Cissy's cheeks matched Georgia's. "Castiel."

"Please remain silent until we finish the ceremony." Giulia's return to inflexibility fell over their lighthearted fangirl rapport like a shroud. Mike hunched into his chef's uniform. Melina and Georgia crossed themselves. Cissy put an arm around Elaine, who rested her head on the housekeeper's shoulder.

Giulia glided to Zane's side, took the holy water flask from her bag, and stopped in front of the window. She handed the bag and flask to Zane and planted herself. With her first flourish of the day she flung apart the drapes. Not-quite-noon sunlight hit the golden area rugs and filled the room.

Two separate gasps from the salt-enclosed corner. Giulia took advantage of her theatrics and spun on one heel.

"Light drives out darkness."

Knowing the sunlight framed her face and blurred her features made this brazen playacting easier.

"*In nómine Pátris, et Fílii, et Spirítus Sancti. Amen.*"

She could've used the help of a haunting setup like the one she'd discovered in Stone's Throw Lighthouse: a hidden speaker with a remote control to trigger ghostly sobbing on cue.

She'd have to do without. She moved away from the kind sunlight into the center of the room. "*Exorcizámos te, ómnis immúnde spíritus, ómnis satánic potéstas, ómnis infernális adversárii.*" Giulia injected authority into her voice.

Fire trucks wailed past the house. She stepped closer to the fireplace, Latin flowing. In the back of her mind a voice whispered, "What's your next line?"

She felt the color drain from her face as she segued into the Credo. As she reached the end of the first section of the rote prayer, the exorcism's words returned to her: "*Váde sátana, invéntor et magíster ómnis falláciae, hóstis humánae salútis.*" She held out her hand and Zane slapped the flask into it.

Something laughed.

Goose pimples erupted over every millimeter of Giulia's skin. With a steady hand she unscrewed the cap and flung holy water in the shape of a cross into the fireplace and finished the ritual.

"*Contremísce et éffuge, invocáto a nóbis sáncto et terríbili nominé Jésu.*" The voice in the fireplace cut off mid-giggle and a thud echoed through the room.

"What the hell is going on in my house?"

Twenty-Four

Everyone jumped.

Elaine said, "Pip!"

Her charming Paul Newman clone stepped onto the salt barrier and scattered it. As he barged between Cissy and Mike to embrace his wife, Mike caught his heel on an uneven floorboard and bumped against the angled bookshelves. With a muffled click, a triangular section of the wall shifted.

Elaine clung to her husband with one arm and pointed to Giulia with the other. "Did you hear it? Ms. Driscoll exorcised the demon! It laughed at her, but then it ran away. We've found the most amazing multitasking detective ever."

Pip pointed to the thin black line in the wall. "Darling, what's that?"

Elaine's mouth opened wider, but no more words came out. With his arm around her waist, Pip walked them both to the crack. He hooked his free fingers around the wood and pulled. The triangle opened onto a night-black space.

"Anyone got a flashlight? Wait. I've got my phone." Still one-handed, he turned on the flashlight app and aimed the light. It revealed a narrow recess, four feet high at the apex and three feet deep. He bent in half to stick his head in. "It looks like a priest's hole." His voice fell dead in the cubbyhole. "Like manor houses in England had back when Henry the Eighth was grabbing all the wealth—"

Elaine screamed. And screamed some more. She took a breath and kept on screaming. Pip soothed. Cissy scolded. Mike, Georgia, and

Melina edged toward the door. Elaine continued to scream in the timbre of nails on a chalkboard.

"Elaine. Sweetheart. Tell me what's wrong." Pip shook her. "Elaine. Elaine. Please stop. Elaine. Talk to me."

He and Cissy dragged her out of the library. Her screams fractured the air until a door closed and cut their volume by three-quarters.

Giulia said to the three remaining, "Do you know anything about this?"

Three headshakes.

"You've never seen the hidden door?"

"No, ma'am," Mike said. Elaine's screams escalated for a moment and he shuddered. "I had no idea. They're bookshelves. I never thought for a second this place would turn into something out of *Young Frankenstein*."

Teri Garr's voice spoke in Giulia's traitorous head. "Put—ze candle—beck." Curse her love of Mel Brooks movies.

The screams quieted at last. Everyone exhaled. Zane sat in the window seat typing into the iPad. Giulia took control of the room again.

"Georgia, would you ask Ms. Newton to come back here when she's finished taking care of Ms. Patrick?"

A tight nod. Georgia left.

"Do you need us?" Mike said.

"No. Thank you."

As soon as he and Melina left, Giulia crouched into the niche and tried to take a picture. The flash didn't provide enough light. She remembered the night vision camera she'd installed with the EVP app.

The glowing green world in the aperture took a few seconds to get used to. She took several close-ups and then six overlapping shots to mimic a panoramic view.

"You wanted to see me?" Cissy said from behind her.

Giulia cracked her head on the angled frame. Her internal "Ow ow ow" didn't make it to her lips. "Yes, thank you. Is Ms. Patrick better?"

Sprays of fine lines radiated from Cissy's sunken eyes and the corners of her mouth. "She's calmer now. Pip is sitting with her. When she's particularly anxious she likes him to read from her favorite childhood book of nursery rhymes." Her expression dared Giulia to judge the household.

"Were you aware of this hidden room?" was all Giulia said.

"Yes. It's on the original house blueprints."

Giulia tried to squeeze more blood from the stone Cissy had become. "Is it possible Ms. Patrick was not?"

The stone didn't yield a drop. "It's possible. The major remodeling of the house was carried out before she was old enough to start kindergarten. The changes she designed after her marriage were decorative only."

Pip's voice came through the intercom next to the door. "Cissy, she needs another one."

Cissy's teeth ground together with an audible crunch. "Ms. Driscoll, thank you for your efforts today. I'm afraid my attention is required elsewhere." She pushed the hidden door until it merged into the wall with a soft *click*.

"We'll see ourselves out."

"No. Elaine wouldn't like that."

Pip from the intercom again, charm fraying: "Cissy, what's the holdup?"

Cissy pressed the lower left button of the six on the discreet box. "Melina, please come up to the library." Then she pressed the button directly above it. "Two minutes, Pip."

"Hurry the hell up."

Melina came running. "Ma'am?"

"Ms. Driscoll and Mr....and her assistant are ready to leave. Ms. Driscoll, about what happened here?"

"We'll contact you with a report."

A brisk nod. "Good." She hustled down the hall and around the corner.

Melina glanced at the corner, then at Giulia. "Please follow me."

Hiccupping sobs followed them to the top of the stairs. Melina cringed until a door closed and muffled them.

On the first floor, Mike and Georgia intercepted the intrepid exorcists at the front door. Mike held out his hand and Giulia shook it.

"I apologize. You're the real deal. I was sure Ms. Newton hired a couple of actors to make Elaine happy."

Georgia shuffled from foot to foot. Mike shot her a look. "Don't nag me, fat boy." Her lips pressed together the way politicians' do when they're caught in a scandal.

"All right." She crossed her arms again. "I owe you an apology too. Everyone here is too invested in keeping Elaine happy—stuff it, Melina. You know it's true. Don't misunderstand me, Ms. Driscoll. Elaine is a sweet woman and an excellent business manager, but she's brittle. I figured Ms. Newton had finally lost her marbles and got taken in by shysters."

If Melina's short straight hair had been comprised of Fourth of July sparklers, it would have spontaneously combusted. "Georgia, you are *cabezón*. Could you not tell these people were honest from the way they spoke with us?"

Georgia's shoulders hunched. "I know. They didn't resort to patter, like that guy from the Christmas party who belonged in a traveling carnival."

"No hard sell," Mike said. "No hand-waving either."

Giulia was not about to discuss her own motives. "What happened last Christmas?"

Melina's face took on a "something stinks in here" expression. "Sandra Sechrest brought a fortune teller as entertainment."

"Without clearing it ahead of time with Ms. Newton." Georgia shook her hands like they'd touched something hot. "Hoo boy, she dragged Sechrest into her private office and blistered the paint."

"Lucky for Sechrest, Elaine thought it was a great idea," Mike said. "I think those three forget they're not untouchable. You know the three I'm talking about?"

"Yes: Sechrest, Hyde, and Pedersen."

"We have a pool going on which one will go too far and trigger the Wrath of Elaine. Up to now she's let them get away with some expense account padding and extras tacked onto supply orders."

Georgia said, "My vote is for Hyde to try and get Elaine to pay her kids' obscene school tuition."

Melina said, "I say Pedersen will marry another empty-brained and large-busted creature. She will then cause such a scandal Elaine will activate a morals clause in the company charter and he will be begging in the streets."

"Dahlia has a morals clause?"

Melina looked disappointed. "I do not think so."

Georgia jumped in. "But it wouldn't surprise anyone if Elaine's mother snuck one in. I've heard stories."

Mike said, "I'd pay money I don't have to find out. My bet is Sechrest will turn off her brain in a Pedersen way and find a gigolo who empties her bank account and goes after her stock."

Giulia said, "You were telling me about last Christmas."

"Right. The fortune teller set up a crystal ball on a velvet tablecloth in the library. He wore a turban and everything." Mike got the lightbulb look. "Maybe he brought the demon into the house."

"Do not forget the Tarot cards," Melina said. "His deck was not the usual design. I disliked the illustrations."

"Melina has a witch phobia." Mike's voice was dismissive. "He let me examine his cards. They were limited-edition watercolors of witches and wizards and black cats."

Giulia hoped Zane was taking surreptitious notes. "Did he promise everyone good fortune, rich spouses, and extraordinary children?"

"Even better," Georgia said. "Sechrest opened and resealed the gifts under the tree and slipped him a cheat sheet. We saw her but none of the other people in the house did. Elaine was over the moon and bought her own Tarot deck from Amazon the next day."

"Ms. Newton threatened us with chameleon poop cleaning duty for a month if we squealed." Georgia shuddered. "She inspects it with a magnifying glass. I never looked at my kids' diapers that closely."

Cissy's voice came through the wall intercom. "Mike, please brew a cup of violet tea."

"It's my own concoction," he said with pride. "Elaine says she's going to talk to the Board of Directors about pairing it with next spring's collection as an add-on." He bustled into the kitchen.

Georgia said, "We should get back to work," and returned to unknown territory via the door behind the staircase.

Melina opened the front door. "Ms. Newton will forget everything until the calamity passes. I will remind her of your good works in this house today when Elaine is quieted."

In silence and in character they returned to Zane's car. As soon as

Giulia buckled herself in she snatched up her legal pad and pen to write up the staff's foyer revelations.

"What is that woman on?" Zane braked for a red light.

"Possibly Xanax."

"I thought Xanax was supposed to calm you down."

Giulia opened her phone, ignored two voicemails, and Googled WebMD. "Major side effects dizziness, drowsiness, depression—this list is brought to you by the letter D. Lots of lower GI stuff."

The light changed. "They'd better not feed it to the chameleons."

"Don't make me snort, please. It's unprofessional. Ah. Here we go: restlessness and talkativeness."

"At least it's not illegal."

Giulia slipped her phone into her messenger bag. "Why would we care, in relation to this case?"

"Heroin, for example, is often cut with fentanyl or morphine. If Elaine was on street junk, I'd strongly suggest we doubt everything she sees and hears."

"I will presume your knowledge of this is not first-hand." Giulia ran her finger down the side effect list again. "Hallucinations are not on the list. Did you bring lunch?"

"No." He turned left. "Primanti's run?"

"Every time we're in Pittsburgh. I'll call Sidney."

After phoning in their lunch orders, Giulia continued writing. "Did you notice the staff calls Elaine by her first name, but their direct supervisor is Ms. Newton?"

"They're fooled by Elaine's looks and giddiness. Anyone who earns an MBA from Harvard at age nineteen is not to be dismissed." He pulled into one of the restaurant's takeout parking spots. "She'll toss them out if they deserve it."

"But with a month's wages and a decent reference. Although Cissy seems to have them well trained." She handed him cash for the three orders.

As they drove back to Cottonwood, Giulia read Zane's iPad notes. "I'd like to get Cissy alone and also Pip alone to see if Elaine really didn't remember the hidden room."

"If she goes off the rails like that on a regular basis, I'm amazed they keep staff for any length of time."

"I'm still boggling at the idea of Cissy inspecting lizard feces under a magnifying glass."

Zane navigated downtown lunch hour traffic. "One of the guys in my fraternity kept a pet tarantula, but I never got close enough to observe its bathroom habits."

Giulia closed the iPad. "Did you know people used to believe if a pregnant woman was frightened by an animal her baby would be born with said animal's characteristics?"

Zane parked in the lot behind DI's building. When they opened the doors, the aromas of fresh coffee and frying bacon mingled with car exhaust.

"Therefore if you get scared by one of Cissy's pampered chameleons..." Zane made the *mano fico*. "Sorry. Not even as a joke."

Giulia made the *corno* at the same time, both ancient hand gestures to ward off the evil eye. "Agreed."

Twenty-Five

Sidney made ecstatic noises over her giant vegetarian Primanti's lunch. All three of them sat at the table in the main office with drinks and piles of napkins.

"Please find clients in Pittsburgh more often." Her cheeks bulged like a chipmunk's.

"I will continue to do my best to keep my staff happy." Giulia kept her bites ladylike. Little Zlatan had begun to object when she ate too quickly.

Sidney drank plain iced tea. "Now I want to hear all about the exorcism. And please don't try to make me believe you found an actual demon."

"Better yet. We found a hidden room." Giulia gave Sidney the condensed version of Driscoll Investigations, Demon Breakers' inaugural breaking. Sidney's only comment about Elaine's castle: "Who'd want to live in a house with all those fancy rooms to clean?"

"Speaking of rooms, we need to know more about the hidden library room. I'm going to sync my phone with my computer." She carted the rest of her lunch in with her and linked the devices. "All set if you want to see."

"Do you have to ask?" Foil-wrapped sandwich in one hand, Zane hovered over Giulia's right shoulder.

"Ooh, night vision." Sidney stationed herself behind Giulia's left shoulder.

In varying shades of green, the pictures showed bricks forming two narrow side walls and a back wall sloping to meet the bricks of the fireplace. Cracked linoleum curling at the edges covered the two-foot-wide floor space.

"Didn't Elaine say her house used to be some kind of a convent?" Zane said. "Ms. D., could this be a punishment room for bad nuns?"

Giulia glanced at him, but the face she saw was "Genius at Research," not "I'm going to attempt humor even though it makes me hyperventilate." She cancelled her Glare of Death.

"Modern convents prefer endless prayers on aching knees or loading the miscreant with extra work. Solitary confinement went out with the nineteen hundreds."

"What are those markings low on the wall where the corner meets the floor?" Sidney pointed.

Giulia enlarged the photo, but part of the corner was cut off. "Let me see if I got that section in another picture." She scrolled through the remaining five. "I see them." She enlarged that section and played with the resolution. "They're words: Elaine…is a…good girl."

Zane whistled.

Sidney erupted. "Her mother locked her in this…this storage niche as punishment? There isn't even room to stand up. There's no air. Was she trying to suffocate her own daughter?"

Zane said, "Can I drive?" Giulia relinquished the mouse and he scrolled backwards through the pictures. "Here's the first one you took with the door wide open. Here's the last one with the night vision app. See the narrow bright green diagonal lines? The artsy bookshelves aren't nailed into solid wood. They're inserted into slots designed with space below for airflow." He added after a moment of silence, "My college girlfriend majored in architecture."

Giulia scrolled through her Muriel notes. "Here it is: 'Elaine's parents bought and renovated the castle.' Cissy said it too. Those bookshelves were new, because Elaine said the library used to be a chapel. Her mother and father found or created the niche and designed it as a punishment room." She stood up. "I need air."

She walked to the window, flung up the screen, and stuck her head out into the heat and stink and noise. A metallic clang and clash and rattle behind her spoke of Sidney's foot meeting the trash can and the trash can meeting the wainscoting. The sounds broke apart her wall of rage.

She pulled her head in. "Any damage to the paint comes out of your salary." But she said it with a smile.

"Totally worth it." Sidney gathered the scattered papers and slammed them into the eighteen-inch-high cylinder. Then she knelt to inspect the wall. "One scrape. I'll come in early one day next week and fix it."

Zane looked from Giulia to Sidney and back again, like a spectator at a tennis match.

Sidney said in a sharp voice quite unlike her usual perky tones, "When you have kids you'll understand." She stood and dusted off her hands. "I almost forgot. I have to get a picture of you for Olivier. Come out into the main office. The light is better."

Giulia and Zane stood side by side against the section of wall between the window and Giulia's door. The light came at them sideways.

"Should I close the blinds?" Giulia said as *The Scoop* burst into the room.

Twenty-Six

Ken Kanning wasted a quarter of a second taking in Giulia and Zane's outfits. He snapped his fingers and Pit Bull, his bald, bearded, tattooed producer, raised his camera and blinded Giulia with its spotlight.

"Scoopers, we're here at Driscoll Investigations to find Giulia Driscoll and her able assistant about to go undercover for their latest client."

As one, Giulia and Zane squared up in Kanning's face. Kanning's monologue faltered and he signaled Pit Bull. The spotlight died and he lowered the camera.

"Mr. Kanning, are you here without an appointment to tell me you've discovered who owns the white panel van that resembles yours?"

Kanning deflated, but only for a moment. "Not yet, but we're working on it." He flashed his gleaming smile at her. "It'd go faster if you'd tell me the name of your current client."

"Once again, it's not going to happen."

He radiated the charm that had garnered him a third season of his cable access show. "Ms. Driscoll, you haven't forgotten how well we worked together only last month. Our two-part Doomsday Prepper exposé garnered us our highest ratings all season."

Sidney opened her bottom desk drawer and hid her face as she searched in it with diligence.

Giulia pretended not to see. "Congratulations."

"You looked terrific in it. You're the Jackie Chan of ex-nun PIs." Kanning added a touch of slyness to the charm. "Speaking of nuns, did you hear your old convent got snapped up by a condo developer? All those poor little old nuns might get tossed into the street. They could use a hero to keep a roof over their veils." He closed the distance between them. "We could work together digging dirt on the developer. Think of the press. Little old nuns are a great humanitarian draw. We could—"

Giulia cut him off. "Mr. Kanning, this is the middle of a workday. Please call for an appointment if you wish to consult Driscoll Investigations. Zane, do you have our hourly rate sheet handy?"

Zane whipped out a half-sheet of paper and slapped it into Kanning's hand as he herded *The Scoop* into the hall.

When the door closed behind the intrepid reporters, Sidney raised her head from inside her drawer. "I'm really sorry. My whole family watched the Prepper episodes. I couldn't keep a straight face in front of him."

"Don't make me assign the next ghost hunting client to you and you alone." She pulled a piece of paper out of the printer tray and wrote down Kanning's teaser about her last convent. "It gives me the crawlies to think Kanning's slimy fingers are digging into my past."

"Wait until he finds out about the Novices forced to be drug mules and the little old nun who built and exploded a pipe bomb a few years back."

Zane's butt hit his client chair. "What?"

"God protect me." Giulia turned to Zane. "Back when Frank was in charge, I went undercover in my old Motherhouse—the huge building where young nuns are trained and old nuns retire to—and discovered some very ugly and very illegal happenings. I'll tell you about it the next time we have to drive to Pittsburgh."

He made a note in his phone. "I will not forget to take you up on that."

Sidney said, "Before we were interrupted, I was taking a picture of you two for Olivier. Pose again please? Thank you. Now say 'Ken Kanning!'"

Giulia said, "That man will drive me to drink."

Sidney's phone *clicked* twice. "Not while you're pregnant."

"The struggle is real."

Twenty-Seven

Giulia exited DI's small bathroom no longer dressed like a church choir mouse.

"Zane, did you notice how expertly Cissy herded us out of the castle?"

"I did." He hung his exorcist clothes on the coatrack. "The path from the library to the front door was as straight as possible, yet Melina had to escort us? Cissy didn't want us snooping while everyone waited for a Xanax to work on Elaine."

"Assuming she's on Xanax. Anyone know how fast they take effect?"

Sidney said, "Olivier might. Want me to call him?"

"No, don't interrupt his workday. I'll email him later. Could you get the phones for about fifteen minutes while Zane and I compare notes from this morning?"

Giulia synced her iPad to bring up Zane's typed notes on the monitor for both of them to read with ease.

"Their body language said ten times more than their words." Giulia pointed to Zane's on-screen comments. "Mike puts on a manly-man face but his eyes shift constantly around the room. When Ms. D. isn't looking at her, Melina stares at her as though she's trying to see into her soul." She looked over at Zane. "She did? I missed that."

"She was good at it. The instant before you might have asked her a question, her eyes shifted to her hands or to Cissy."

"Brr. There are too many people in this case who want to get into my head." She returned to the screen. "I'm not seeing much about Georgia."

"Her vibes were too normal. She didn't trust us, didn't want to believe anything was really haunting the place, but she was crossing her fingers we were all wrong and she was right."

Giulia tapped a pen on her legal pad. The random blue dots didn't form into a cryptic answer from the stars. Rowan would be disappointed in her new student's inability to read a supernatural message in them.

"Did you see anything out of the ordinary?" she finally asked.

"Well, the hidden room."

"You know what I mean."

"At one point in the library I wouldn't have sworn I didn't feel a possible cold spot."

Giulia laughed. "You sound like the fine print on a TV commercial for the latest wonder drug."

Zane gave her a one-sided grin. "That entire sentence was a disclaimer, wasn't it? If pressed, I'd have to say no. I didn't see anything ghostlike. But that laugh...Why did you hone in on the fireplace?"

"It wasn't pre-planned. When I saw those velvet drapes, I knew they were meant to be flung open with all possible drama. But when I walked the circuit of the room, the fireplace called to me—you know what I mean. Those angled bookshelves draw the eyes to it as the centerpiece of the room." She flipped to the layout she'd sketched in the car. "If I were to learn that the altar in the former chapel stood where the fireplace is now, well, I'd head back to Rowan first and my parish priest second."

Zane dragged her keyboard onto his lap and took over. Giulia opened her phone and bookmarked a woodworking site on Etsy with a "Genius at Work" plaque for sale. Zane needed a one year at DI anniversary memento.

Her cell phone rang. The collision shop popped up on caller ID.

"Giulia Driscoll speaking...yes...yes, please...Saturday morning is fine. Thank you."

Zane said in an absent voice, "You agreed to an exclusive partnership with *The Scoop*?"

"Zane, if you continue to tell such monstrous lies, the ground will open up and the devil will drag you straight down to Hell."

In the same preoccupied voice, Zane said, "*Deadly Blessing,* 1981, early Wes Craven with Sharon Stone and Ernest Borgnine. Controversial ending...Aha. I am invincible."

Giulia said, "*Goldeneye,* 1995, yet another movie in which Sean Bean dies."

"He's his own trivia category. Here you are, ma'am—er, that is, Ms. D."

Archived blueprints of each floor of Elaine's house filled the screen.

"Zane, you're amazing."

"Full disclosure: the house came up a couple of times in my hunt for Dahlia's finances. I got curious and poked around historical floor plan sites."

Giulia enlarged the second floor blueprint. "Honesty does not tarnish your genius." Her mouse searched the image. "What's this overlay?" She clicked and a pop-up appeared. "Maybe I'm more than a stage psychic. When the nuns turned whatever the library started out as into a chapel, they bricked up the fireplace and added an altar where the hearthrug is now."

"Ms. D., are you saying Elaine's parents had a sacred space cleansed—"

"Deconsecrated."

"Deconsecrated, but a malevolent presence still latched onto its residual energy?"

Giulia stopped clicking. "The possibility must've been in the back of my mind." A second later: "No. It's too pat." She double-clicked the corner section and a second overlay appeared. She read, "'During Prohibition the wall in this corner was cut open and fitted with a hidden door for bootleg liquor storage.' Pip the Wonderful missed his mark by one ocean, one continent, and about five hundred years."

Zane returned the keyboard to the desk and tapped the iPad screen and a video icon in the upper right corner. The screen went black. Giulia's voice reciting Latin came through the speaker.

"When everyone was watching you, I wormed my hand into your bag and started recording. I figured you might want to use it for practice in case we add it to our list of services."

Giulia made a face. "I had to wing the ritual once. Could you tell?"

"No."

"Good. I recited the Nicene Creed until I got myself back on script."

Her voice on speaker increased in volume and intensity as she neared the rite's climax. The recording picked up faint fire truck sirens and then laughter with a brief echo.

Giulia's core temperature dropped at least two degrees. "We did hear it."

Zane said, "You doubted it?"

A barely audible splash of water punctuated Giulia's final words and the laughing voice cut off.

"Like someone flipped a switch," Giulia said.

"Or like your words and the holy water sent it back to the underworld." He hunched his shoulders when Giulia stared at him. "It's the logical conclusion."

Immediate rebellion opened Giulia's mouth. "No. Number one, I don't accept a demon lurking in the fireplace like a demented Santa Claus. Number two, I'm not a trained exorcist. Number three, if a fifth-rate demon was squatting in the fireplace, are we to believe it chose to practice its evil laugh in Elaine's house just in time for me to swoop in and intimidate it?"

Zane pushed himself into the back of the chair. "Ms. D., does being a former nun mean you're not duct-taped to official doctrine anymore?"

Giulia made a note to ask Frank if she came across as intimidating without meaning to.

"If you're asking whether or not I have an open mind, yes I do."

Zane kept a few extra millimeters of distance between them. "I think maybe there was something in the house."

"Come on."

"All the whisperings and laughter and noises Melina, Georgia, and Mike talked about. Here." He took the keyboard again and paged up through his notes. "One person hearing voices is cause to check their hearing or their room for what they might be smoking. Everyone in the house reporting unusual phenomena is cause to call for backup. Enter the new and improved DI."

Giulia made a conscious effort to keep her voice non-aggressive.

"When Stone's Throw Lighthouse called us in, the source of the ghostly moaning turned out to be a hidden speaker with a remote switch."

At least Zane didn't try to back away farther.

"I'll concede that one, but we shouldn't dismiss the supernatural possibility."

Giulia started to speak, but he overrode her.

"And if we accept that possibility, the next logical step is we accept your own power—"

"I'm done listening to this." Giulia unhooked the cord connecting the tablet and the PC.

Zane's hand went out to Giulia's, but he stopped short of touching her. "Sidney may still be reacting to ghosts like she's ten years old, but you aren't, right? You're not lying through your teeth to the client."

Giulia forced herself to remain seated. "Correct."

"Then, logically, the Catholic Church's rules aren't the only rules. We came to the castle today with the intention of helping the client. That's a form of power. Your aura, for lack of a more precise term, covers me as your assistant. Thus whatever was in the fireplace recognized and reacted to it." He raised his pale eyes to hers. "It's syllogistic reasoning without a fallacy."

"Don't throw big words at me, mister. I'm a teacher." What Giulia really wanted was to run far and fast from this conversation. However, she also didn't want to spook Zane.

Ha, ha. Spook.

"Let's table this discussion for now, please."

Zane's Adam's apple jumped with the force of his swallow. So much for not spooking him. At least he didn't revert to skittish rabbit mode. Giulia dreaded the thought of bringing him out into standard communication with fellow humans again. She spared a fleeting curse for the telemarketing hell he'd come to DI from.

"How close are you to getting into Dahlia's real numbers?"

Zane popped out of the chair like his butt had hidden springs. "A nanometer away."

"Wait." She opened her notes from the Dahlia interviews. "If you need more impetus, Ms. Sechrest gratuitously shared her opinion of MIT grads. According to her, they think only of how to take advantage of anyone not in their exclusive geek club."

A touch of evil infused Zane's smile. "I'll finish this now."

Alone in her office, Giulia called her husband. "I need an honest answer. Am I too intimidating?"

Frank groaned and repeated the question to his partner over the sound of the police radio in their car. He must have held the phone to Nash VanHorne's mouth, because she had to pull the receiver away from her ear.

"Oh, dude, that's almost as bad as 'Does this dress make me look fat?'"

Twenty-Eight

The next morning Giulia stopped in the office before what promised to be a grueling day of driving and interviewing another round of suspects. The phone rang. Weird, on a Saturday. She decided to pick up rather than let the machine get it.

"Ms. Driscoll?" A voice whispered. "It's Mike Davenport from the castle."

"Could you speak up, Mike?"

"I can't. I don't want anyone to hear me. I couldn't tell you yesterday with everyone hanging all over you, but Elaine's been in a bad way for more than a month." He spoke faster and must have blocked the mouthpiece with one hand, because she had to plug one ear to understand him. "Two and three nights a week she's gotten me out of bed in the middle of the night to make her this hot milk and Bailey's concoction the cook when she was a kid used to brew for her. She's not sleeping and she jumps at every noise. She takes Xanax, you know, and Bailey's shouldn't be mixed with meds. I worry she's going to OD."

Click.

Knock, knock-knock knock, knock.

Giulia stared at the phone for a moment before her brain connected the "Shave and a haircut" raps with the office door. Did the entire world think private investigators kept office hours seven days a week? Curse you, Raymond Chandler.

The frosted glass showed only a tall male figure on the other side. In theory, a thief wouldn't knock first. In reality, she prepared to administer her never-yet-failed disabling technique as soon as she unlocked the door: Foot to instep, heel of hand to nose. Bam. Temporarily blinded assailant disabled.

"Ms. Driscoll. I'm glad I caught you here on a Saturday. I took a calculated risk." Pip stepped over the threshold and owned the room. His gray three-piece suit fitted him like it was hand-tailored. It probably was. A repeating pattern of white dahlias on his tie accented his pale green shirt. Giulia was again glad she wasn't cursed with clothing envy.

"Mr. Patrick, I'm about to head out to a full day of appointments."

"I'll only keep you a minute. I'm headed to work myself."

"Let's walk to my car together."

The Smile appeared. "An efficient vendor who bills by the hour? I thought the species was extinct."

Giulia searched her arsenal of Polite Smiles and produced Number Three. A much better choice than kicking him in his condescending yet charming shins. She led the way down the narrow stairs and into the parking lot.

"How may I help you?" she said when they stood by her temporary vehicle.

He may have picked up on her frost, since he didn't comment on the Clown Car. "I wanted to let you know Elaine is back to her old self. She filled me in on yesterday's adventure." He winked. "About the official letter too. Nice put-up job to soothe the help."

Maybe she could pretend to trip over something and get in one good strike to his shins after all. "The letter is genuine. Driscoll Investigations is not in the habit of lying to our clients." Giulia had always been a quiet supporter of opening the priesthood to women. This conversation might turn her into a sign-waving radical, if only to become a priest and a sanctioned exorcist.

The charm never faltered. "I apologize. Sometimes Elaine is a little too trusting." He leaned his six-foot-plus self over her and lowered his voice. "Did you sense anything in the house?"

Giulia parried. "Why?"

"I've heard things myself, you know. At first I thought we'd been invaded by those scrawny black squirrels. Do you have them here in Cottonwood?"

Giulia knew those squirrels. Back in the day, she and her fellow

Novices had spied on the oldest nuns to try and catch them painting the squirrels to match their habits.

"We do. You heard noises in your attic?"

"In the attic, between the walls, and in the basement. It's an old house. At first I dismissed it all when an exterminator found one hole in the roof and took out a single squirrel nest. But the noises persisted. Elaine began to hear them too. Did she tell you about the knickknacks?"

The Saturday coffee shop regulars began to appear in the parking lot.

"Knickknacks?" The open door released the aromas of almonds, bacon, and vanilla bean coffee. Her caffeine gene poked her.

"Elaine is into antique glass and china figurines." A shrug conveying how men weren't wired to understand the attraction. "At least they're valuable and not only dust collectors. A few have disappeared. One of them vanished as soon as she turned her back to it. It reappeared three rooms away under a chair."

The Knitting Women exited their taxi, flowered bags in hand, all talking at once. When their leader opened the door, they chorused, "Bring us almond croissants or we'll cover the chairs in granny squares!"

Their traditional call to arms stopped Pip cold. Giulia spent the moment chasing the memory Pip's story pinged in her brain, but it didn't surface.

He reoriented himself. "The Bible incident unnerved the entire household."

"I was informed if it yesterday." Now she had it. From her research on ghostly phenomena, Joe Nickell's *The Science of Ghosts*. Specifically the chapter on children palming small items from shelves or mantelpieces, drawing a parent's attention to the gap, and the moment the parent wasn't looking, tossing the purloined object. "Look," the child would say, and the parent saw the object flying through the air. Instant haunting.

"Do you know if any object teleportation occurred in the library?"

"Yes, I believe something happened, but only once. I don't recall which china dust collector was involved." His brow contracted and a hint of crow's feet appeared at the corners of his sky-blue eyes. "Cissy said you banished a demon. I think you may have saved Elaine's life."

Giulia didn't want a maudlin Prince Charming on her hands. "I assure you there will be no extra charges on the bill."

Score one for unexpected tactics. Pip remained speechless for three whole seconds.

He managed a weak laugh. "Ha, ha. Good one." He glanced at a Rolex peeping out from his sleeve. "I have an early appointment as well. Thank you for your time."

"One thing, Mr. Patrick—"

"Pip, please. Everyone calls me Pip except the staff. My collection of different editions of *Great Expectations* takes up an entire bookshelf."

"Pip, has Elaine been able to tell you why she was unnerved at the sight of the hidden door?"

His slight head bob indicated an apology for not doing his homework. "I didn't want to push her. When she told me what happened in the library yesterday, she didn't go beyond the laughing voice in the fireplace choking off and the strange thump or knock or whatever the concluding noise was."

Giulia checked her phone. "I have to get on the road myself. Thank you for your information."

He shook her hand with great heartiness. "You're doing Elaine a lot of good. I was worried she might have been imagining the voices, and I admit I wasn't thrilled when Cissy told me she'd hired you. I see now she was right. Keep at it." He upped the dazzle of his smile to a thousand lumens, jumped into his Porsche Boxter, and roared away into the sunshine.

She made a note into her phone to add Prince Charming to Zane's list of Dahlia suspects.

Twenty-Nine

Elaine's former guardians lived in a condo complex near the railroad. Servant's quarters compared to the castle.

Giulia's probe into their past and present finances had revealed two credit cards a whisker away from being maxed out, but nothing extreme otherwise. Perhaps there had been catastrophic medical expenses and they were too proud to ask Elaine for a bailout.

A border of pink impatiens drooped along the front of their condo. The brown siding needed a power wash. The door might once have been the color of parsley, but it had weathered to the seasick green of old hospital walls.

The older man who answered the door liked beer more than push-ups. A friend needed to give him a heart-to-heart about his comb-over. His dentures needed refitting.

To say Caroline and Thomas Emerson welcomed Giulia into their home would be stretching the definition of the word. Thomas offered her a cup of coffee from an old-fashioned percolator plugged into an outlet on the kitchen counter. When she declined he took up a dish towel and finished drying breakfast dishes for two. Caroline made big nodding motions with her head toward a kitchen chair as she continued giving advice over the phone.

"Honey, black flies sting. You know that...Honey, are you sure you should wear your contact lenses? How clean are the bathrooms?...Please try to give us a call once a week. We want to know all about your summer...I love you too. Kisses from both of us...Bye, honey."

She set down her cell phone. "Our youngest daughter is starting her first session as a camp counselor up in the Adirondacks. Please have a seat, Ms. Driscoll."

With a smooth bit of sleight of hand, Thomas put juice glasses in a cupboard and withdrew a 750 ml bottle of bourbon. He added a generous splash to his coffee cup and whisked the bottle back into its niche.

Caroline's formal smile became stiffer. "How can we help you?"

Giulia produced the same cover story she'd used in her Dahlia interviews. "We've been hired to look into Dahlia's profitability management since Elaine assumed control."

"How terrible," Caroline said. "After all Elaine's done to make Dahlia a success. You'd never think someone as young and sweet as she is would succeed in business, but Elaine was always older than her years."

Thomas took a swig of his doctored coffee. "Yeah, if she didn't wear those fancy clothes she designs, you'd think she wasn't legal."

Giulia pretended to consult her notes. "I understand you were named her guardians in her mother's will."

"My poor sister." Caroline's stilted expression didn't alter. "We moved in with Elaine when she was released from the hospital. Have you met Elaine's housekeeper? Oh, good. Then you know what a treasure she is. As soon as the police gave her permission, she brought in those people who clean up after fires and other disasters. We never would've been able to tell five murders had taken place in the house."

Thomas picked up the story. "Elaine wouldn't go into the kitchen or dining room for weeks. Kid kept saying she couldn't walk over her parents' blood."

His wife interrupted. "Anyone would've had problems returning to the house after such a tragedy. We found her an excellent child psychologist."

Thomas made further inroads on the spiked coffee. "Yeah, but we had to drag her to the appointments sometimes. He told us the kid had regressed to about age four. She didn't want to leave her room and refused to go to sleep unless all the upstairs lights were on." An attempt at an indulgent chuckle. "She was a handful."

Their dog and pony show was wasting valuable time. Giulia tried her first poke. "Having cousins her own age in the house must have helped her recovery."

Caroline's mouth stretched taut, like a thin rubber band. "Our children were older than Elaine by ten years and more. I often had to read nursery rhymes to get her to sleep. At age nine and ten. None of our children decided to return to infancy when bad things happened. On top of Elaine's issues, we had to deal with Cissy Newton's meddling, interview for a new cook and maid, manage the finances, everything. We found a combination governess and glorified babysitter to coddle Elaine through her childhood."

Giulia possessed one superpower: the ability to blend into any scenery. She used it now to become...

Secretarial Pool Woman!

See her eager naiveté! Marvel at her pathetic eagerness to please! Gaze in awe at her efficiency!

Her pen touched the next line in her legal pad. "Your children are fortunate their parents are still living." In those nine words, she conveyed the impression hers were not.

Condescend to her misfortunes! Indulge in guiltless schadenfreude!

Caroline's demeanor shifted the least bit. "We taught them to rely on their skills and not to expect handouts."

Giulia wrote, "Elaine refused to set her cousins up in business? Caroline and Thomas mismanaged the money they received as Elaine's guardians? Elaine is much more ruthless than she appears?"

Thomas' phone dinged. He checked out of the conversation and began texting.

Caroline's lips pinched.

"Hey." Thomas looked up. "There's a horse called Hickory Dickory Dock at eleven to one odds. Want to go in on a bet with me, detective?"

With a shy smile, Giulia refused.

Caroline said in a brisk voice, "Is there anything else we can help you with?"

Secretarial Pool Woman infused a smidgen of guilt into her posture as though she'd been caught wasting her employer's time. "Yes, please." She asked the same questions about Dahlia as now run by the Board of Directors plus Elaine.

Thomas switched from texting to calling and disappeared into a room with a door to close.

Caroline's posture could only have gotten more rigid if she'd been strapped to a backboard. "To be honest, we weren't involved in the business. I'm a nurse and my husband was in sales. We knew our most important job was being surrogate parents to Elaine."

"You mentioned hiring a governess."

"Oh, my, yes. We weren't the homeschool types. We also found her a more advanced tutor when she was ready for higher education. Did you need their names, dear?"

Bravo! Secretarial Pool Woman's mesmeric powers had accessed the hidden reservoir of condescension in her adversary. Super Saiyan Level activated: Wallpaper Woman!

"Thank you, no. Ms. Newton was kind enough to let me have their names. She's been extremely helpful."

"She didn't ask you to call her by her first name?" Caroline's spine abandoned the backboard. Giulia was now "the help." "If you interact any further with Cissy, you'll realize she takes her managerial duties to heart. Several times over the years she forced me to assert my authority when she and I disagreed about what was best for Elaine. She chose to forget we were Elaine's legal guardians and she was merely the housekeeper." A shake of the head. "Too many people liked to pamper Elaine when what she needed was a good, stiff dose of reality."

"Have you met Elaine's husband? He treats her like a princess." Wallpaper Woman sighed like a teenage girl reading a romance novel.

"Certainly we know Pip. They met at a Christmas Ball we insisted Elaine attend." Thomas returned to the room, but Caroline ignored him. "People in her position are expected to attend certain formal events. The ball in question was one of only two she agreed to leave the house for."

Giulia underscored the words. Any history about Pip would shorten Zane's search.

Caroline continued: "We had the family lawyer run a background check on him when his intentions became serious."

Thomas coughed one comment: "Gigolo."

Caroline's voice trampled the cough. "Thomas, you don't know that."

"He's a fool if he doesn't, and Pip's no fool."

Caroline said with a return to stiffness, "Pip is a very well connected young man. His family traces its ancestry all the way back to the first colony in Jamestown."

"Detective, my wife thinks she's too proper to say it, but he's got women on the side. Look at his teeth."

"He's not a horse, Thomas."

"No, but he sure is a stud." Thomas laughed heartily enough for all three of them. "Think about it. Elaine is a china doll, and Pip with his asinine name is a Golden Boy who loves competition in everything: work, women, sports. Once he captured his prize of a rich wife, he set himself a new goal."

Giulia made her voice sweet and neutral. "Are you saying Elaine's husband is planning to file for divorce?"

Caroline swooped. "Thomas, stop planting baseless rumors."

"Carrie, if he didn't marry her for her money, I'm Donald Trump." To Giulia: "Of course he's not going to divorce her. The family lawyer is too smart not to have had them both sign an ironclad prenup. Elaine plays princess in her castle. Pip caters to her fantasy inside it and does what he wants outside it. Everyone's happy."

"But Elaine isn't a child in an adult's body." Giulia didn't feel obliged to mention her personal opinion on this. "She runs the family business remotely from her house. Many people telecommute these days."

"They have to accommodate her," Thomas said. "She owns the business and is majority stockholder."

"Be fair," Caroline said. "She has the business acumen to keep it profitable or the Chief Financial Officer and Belinda and Arthur's personal assistants would've found a way to oust her. The stockholders—"

Thomas' groan cut her off. "If Elaine had only given us stock."

Caroline said with a large smile at Giulia, "But she didn't. There's no point in pining over what we don't have. Ms. Driscoll, if there's nothing else we can help you with..."

Thirty

Halfway to the second appointment, a white van glued itself to the Clown Car for a quarter mile before passing her on the right. Its vanity plate—THESCOOP—replaced her momentary panic with anger. Were they following her hoping to capture her next brush with death in real time?

She pulled into the nearest parking lot and called Frank. "I need everything you know about dashboard cameras."

Next she left a message on the phone of Elaine's first governess/tutor to say she'd be a few minutes late.

Then she drove to the nearest non-chain electronics store. The owner's assistant installed the camera for her for an additional thirty dollars and she made it to her appointment only fifteen minutes late.

Veronika Graser wore the boho look well. Her lilac blouse and hemp sandals appeared to be handmade. If Giulia hadn't learned about Graser's childhood train accident from her research she wouldn't have noticed her slight limp under her flowing multi-tier cotton skirt.

Her smile of greeting was the most genuine of all the Dahlia and ex-Dahlia connections.

"Welcome to the Spin Cycle. Your phone call came at the perfect time. My latest dye creation hit critical mass way sooner than I calculated. If I hadn't put it through the rinse baths when I did, I'd be trying to figure out how to weave Pepto-Bismol pink wool into Christmas crafts."

The country bouquet of sheep dung competed with the heavy aroma of honeysuckle flowers from two massive bushes at the corners of a huge renovated farmhouse. Giulia chatted about sheep fiber versus alpaca fiber (thank you Sidney's family alpaca farm) as they walked up a cobblestone path.

No ghosts. No demons. No disembodied laughter, unless a smart-aleck entity had latched onto Giulia and wanted to mess with her by possessing the sheep during this interview.

Giulia made the *corno* as soon as the thought formed. Generations of superstitions weren't sloughed off after a mere ten years of teaching.

Her enjoyment of a routine interview must have communicated itself. Graser's expansive gestures increased as they entered the house.

"We bought this old place six months before we got married. Nothing like gutting and restoring a house to prove whether you can live with someone. All the wood is reclaimed. We're replacing the area rugs with ones made from our own wool. Do you weave?"

"I've tried spinning, but it was less than successful." Giulia did not have grateful memories of the drug-addled Doomsday Prepper camp case, despite being able to honestly say she'd spun wool. Once.

"You need to try again. Once you get the hang of it you'll never buy a mass-produced sweater or scarf again. Let me show you our looms."

She led Giulia to the back of her house. A wide sun porch held three looms of varying sizes. Two older women sat at the larger looms. Twin toddlers played with a toy farm set in a shady corner. They held out their arms in sync when Graser appeared, and she interrupted her tour guide speech to run over and hug them.

"Mama has to talk to this lady now. You play nice and then we'll all feed the sheep."

The twin girls toddled over by the older of the weaving women, who plucked several bright dangling threads out of their reach.

"This is my mom and my aunt. They're wizards at weaving. They taught me, and they're going to teach Siobhan and Annie as soon as they remember threads are for weaving, not eating." She made an indulgent face at the girls as she said it. "The grand tour is now complete. I'm all yours. Come see the sheep while we talk."

Giulia complimented the fat, fluffy woolbearers and opened with the same unspecific statement about Dahlia, Elaine, and the Board of Directors. Graser leapt to the same conclusion as everyone else.

"Elaine's been running Dahlia for three years and now they're trying to seize power? They ought to have more sense."

A wail from the sun porch interrupted her. Graser ran inside and came out with a tearful twin clinging to her with one hand and clutching a homemade Pippi Longstocking doll in the other. Subdued wails followed them.

"Siobhan wanted Annie's doll. Annie didn't want to relinquish it. Siobhan is developing a mean right hook."

Giulia made a sympathetic pout at Annie. "Siobhan is now regretting the use of violence as an initial means of achieving her goals?"

Graser laughed. "Got it in one. We were talking about Elaine running Dahlia, right? I was Elaine's tutor starting a few months after her parents' deaths up to her fifteenth birthday, more or less. Sure, it took her a while to adjust. Do you know anything about trauma recovery?"

"A little." Giulia attached mental blinders to focus on Graser's face and not be distracted by the adorable baby.

Graser kissed Annie, who imitated a lamprey around her mother's neck. "Elaine's aunt and uncle hired me, but Cissy the housekeeper was the brains behind the place. Is she still there?"

"She is, and I agree with your assessment."

An airplane flew high overhead, the only sign of civilization Giulia had seen since arriving.

"Elaine had a lot of rough nights. A lot a lot. The only way she'd go to sleep was if I read to her. She had to see a child psychiatrist once a month for a year, and those nights were the worst. No, Annie, you can't play with the sheep. You'll get poop all over you."

Annie pouted some more but settled back against her mother's neck.

"I'm telling you this to highlight what an accomplished business leader Elaine's become. *Some* people seem to think she's still that traumatized little girl. You know she's a classic agoraphobic, right?"

"I'm not familiar with the medical definition, but she came to our offices earlier this week."

"Did she ask if you had any Constant Comment tea?" Graser sat on the grass to let Annie pick wild daisies.

Giulia smiled. "I keep a stash of tea and she noticed the Constant Comment right away."

"Back then she thought tea made her look grown up. She'll force herself to go out of the house in unavoidable circumstances, but here's the important thing: she doesn't need to be in Dahlia's offices to run her company."

Annie handed Giulia a bouquet of tiny daisies with squashed stems. Giulia accepted them with gravity. "Thank you, Annie. They're beautiful."

Annie rewarded Giulia with a miniature copy of her mother's smile and dived back into Graser's arms.

"Elaine has a first-rate business head," Graser continued. "By the time she was fifteen she'd progressed beyond my capabilities. My field is Early Childhood Education. I'm still a private tutor, but I stick with K through five."

Annie balanced on her mother's legs and gathered buttercups and more daisies.

"I was the one who recommended Elaine's aunt and uncle find her a new tutor. I didn't expect to be packed up and tossed out the next day." She managed to convey cynicism and ruefulness in a single gesture. "I don't know if you've met her aunt and uncle, but if you ever do, don't turn your back on them."

Giulia picked up on the cynicism. "The next day? What did you do for money? Did you move into a hotel?"

A hand wave. "Practically the next day. They gave me a week's notice, but I'd been saving. Even with room and board at the house decreasing my salary, I made darn good money all those years. I wasn't going to end my days a mad governess in someone's attic. No gothic novels for me."

Giulia tipped her head in approval. "I taught high school for ten years, but my severance package bought me lunch at McDonald's."

Graser opened like a flower to the sun. Giulia had long since stopped wasting useless guilt on deliberate information sharing to draw out a client. Or a witness. Or to suss out a red herring.

"That's criminal. Where did you teach?"

"The Catholic school system."

A groan. "You poor thing. A friend of mine got a position right out of college in Philadelphia's parochial system. Too much student loan debt made any teaching job better than 'Do you want fries with that?' She escaped after three years." With her hands over Annie's ears she whispered, "They treated her like a second-class citizen because she wasn't a nun. If this one wasn't in my lap, I'd tell you exactly what I think of the parochial system and Catholics in general." She tickled her daughter until the toddler collapsed giggling on the grass. "After my Elaine years I started working for Kaplan, the tutoring company. One day this hot guy dragged in his little brother and I reeled him in like a large mouth bass. The hot guy, I mean."

She stood, swooping Annie onto her hip in the same motion. "I need to go inside and show Siobhan I still love her."

Giulia kept pace with the taller woman. "Have you met Elaine's husband?"

"Oh, Pip." Graser's free hand fluttered over her heart. "What a lady killer. Don't get me wrong, he and Elaine are perfect for each other. I met him at their fairy-tale wedding." They entered the sunroom. "Siobhan, come tell Annie you're sorry."

Giulia began her exit strategy before her pregnancy hormones derailed her day of interviews. In a perfect world, she'd ditch her to-do list and spend all day playing with the twins.

"I'll walk you to your car." Graser balanced a twin on each of her hourglass hips. "My husband works for Pip's marketing firm. We had no idea until their wedding. We don't breathe the rarefied air of upper management, natch. He crunches data and is my personal marketing wizard in his spare time."

Giulia made certain Annie saw her bouquet of daisies in a prominent place on the car's dashboard. The little hands clapped.

Graser beamed. "You made her day. About Dahlia. You can trust me on this: Elaine would have no problem whatsoever running the company as long as she stays in her mansion. She has Pip to run her errands and Cissy Newton as her personal privacy fence." She nuzzled Annie's chubby neck. "You and your sister are going to grow up strong, talented, independent women. You won't need a cross between Mary Poppins and the good Terminator from *T2* to function."

Her daughters kissed her cheeks.

"It's all about the proper parental involvement, don't you agree? If

Elaine had had a normal mother instead of a surrogate bodyguard, she might have turned out differently. Still, she has everything any woman could want. I wish I had her life."

Siobhan flung her arms around Graser's neck. A moment later Annie did the same.

Graser squeezed her daughters. "No I don't, after all."

Thirty-One

Giulia sat in the rental car eating the hot dog Zlatan demanded for lunch and reading the dashboard camera manual.

Her phone's memo cache was ninety-five percent full. She'd have to bring the tablet to the second tutor's interview.

She finished the hot dog and programmed the camera to take a picture when the car shuddered. "Shuddered" should've been in the three-language manual, none of whose languages resembled grammatical English, including the "English" section.

If the anonymous van came at her from front or side, all she had to do was spin the camera's swivel mount in the proper direction. A good use of a few extra dollars, assuming she wouldn't be occupied with not plunging over a bridge.

"It's pronounced 'Vagh-ner' like the composer, not 'Wagner' like the power tools."

Elaine's college tutor, a pre-Captain America Steve Rogers, let her into his loft apartment.

First a young Paul Newman, now him. This case was as close as Giulia would ever get to movie stars. If only the tutor's first name had been Steve.

"Thank you for taking time to see me, Mr. Wagner." She pronounced it correctly this time.

"Anything for Elaine. She's the only woman who understood me outside of my advanced differential equations professor at MIT."

She followed his Ralph Lauren acorn-brown suit into an open

room decorated in blues and ivories with accents of rust red. The red should've looked like dried blood, but instead the overall effect was of fall mums against a blue sky.

Giulia resolved not to like Clark Wagner too much.

"You picked the right day to set this up. My usual schedule is four ten-hour workdays, which makes every weekend a long weekend. Nice, isn't it? Have a seat. Would you like a glass of water or a Coke?"

"Thank you, no." Giulia sat at a trestle table with stained glass inserts and brought out her iPad. "We've been hired to look into Dahlia's business practices under Elaine Patrick's management."

Wagner sat facing Giulia. "Someone still thinks Elaine can't possibly be a success from the confines of her home? Please. Are you familiar with my credentials?"

Giulia played straight man. "I know you received a master's degree from MIT."

"Beavers rule." Even his grin was worthy of Captain America. "False modesty is a waste of time. I'm pretty damn smart, Ms. Driscoll. I also have a knack for spotting entrepreneurs who have what it takes to be successful."

He jumped out of the chair and rifled through the newspapers in a magazine rack. In a minute, he brought over a yellowed business section with a banner headline: The Next Hot Start-Ups. "Third one down. We're going to give Google a run for its mountains of money. I guarantee it." He plucked the paper from her hands and returned it to the rack. "When I first came to the castle I was twenty-five and she was fifteen. Elaine was in major withdrawal from the loss of her first tutor and wouldn't come out of her suite of rooms for two days." The grin reappeared. "Nice to be rich and able to do whatever you want, isn't it?" He watched Giulia type. "Want me to slow down?"

"You're fine. Thank you."

"Cool. I get into a rhythm when I lecture and altering it interferes with my synaptic connections."

Giulia tried harder not to like him.

"Veronika, the former tutor, ended up saving my job. She left me an 'Elaine 101' manual. While her parasites—sorry, her aunt and uncle—were trying to convince the house manager to force Elaine's door, I gave myself a crash course in all things Elaine."

Giulia typed, "Do NOT smile. Do NOT smile."

"No, go ahead. Enjoy the image." Wagner leaned forward. "The house was a cross between a chaotic sitcom and an amateur rugby match. When I finished the manual, I slid a paper under Elaine's door with a college freshman level statistical analysis problem. An hour later she came out of her room with the problem solved and asked Cissy to make her a cup of that orange tea she drinks by the gallon." He preened in the way a champion hoists a trophy.

"In your opinion, therefore, Elaine is capable of running Dahlia."

"No question. Why else would I have called in favors and pulled strings to get her enrolled in Harvard's MBA program at sixteen? Besides, money talks." He winked.

"Elaine was also a notch in their inclusivity lists."

"You bet she was. Admitting her was a slam-dunk for Harvard. Neither of us cared about that aspect, though. Once we removed the stress of leaving the house, she aced most of her classes. The only 'B' she got was because her keepers nagged her all semester to go to this ridiculous Christmas costume dance."

Again with the Christmas ball. "Which involved the usual anxiety factor of going out into a crowd."

The door opened, and a statue from ancient Rome come to life walked into the apartment. His curly black hair brushed the lintel. His nose ought to have caused sculptors to stalk him on Facebook. His pecs under an Orangetheory Fitness polo announced "personal trainer inside."

"Darling, I have the most succulent tomatoes to grill—oh."

Wagner stood. The top of his head reached no higher than the newcomer's collarbone. They shared a "we're in front of a stranger" kiss.

"This is Ms. Driscoll of Driscoll Investigations. She's here about Elaine."

The Nose looked from Giulia to Wagner and back again. "*The* Driscoll Investigations? Stone's Throw Lighthouse B&B Driscoll Investigations?"

Polite Smile Number Two appeared (the one which masked her desire to beat her head against the nearest wall). "Yes, we were able to assist Stone's Throw earlier this summer."

The farmers' market bag hit the table with too much force for the integrity of the tomatoes. "Oh my God, I am such a fan. Clark and I stayed there last Christmas." He pumped Giulia's hand. Giulia got the strongest sense he wanted to ask for her autograph.

Wagner's heartthrob attractiveness increased exponentially when excited. "I didn't think to make the connection. We're on the Stone's Throw mailing list, and she sent flyers for Halloween. Brad, did we save it?"

Brad searched a basket on the kitchen counter. "Yes, we did." He passed it to Wagner and retrieved the bag of tomatoes on his way to the balcony.

Wagner spread open the booklet-sized mailing. The cover matched the B&B's home page with screaming capital letters and translucent ghosts. "We must go back for a haunted weekend now. We'll be minor celebrities because we know Driscoll Investigations."

Giulia's polite smile became strained.

Brad called from the balcony, "Halloween is probably booked, but maybe for our anniversary in February."

Wagner grimaced. "Please don't think we were married on Valentine's Day. It's too cliché for real life. We chose Imbolc because my parents still call it Candlemas and think witches practice human sacrifice on that night and on Halloween."

Brad poked his head inside. "By way of explanation, his parents send money to *The 700 Club*. Ms. Driscoll, would you like to share our lunch? We have plenty."

"Thank you, I already ate. Mr. Wagner, about Elaine's education and her assumption of Dahlia's leadership—"

"Oh my God, I just figured it out." He stabbed the Stone's Throw flyer with a long index finger. "Elaine thinks her castle is haunted. No, wait. Cissy thinks the castle is haunted. Tell me I'm right."

"We don't divulge our client's information."

Brad said from the balcony doorway, "Don't pout."

Wagner wiggled his fingers at him. "Aren't you supposed to be on lunch duty today?"

"Unlike some brainiacs, I can multitask." He carried in a plate of roasted plum tomatoes covered with chopped scallions and melted cheese. "I'll slice the bread."

Giulia's stomach rumbled—silently, thank goodness—as little Zlatan decided he liked the aroma of cheese-slathered tomatoes.

Wagner poured drinks for himself and Brad. "Ms. Driscoll, it wouldn't surprise me if the castle harbored a resident ghost. It's one of the oldest houses in Pittsburgh. Elaine's mother and father spent a small fortune renovating it, but what if the original builders had been freakazoids?"

Brad brought Italian bread and ramekins of herbed oil to the table. "What if your Elaine has a modern-day instance of the ancient custom of walling people alive in house and bridge foundations?"

Wagner dunked bread. "You have a seriously twisted mind."

Brad's smile was almost as charming as Clark's. "And you love me for it." He emphasized his point with his fork. "I'm not addicted to the SyFy channel only for the *Sharknado* movies. Wouldn't you haunt the house where you'd been forced to reenact the loser's role in 'The Cask of Amontillado'?"

Wagner popped a tomato in his mouth and spoke around it. "I can envision several centuries of anger as a result, yes."

Brad speared a tomato. "Ms. Driscoll, are you familiar with the admittedly barbaric practice?"

In her cloistered Canonical Novice year, a restless Giulia unearthed an ancient volume of church history describing something similar in the life of Saint...Saint...The name refused to come.

"This isn't the first I've heard of it, but it's been a while."

Brad swallowed the tomato whole. "I'm researching legends and their cross-culture assimilation for my master's degree. This practice is ancient enough to cause a cage match among multiple cultures over who began it."

Giulia gave the derail its head as she watched Brad and Clark interact. The former unpacked immurement rituals of a dozen religions and cultures. The latter interjected variations on "creepy," "disgusting," and "sick puppies."

She never sensed they were putting on an elaborate show for her benefit. Their banter was not accompanied by shifting eye movements or twitching fingers.

"What about residual energy?" Wagner finished off his fourth tomato.

"Remember the curse on King Tut's tomb." Brad took the subject further afield.

Wagner narrowed his spectacular eyelashes at Brad. "You're doing it again."

"...the cow's head and painted vase discovered less than a decade ago—What?"

"Leading your dinner companions down a rabbit trail of fascinating trivia. We're supposed to be discussing ghosts in Elaine's mansion."

"Mmph." The bread in Brad's mouth precluded intelligible speech. He handed his phone to Wagner. "Ak-kk."

Wagner translated. "He wants to show you his apps."

Brad forced down the mouthful. "Make it test the ghost voices."

"I'm not sure if Elaine would jump all over this or build a fort with her collection of nursery rhyme books if she heard it." Wagner held the phone to Giulia's face. "Say something."

Giulia spoke with precision. "I am sorry to disappoint you, but I already downloaded a similar app."

A familiar robotic voice spoke from the phone: "Load Hiss Apple."

Everyone laughed.

"Ghosts write bad haiku?" Wagner said.

"As long as I'm not destroying your belief in another plane of existence," Giulia said, "EVP recorders are notoriously unreliable."

Brad raised his eyes to the ceiling. "You're going to cite Joe Nickell."

"Well, yes. His years of research have indicated EVP is most likely caused by picking up random words from TV or radio."

Brad countered: "What about spirit box sessions? Have you listened to some of those on YouTube?"

Wagner gathered the dishes. "I don't care if they're real or elaborate party tricks. I'd bet a week of Brad's cooking Cissy Newton has five of those apps on her phone and checks them every time she goes to a different floor. She's such a mama bear when it comes to Elaine, she'll work herself up to thinking the castle is the Amityville Horror and Winchester Mystery Houses combined."

Brad shook his head at Giulia and said to Wagner's back, "Clark, you're being naïve."

Wagner turned toward him from the sink, a dishtowel in one hand and the long-handled grilling fork in the other.

In a sweet voice, Brad said, "This detective wouldn't be here if someone hadn't thrown you under the bus."

Thirty-Two

"Well, butter my butt and call me a biscuit."

Giulia attempted to hide behind her iPad screen.

Wagner slammed the grilling fork on the counter and flung the towel next to it. He took three steps to the table, snatched his phone, and pounded the keypad. "Here is a snapshot of my current financial status." He shoved the phone under Giulia's nose. "Please take note of our current rent payment, my car loan status, and my monthly student loan payment. My savings balance is at the bottom of the screen. If you click on my checking account, you'll see my take-home pay. Is that enough to satisfy your masters or would you like me to add the bonus structure at my place of employment?"

Giulia noted the figures.

"Brad is no hourly grunt either. Tell the detective."

At Wagner's peremptory gesture, Brad ran through a similar list. "I'm a personal trainer to several Carnegie Mellon Tartans and a long list of alumni as well as the Pittsburgh Hornets."

"He charges seventy-five bucks per hour because he's worth it." Wagner took back his phone. "Let me assure you we can more than afford our upscale residence. Our most expensive habit is gourmet cooking. It stands to reason I'm dying to oust Elaine from her own company. I must be working with Pedersen because I have a gambling habit. No, I cut a deal with Elaine's aunt and uncle because they offered to bankroll my secret startup." He sat next to Giulia. "Have any of the Dahlia people said snide things about Pip? Don't bother. I know they did. Don't believe them. Pip is a walking vanity plate, but he's good to

Elaine. Sandra Sechrest hates him. Speaking of Sechrest, I bet she neglected to mention she lost her sugar daddy when Elaine's father was murdered."

Giulia loved it when the correct answer was also the honest answer. "I didn't know. Please tell me more."

Brad said from the sink, "Those words are the equivalent of a starter's pistol."

Giulia imitated a sparrow eyeing a particularly tempting worm. Wagner did in fact lean forward in the position of a runner waiting for the signal to start.

"The cook at the castle is Elaine's cousin. We shared a common hatred of the Steelers and a common love of brewing IPAs in small batches in the cellar. During our many late nights crafting seasonal ale, I taught him poker strategies and he dished on the Davenports. There's a family legend of Elaine's mother sacking a maid who compared her in a certain flowered dress to that particular style of sofa." He snickered. "The stories he told me about Mama D. No male alive would blame Daddy D for getting some on the side, but Sechrest? You'd think the man would find a plump, easygoing type whose skills began in the kitchen and ended in the bedroom." He waited until Giulia finished typing. "You've met Sechrest already, right?"

"Yes."

"Okay, then. You know whereof I speak. Daddy Dahlia and his efficient personal assistant romped at will for six years. She thought he'd divorce his wife and make her Queen of the Dahlia empire." A snort.

Brad leaned his chin on top of Wagner's head. "Have you ever watched *The Scoop*?"

Giulia hoped her smile wasn't too much like a grimace. "Once or twice."

Wagner said, "They could milk Dahlia for a month's worth of episodes."

"For sweeps week," Brad said.

"They'd smoke the competition. Take Elaine's aunt and uncle and their four waste of space spawn. If the reason you're here isn't Sechrest scheming to seize power, it's Elaine's aunt. Ruthlessness is in the Davenport female DNA."

Giulia, typing: "I wouldn't have said Elaine knew the definition of ruthless."

Tandem laughter stopped her fingers.

Brad took the chair on Giulia's other side. "I never get tired of this story."

Giulia interlaced her fingers and bent them backward until the knuckles cracked. "Hit me."

Thirty-Three

After his one-eighty from charming intellectual to wolverine at bay, Wagner now became a kid around a campfire.

"Remember how I said the only time Elaine didn't ace a class was the Christmas after she turned eighteen? Auntie and Uncle nagged her for a solid month, from October first to November first. She had to attend, they said. Elaine couldn't shirk certain obligations, they said. They hinted if she couldn't manage a simple party they'd force her to go back to a shrink for her agoraphobia."

"Ouch, right?" Brad said.

"They finally played the marriage card. It'd do Elaine good to meet other young people. What they meant was 'young men of similar social standing and bank balances.'"

Giulia shammed ingenuous. "Elaine's aunt may have known what Elaine needed in this particular case."

Wagner made a rude noise. "Not by the hair on her chinny chin chin. Not that Aunty Caroline would've allowed a single hair out of place on her expensively coiffed head. She knew they'd be suspected of keeping Elaine from a fulfilling life if they let her stay tucked into her turtle shell."

"A classic Catch-22."

"I do love encountering adults who read. Exactly. They nagged and wheedled and did everything they could to wear her down. Finally they thought to mention the fancy affair was also a Dickensian costume ball. Elaine is a terrific seamstress. She designed the tuxedos for our wedding." He gathered himself. "Guess what costumes she created for auntie and uncle?"

Giulia cudgeled her brain. She hadn't read Dickens in years. "Bob Cratchit and...I don't recall his wife's name."

"Please. How pedestrian. Elaine locked herself in her sewing room for two weeks. The morning of the ball she presented them with their identities for the night: The Golden Dustman and wife." He opened his hands and raised his eyebrows.

Giulia reveled in another opportunity for honesty. "I must not have read that book."

Wagner collapsed like a Serie A soccer player. Giulia typed, "Do not be taken in by his charm."

The typing appeared to unnerve him. He traced the stained glass designs in the table.

"Please explain the significance of the Golden Dustman," Giulia said.

"Right. Two of the characters in *Our Mutual Friend* are the downtrodden employees of the hero's reprehensible father. When the father kicks it, he leaves his fortune to said honest employees. They have no clue how to fit into society, including how to dress. Just a minute."

He ran to the living room end of the open floor plan and returned with a MacBook Air. "I took a picture without them seeing." He scrolled and clicked. "Enjoy." He slid the laptop over. A full-length photo of Caroline and Thomas Emerson assaulted her eyes.

Caroline wore an off-shoulder fuchsia dress trimmed with canary-yellow ruffles at the bodice and short sleeves cut at the right length to showcase her Bingo Lady arms. An ostrich feather fascinator bobbed over her head. An emerald cut citrine glittered on her spare bosom. Matching oversize urine-yellow crystals dangled from her earlobes. Fuchsia was not her color.

Thomas was a vision in black. Black frock coat and black trousers tucked into knee-high black boots. A pea-soup green shirt peeped out from behind a black vest and a black bow tie. A gleaming black top hat and black gloves completed the outfit. False mutton chop whiskers clung to his cheeks. His nose, not yet as neon red as when Giulia met him, wrinkled as though he was trying to stifle a sneeze. Pea-soup green was not his color.

The fuchsia and pea soup clashed in the worst way. The green made Thomas look jaundiced, the fuchsia made Caroline look bilious.

"Oh dear," Giulia said.

"Told you. I helped Elaine carry the outfits and snagged a first-row seat for the entertainment. Elaine told them all about the characters when she presented the costumes. It wasn't only the electric pink and puke green making aunty and uncle look sick. Despite Elaine's obvious intelligence, they still thought of her as the nine-year-old hiding under the bed because she didn't want the child psychiatrist rummaging around in her brain."

Giulia returned the laptop. "The costumes forced them to see the adult Elaine."

"Not only Elaine as a functioning adult—sort of—but an Elaine who wasn't afraid to remind them of their subservient position in her house." His face was the epitome of schadenfreude. "They walked on eggs for the next three years. I overheard some colorful complaints when they thought no one was around."

Brad said, "His favorite was 'pampered little spiteful bitch.'"

"True. Now you see what I mean when I say all Davenport women are born ruthless." He snapped shut the laptop. "When Elaine was prepping to take charge at Dahlia, the Board of Directors summoned me. I had to show them Elaine's transcripts, her thesis, and her professors' assessments. Finally, those three demanded my personal guarantee Elaine had earned her degree and not bought it."

"Your guarantee?"

His animated face grew dark. "Their lawyer said he could get me blackballed from the teaching profession. Not in those exact words, but I understood him."

Giulia was unsurprised. "Since Dahlia has continued to be profitable, you've been justified."

"I'm seldom wrong. *Cherchez la femme*, detective, look for the woman. In this case, you want *la belle dame sans merci,* and I do mean that literally. Between Sechrest and his wife, I wonder if Daddy Dahlia wasn't the walking dead years before his official death."

Giulia typed like a diligent secretary. "A moment ago you tried to convince me Elaine's aunt and uncle were the ones to suspect."

A coy smile. "I'm not a licensed private investigator. I wouldn't dream of telling you how to do your job."

Thirty-Four

"I don't trust the way Clark Wagner kept pushing Caroline and Thomas Emerson at me as the prime suspects."

Giulia dictated into her phone as she drove on the Turnpike. Traffic was heavy but flowed well.

"Zane may have discovered a Daddy-Sechrest connection in his research, but if the affair lasted several years, Elaine's father must have concealed it well. Sechrest struck me as wanting power, but not necessarily as a saboteur. Thomas and Caroline's obvious hunger for the lifestyle they can no longer afford is more—"

The Clown Car jerked forward. Giulia snapped to attention. A two-tone VW Bus rode her bumper.

Camera. Did it turn on at the contact?

The VW knocked against her again. She glanced in her side mirror. One car too close on her left. A several-story drop into the Allegheny River on her right. Her wannabe assassin knew how to time his attempts.

The VW smacked her harder this time. The steering wheel jerked in her hands. A Honda passed her on the left but an Audi took its place, going way over the speed limit.

This time the VW stayed on her bumper, pushing her toward the guard rail.

The Clown Car was smaller than the Nunmobile. Giulia hit the gas and swung into the left lane without signaling.

Multiple horns. A hand emerged from the Audi's window and flipped her off. The VW sped up and weaved in and out of traffic too fast for her to catch the license plate.

She eased up on the gas until she returned to the speed limit. The Audi roared past her. Its tinted windows concealed any parting gesture from the driver.

Her hands trembled. She anchored them at the ten and two positions on the steering wheel and glanced down at the gearshift. Her phone was still there. Upside down, but there. She raised her voice in the hope the voice memo function was still recording and enough space remained.

"It's four p.m. on Saturday, July twenty-second. I'm two miles from the Cottonwood exit on the Turnpike. A tan and blue Volkswagen bus just tried to run me off the overpass. In health news, my adrenal gland is functioning in top shape. In pregnancy news, I'm surprised Zlatan isn't sending psychic complaints about how I'm disturbing his naps. Maybe he is and Jasper is looking up my phone number right now." She signaled and exited. "Given the choice as a way to keep alert, I'll take coffee over near-death experiences any day."

Thirty-Five

Giulia sat in the little car for several minutes before she trusted her legs to get her up the two steps from the garage into the house.

Frank wasn't there. She gave up trying to remember and opened the calendar on her phone: 4-7 p.m. Coach kids' soccer. YMCA.

She could postpone telling Frank about the latest car incident until she got a handle on herself.

If this kept up, she might as well stock up on hair dye, because Zlatan would be skydiving or in a demolition derby by middle school.

She called Sidney. "I hate to ask this with zero notice on a Saturday, but are you open to overtime?"

Sidney laughed. "You're worried that the parents of a six-month-old have plans for a wild weekend of partying? Olivier, listen to this." Olivier laughed even louder. Sidney said into the phone, "What do you need?"

"Our hive mind. My iPad is full of notes from today's interviews. If this were a workday, I'd beg you to stop whatever you were doing and huddle with me."

"Come on over. The August blowout sale from Christmas in July was light today. Mom and Dad don't need me."

"You're the best. I'm calling Zane next."

Giulia held a box from The Garden of Delights in front of her face when she rang Sidney's doorbell. The squeal of joy informed her the offering was acceptable.

"Tell me they had berry tiramisu, please please and please again."

"How could you doubt me?" Giulia followed the box inside the cottage.

The doorbell rang again while she was unpacking. Olivier opened for Zane as Sidney set out plates, napkins, and forks.

"Do I see an offering from The Garden?"

Giulia held up a plate with slices of pie, rounds of shortcake, and two kinds of tortes. "Raspberry lemon meringue included."

"I love my job." He looked relieved when the door closed. "Sidney, what do your hulking beasts have against males?"

Olivier answered. "I've narrowed it down to a six-thousand-year-old collective memory from when humans first gave their species a curfew. Or their less-remote ancestors watched too many episodes of *The Donna Reed Show*, and they blame men for the oppression of the female sex as a whole."

Zane picked up a piece of meringue-covered pie and bit into it without taking his gaze from Olivier.

"Don't fall for his delivery," Sidney said. "He likes to impress people with obscure facts."

"I wish I could impress the woolly varmints with my big words. Who targeted you?"

"Belle and Vixen. I know to keep outside of their spitting range now."

Giulia opened her laptop. "Wait a minute. Where's Jessamine?"

"Modeling our cuddly new felted blankets."

"In this heat?"

"Mom and Dad cranked the air conditioning in the gift shop." She raised a spoonful of her all-natural, honey-sweetened tiramisu. "Here's to spoiling our dinners."

"Adulthood has its privileges." Giulia claimed the peach shortcake. "Olivier, they didn't have any margarita pie left. I took a chance on chocolate hazelnut torte."

Olivier clutched the plate with its generous square of chocolate decadence. "An hour ago I was waving a jar of Nutella at Sidney to convince her to make filled pancakes for breakfast tomorrow. You must be psychic. "

The staff of Driscoll Investigations laughed. Olivier paused in his chocolate worship. "What did I say?"

"I'll tell you later, sweetie," Sidney said. "DI hive mind, activate!"

"*Wonder Twins*," Zane said. "I have it queued up after I finish *Underdog*."

Olivier sang the first line of the *Underdog* theme. Zane joined in as he booted his laptop. As they finished their mostly on-key serenade, Zane set his laptop in front of Giulia. Two spreadsheets, a PowerPoint, and an annual report filled the four quadrants on his screen. "I have accessed Dahlia's financials."

Giulia knelt and bowed her face to the floor. Sidney gasped and giggled. Giulia raised her head and got to her feet before Zane keeled over in shock.

"When I die and my many sins are weighed against me, channeling your skills away from the creation of a criminal empire should even the balance."

A pause.

"Zane, breathe."

He inhaled. His pale eyes followed her lip movements.

"Zane, you've seen me make a joke before."

"Not one that good."

Sidney fell off her chair.

Thirty-Six

"Everyone was right, whether they liked to admit it or not," Giulia said. "Elaine is successfully running her family business."

Giulia, Sidney, and Zane crowded next to each other at the kitchen table paging through screen after screen of reports. Olivier had finished his torte and left to help with Jessamine.

"They've only posted a loss twice in the last fifteen years," Zane said. "Neither time after Elaine took over."

Giulia wrote essentials on a fresh page of her legal pad with her right hand and conveyed shortcake into her mouth with the fork in her left.

Zane nodded across Giulia at Sidney. "I'm not the only star of this show."

"I blame the bad influence of *The Scoop*." Sidney opened her own laptop. "Have I mentioned lately how awesome our work network is? Logging in from here is almost as fast as when I'm in the office. Anyway, Ken Kanning would make you even more inappropriate offers if we gave him all this dirt. Listen: Pedersen the CFO and his two ex-wives and two alimony payments every month? He had to get his first marriage annulled to marry the trophy wife, and he forgot the rule about complaining online."

"The internet is forever?" Giulia said.

"Yes indeed." She swallowed another mouthful. "My God, their desserts are good. Way back when Facebook first opened to the world he griped on it about how much he had to bribe the Annulment board." She patted Giulia's hand. "Don't be shocked."

"I'm not. I haven't been that starry-eyed in a long time."

"I'm proud of you. Pedersen promptly married his mistress, who dumped him within a year for—wait for it—his son's college roommate."

Giulia stopped writing. "You're kidding."

"I may be laughing, but none of this is a joke. Next we have Sandra Sechrest. Did you know she and Elaine's father had a six-year affair?"

"Vagh-ner the tutor let that one drop when he assumed Sechrest accused him of being the power-wresting mastermind."

"*Tsk*. Weren't any of these people taught to play nice way back in kindergarten? Sechrest also has an expensive divorce under her belt, but it happened years before she joined Dahlia."

"If she's behind the power grab, what about debt as the reason?" Giulia said.

Zane finished his pie and looked with sadness at the empty plate. "I vote for revenge. What if she had a humiliating catfight with Elaine's mother at the company picnic?"

"Ooh, with a private video on YouTube," Sidney said. "Except I couldn't find any evidence Elaine's mother knew about the affair."

"From everything I've heard about her, she knew," Giulia said.

"But didn't care?" Zane said.

"I'm sure she cared."

"She didn't want the scandal, then," Sidney said.

"No, I don't think scandal was her issue," Giulia said. "She wouldn't have wanted the distraction from business." She drew arrows between both names on the legal pad. "Are you now going to tell me Konani Hyde was also sleeping with Elaine's father?"

"Nope. Even better." Sidney's joy almost matched her reaction to the tiramisu. "Again, thanks to angry people on Facebook. One Christmas Mr. Dahlia pounded a lot of something called bourbon slush at the company party and got handsy with Ms. Hyde. Her exact post: 'The old goat stuck his scrawny hands under my skirt.' Three exclamation points. When her friends expressed outrage, she fed the flames: 'He kneaded my tush like it was a two-handed stress ball.' Five exclamation points."

Whimpering sounds came from Zane's head buried in his arms.

"I'd love to know if she blew him in to Elaine's mother," Giulia said.

"Funny you should ask. In an update to the conversation, she hints how Elaine's dad is scared she'll do exactly that, and he's treating her like she's a rare and fragile piece of art."

Giulia drew more notes and arrows. "Wagner was right. If Ken Kanning had access to this, he'd rule sweeps week."

Zane took his plate to the sink. "I'm making a side trip tonight to pick up more pie. My girlfriend will be almost as happy as I am."

Giulia's spoon *tinked* on her own plate. "I'm out of shortcake."

Sidney mimed playing the violin and hummed Barber's *Adagio for Strings*. "Aren't we supposed to be working? Hyde also posts a lot about the Meadow Schools."

Zane double-clicked. "Hyde's kids both go there. If you can afford to send yours, Ms. D., Sidney and I would like to renegotiate our salaries."

Giulia spread her hands. "If you require proof of my financial assets, I will be happy to reveal my bank balances." She gave Zane a Mr. Spock eyebrow. "Even though you could find them on your own."

Zane's skin paled to translucence. "I swear by all the gods, I've never even thought about hacking you."

"I'm pleased you continue to use your talents on the side of justice."

Sidney gathered the rest of the plates. "Zane, you're scarier than any fake ghost we might unearth."

His confusion appeared genuine. "How am I scary?"

She stacked the dishes in the sink and ran water over them. "Seriously? Giulia, explain to the human computer, please."

Olivier opened the front door with a crying Jessamine in his arms.

Sidney turned off the water. "Mama to the rescue—Whoa." She picked up her daughter by the armpits. "Someone needs a fresh diaper."

Jessamine's cries faded as Sidney took her to the little bedroom off the living room. Coos took their place in between Sidney's running monologue.

"No young lady should smell this bad. Did the customers still think you were adorable after this poop explosion? Oh sure, smile at me as I wipe your butt. You know exactly how to get around me, little lady."

Olivier poured himself a glass of water. "Nobody told me the odoriferous side of parenthood would be this intense."

Giulia said, "I thought you had two younger brothers."

"Mom was the diaper queen. I emptied trash and mopped floors." He glanced down. "I know what I'm doing after breakfast tomorrow."

"Trading diaper duty for floor mopping." Giulia scribbled in the upper corner of her current sheet of paper. "I think I'll propose this deal to Frank."

Zane said, "Wait, Ms. D. We got sidetracked. How am I scary? I'm your garden-variety geek, with muscles. A center-cut pork chop on the grill has more to fear from me."

Giulia packed her legal pad and tablet. "You are the destroyer of everyone's secretly cherished illusion of online privacy." She waited for the light bulb to appear over his head. "One more thing for Monday morning: Cissy Newton. Wagner emphasized her eccentricity while admitting her extreme overprotectiveness of Elaine. I would hate to learn our client has secretly bought massive amounts of Dahlia stock and wants to create a leaner, meaner regime to boost her dividends."

Thirty-Seven

Contact with humans who weren't trying to kill her had reduced Giulia's pulse to a non-daredevil rate. She still drove home with one eye on the road behind her. No *Duel* copycat vans of any color followed the Clown Car.

When she pulled into a still-empty garage, a text from Frank pinged her.

Running late. Will pick up pizza & chicken wings.

Zlatan approved of chicken wings. She brought the dash camera inside. Ignoring the garden's need for water and the junk mail in the mailbox, she connected the camera to her laptop and started the upload process.

The first photo caught the VW's grille and windshield. The second was all windshield as the VW crowded up to the rental car. The third and fourth were blurry, probably the fault of her wrestling the steering wheel for control. The fifth captured only half of the VW's front end as she changed lanes. The last framed the Audi owner's explicit hand gesture dead center.

She enlarged all the photos except the last, looking for any distinguishing marks on the vehicle or a clear shot of the driver.

Nothing. Not even a bumper sticker or windshield decal. If only Pennsylvania required license plates on the front of vehicles as well as the back.

The door from the garage opened. "I come bearing gifts of hot sauce and garlic."

"Enter and approach the Table of Offerings."

Her husband appeared in the living room archway. "Is the Table of Offerings supplied with the Beer of Refreshment?"

Giulia stood. "If the suppliant will pace slowly toward the Table, one will magic itself out of the fridge by the time you get there."

Frank's sneakers stopped squeaking when he stepped from the hall to the rug. "The real estate agent forgot to mention the house had magical properties."

Giulia came into the room carrying a Murphy's Irish Red as Frank set down the pizza and wing boxes behind Giulia's laptop.

"Why are there dash camera close-up pictures on your screen?"

Giulia knew that tone of voice. She'd heard him use it on suspects back when they owned Driscoll Investigations together.

"I called you about them this morning, remember? I thought I should buy one after the incident with the white van Ken Kanning swears wasn't his." She set the beer next to the pizza box.

Frank clicked the back arrow and scrolled through the series of photos. "I don't see a white van." His dormant volcano voice indicated imminent eruption.

"Did you see the anatomical suggestion from the guy in the Audi?"

"Honey, please explain these pictures to me."

A final attempt to cap the volcano. "It's simple. A VW bus was riding my bumper on the Turnpike. Merging left was my only option. The Clown Car zipped into the left lane and foiled the bus. I didn't think to signal. Thus the explicit hand gesture."

Frank clicked through all the photos in order again. "Now tell me what you're not telling me."

Giulia surrendered her volcano-capper card. "I set the dash cam to take pictures at car-to-car contact. The VW tried to run me off the overpass into the Allegheny. There was just enough space for me to merge to the left. I cut off the Audi, the VW couldn't follow, and I kept moving until he cut off even more drivers getting away."

Vesuvius' pyroclastic cloud had nothing on a Driscoll husband whose wife was in danger. Giulia had heard stories from her sisters-in-law.

Frank let loose with a string of Irish profanity. Giulia understood about a third of it, and what she caught wasn't in the vein of "May the cat eat you and may the devil eat the cat."

She stood by the coffee table, wanting pizza, wanting not to have this discussion again, wanting a magic button to defuse the Driscoll volcano.

Frank stopped. One second he was damning every murderous driver of vans to eternity up the devil's nether regions. The next second he enveloped Giulia in a massive hug.

"*Muirnín,* drop this case. Please drop it. We don't need the money. You have plenty of other clients." He kissed her hair, her ear, her neck, which was as far as his own neck could bend without letting her go. "Use the baby as your excuse."

Giulia kissed his scruffy cheek. "I have a handle on it."

"No, you don't." Vesuvius rumbled again.

"I beg to differ."

He shifted his hold to her shoulders. "You don't because they've changed the rules. The white creeper van is obvious. A hippie van isn't. Too many people are restoring them to relive their wild youth. Easy to hide. Easy to ditch."

"And easy to dodge. Look at my pictures. They showed their hand when they tried to make me create a new exit off the bridge."

His hands tightened. "Exactly what I mean."

"They couldn't even come up with a new way to scare me." She filled her voice with confidence. "Whoever's behind the wheels seems to think women can't drive well under pressure." She reached up and squeezed his hands. "You know I work best under pressure."

Frank cursed again.

"Don't try to disguise blasphemy. Your grandfather teaches me something new and colorful to say every time we visit."

Frank's neck muscles bulged. "Don't deflect me. I didn't sign up to become an eligible widower."

Giulia said in all seriousness. "And I have no plans to make you one. You tell me all the time you have confidence in me. Are those merely empty words to shut the wife up because you want to watch ESPN in peace?"

His teeth clenched with an audible crunch. "No."

She crossed her arms. "Then I will continue to work this case as I think best." He opened his mouth but she continued, "If I need you for action or extra backup, I promise to call. As long as your action doesn't involve shooting or arresting someone in my case. Well, not without cause."

Frank's short ginger hair threw off sparks. Giulia waited and watched his face as the cop fought the husband.

"I'm not happy," he said at last.

"I understand."

"Why didn't I marry a woman whose only hobbies were knitting and housecleaning?"

"Because you couldn't resist my sauce." She returned to the kitchen. "I'll bring plates and a lot of napkins."

Thirty-Eight

At nine the next morning Giulia said to Frank, "You know, dear, church would be an excellent use of your Sunday after yesterday's blasphemy session."

Frank protested. "How can you be sure I blasphemed if you couldn't understand all the Irish I used?"

Giulia didn't dignify his sophistry with a response.

Frank went to church.

Her phone rang as they drove home.

"Ms. Driscoll? This is Cissy Newton. Do you have a few minutes to meet today? I realize it's Sunday."

Giulia covered the mouthpiece. "Client wants to meet. Okay if I use the kitchen instead of going into the office?"

Frank shrugged. "I can manage it."

Giulia said into the phone. "Can you be at my house in—" she checked their location "—any time after eleven thirty?"

A brief hesitation on the other end. "I'm calling from your front porch."

Giulia facepalmed. "I see. We'll be there in seven minutes." She ended the call. "My client is stalking me. She's at our house now."

"Good God." He turned left. "Please take note of the lack of blasphemy in my remark."

"This pleases me."

"What's up with this woman? She thinks you're not earning your fee if you take a day off?"

"She's protecting her cub." Giulia cast a longing look as they passed a Starbucks. "Now I won't have time to make coffee."

With glee in his voice Frank said, "Offer it up?"

Giulia hit the back of her head against the headrest. "I've created a monster."

"I love it when you feed me a straight line. Oh, look. We have a squatter on our top step."

Cissy Newton rose when Frank hit the remote and the garage door opened. Today she wore khakis and a pink shirt with the sleeves rolled up to the elbows. Her sneakers matched her shirt. Giulia wondered if the woman secretly longed for *Sex and the City* shoes and was forced to settle for the complete line of Keds.

Giulia opened the front door from the inside. "Good morning. Please come inside. May I offer you coffee or tea?"

"No. This isn't a social visit." She preceded Giulia into the kitchen.

The smile Giulia aimed at her back did not qualify as "polite." She refrained from showing any of her irritation at Newton: 1) taking over Giulia's own house, and 2) choosing to forget about the iced tea Giulia served in the kitchen at their first meeting. The convent wasn't far enough in Giulia's past to make her forget how much she hated people taking power out of her hands.

Secretarial Pool Woman to the rescue! Giulia dragged her superpower out of hibernation. When Cissy sat at Giulia's kitchen table, Secretarial Pool Woman sat opposite her with a bland smile on her face.

Cissy said, "Elaine and Melina assure me the demon has left the house."

Giulia did not think "Elvis has left the building." Not at all.

"However, we are still hearing noises."

Giulia reached over to the refrigerator and removed the memo pad and its attached pen, leprechaun magnet and all. "Please be specific. What types of noises? At what time do the noises occur? In which areas of the house?"

Cissy recited like a student at an oral exam. "Two days ago, knocking on the cellar walls. Also two days ago, whistling in the hall opposite the library. One day ago, more knocking, this time in the sewing room. Also one day ago, all my chameleon cages were out of place. Food, water, bedding, and scat were strewn all over the floor. Also one day ago, both Melina and Georgia found the linen closets on the first and second floors in complete disarray." She paused for breath or emphasis. "This morning Mike woke me up much too early for Sunday breakfast and made me come down to the kitchen. We both heard the patter of footsteps. Elaine surprised us as we were listening. She hasn't been sleeping and came to make herself some tea." Anger flashed across her plump face, obscuring the freckles. "I do everything I can to keep Elaine free from unnecessary worry, and she chooses that particular moment to want tea. We had to tell her everything. She made me wake up Melina and Georgia to tell her what they'd heard and seen. Melina took charge of the telling. It was she who convinced Elaine the demon hadn't returned and these sounds were from something else."

Giulia watched her hope of one peaceful day this week flutter out the kitchen window. Emily Dickinson was right: hope was the thing with feathers and it knew how to use them.

Cissy went on, "Elaine sent me here with a request. She would like a Ouija Board session with you today. Muriel and I agree, although Melina insists Ouija Boards open the sitters to demonic possession." For the first time, Cissy's efficiency cracked. "You've realized by now that I was Elaine's guardian before Pip came into her life."

Secretarial Pool Woman also had a talent for stating the obvious. "I understood Caroline and Thomas Emerson were appointed Elaine's guardians after her parents died?" The hint of a question at the end encouraged the listener to explain to poor little Secretarial Pool Woman.

Cissy obliged. "I'm not referring to the legal documents which installed Elaine's aunt and uncle in the house." Censure hardened her voice. "Elaine's parents were both neglectful and strict. They focused on keeping Dahlia profitable. I would haunt the castle after my death to protect Elaine if I believed in ghosts, which I don't. Maybe." The hard shell fell away. "About the Ouija Board. Elaine owns one, but if you prefer to use your own, we'll defer to you."

Giulia sent Secretarial Pool Woman on vacation.

"Driscoll Investigations does not use Ouija Boards." She didn't apologize. Weakness and deference were the vacationing alter-ego's territory.

For an instant, Giulia thought Cissy was going to lecture her on proper employee deportment. Instead, in a drastic shift of gears, she resettled herself in her chair. "If you're immovable on this, I'll try to convince Elaine. But for Muriel's and my benefit, I have to ask: what are we paying you for?"

Such an offensive remark didn't deserve even the minimum of polite smiles.

"Ms. Newton, the contract we both signed specifies Driscoll Investigations will use its experience, skill, and judgment to the best of its abilities. If these terms are no longer acceptable for the resolution of your case, perhaps we aren't the agency you need."

"No." She gripped the table edge. "You must help Elaine. I apologize for my last remark. It doesn't matter what I think. Elaine wants you. Elaine believes in you. Why won't you do as she asks?"

What popped into Giulia's head: because adults don't alter their convictions merely because someone waves money at them. What came out of Giulia's mouth: "We are conversant with several methods of contacting spirits. We focus on efficient eradication."

"That's what I'm asking." She stood and paced to the window.

"I heard you ask for a Ouija Board session."

Cissy turned from contemplating Giulia's garden. "What's the difference?"

"Ms. Newton, some Ouija lore insists the board is only a game for teenage slumber parties."

Cissy picked up Giulia's collection of kitschy salt and pepper shakers one at a time. "As do I."

"Then you're here to humor Elaine."

"No." She set down a Minnie Mouse and picked up Mickey. "Well, yes."

"Ms. Newton, you're due a report from us. It's not at final draft yet, but this is what we've learned."

As Giulia spoke, Cissy examined every salt and pepper shaker on the windowsill.

"Mr. Pedersen has a gambling problem and divorce-related debt, but his driving force is power. Konani Hyde has expensive tastes, including her children's private school."

Cissy moved on to the salt and pepper pairs along the top of the stove.

"The Emersons are pining for the life they lived as Elaine's guardians. We're completing our research on them, but preliminary findings indicate heavy gambling debts."

Cissy rubbed a thumb over the face of a salt angel.

"It's our opinion neither of Elaine's former tutors is interested in Dahlia."

The angel took its place next to the pepper devil. "Then the Board is trying to take it all away from her."

Giulia, eighty-seven percent a non-violent person, debated whether she could heave the vase of toad lilies on the table far enough to hit Cissy in her stubborn head.

"It was our understanding such a situation existed when you hired us."

Cissy picked up the devil. "I was almost certain, but I needed outside help. When Elaine came to you, she gave me an opening. She thinks Muriel and I hired you as her personal ghost busters. We don't want to worry her about the snakes in her company." Her thumbs rubbed the devil's face and wings. "The ghosts are making her nervous, but we can handle her while you stop whichever one of the three is trying to steal her company."

Her hands turned the pepper shaker over. She looked down at it as though seeing it for the first time, brought up one hand to push her hair away from her face, and inhaled the spilled pepper.

She sneezed for fifteen seconds by the kitchen clock. Giulia guided her to her chair and handed her napkin after napkin. It took Cissy another minute to blow her nose and wipe her eyes. When she blinked them clear, she bent to the floor and brought up the pepper devil.

"He isn't even chipped."

She sneezed again. The ceramic figurine rolled out of her hand. Giulia caught it before it smashed onto the glass table.

"This set was a Christmas gift. He's cute, isn't he?" She turned him from side to side. "You'd never think this devil would do anything more evil than sneak pepper into your dessert."

Cissy smiled. Giulia didn't.

"Because I'm refusing a client's request, here is the explanation. In my professional opinion, Ouija Boards are dangerous. We will not use them in our investigations. However, if a Tarot reading is an acceptable substitute—"

"Yes! Oh, definitely yes." Cissy's phone was in her hand before the last syllable left her mouth. "Elaine has been fascinated by the Tarot since she was a little girl. Elaine, it's Cissy." She spun Giulia's ultimatum into the promise of fulfillment of Elaine's fondest desire. She put her hand over the phone. "Is three o'clock all right?"

Giulia thought fast. "Closer to midnight would be preferable. Reading the cards is more propitious at night."

Cissy conveyed Giulia's message. Giulia heard Elaine's excited voice even through the phone pressed to Cissy's ear.

"Elaine chooses eleven thirty," Cissy said after hanging up. "I know I said I didn't believe in ghosts, but I'll admit only to you I'm worried. One of the ways I've always looked after Elaine is to read whatever she reads, in case she has questions or is troubled by a story."

Giulia refrained from pointing out Elaine's current age was twenty-four, not seven.

"Ever since Pip and the staff first pointed out the noises, Elaine's been reading ghost stories and true-life hauntings." She sniffed and blinked, but didn't sneeze. "What if it's not the house, but Elaine who's haunted?"

An underused movie plot device. Giulia would know, since her limited movie time wasn't exclusively spent on Godzilla. She'd have to ask Rowan about someone becoming convinced they were personally haunted. There couldn't be that much difference between a ghost and a demon riding your back. She'd evicted the fireplace demon, after all. Assuming a demonic presence had actually inhabited the fireplace.

"The library fireplace hasn't been anything but a fireplace since your ceremony," Cissy said. "Elaine says you should be on Angie's List."

Giulia stood. "Then please let her know I'll be at the house at the agreed time."

Cissy's effusive thanks lasted all the way to the front porch, when she stopped. Giulia backpedaled to avoid stepping on her heels.

"How could I forget poor Scarlett?" Cissy picked up a huge openwork cage with a miniature dinosaur inside. "Scarlett is a veiled chameleon and she loves garden bugs. Place her in her cage right in the center of your garden and you'll never have to resort to commercial pesticides again."

The lizard's protruding eyes swiveled independently. One stared at Cissy, the other at Giulia.

"Make sure to mist the foliage in her cage when you water the garden, and she can stay outside until the temperature drops to about fifty degrees." She held the cage out until Giulia took it. "Here's a booklet I wrote about care and feeding and everything you need to know." She set a folded five by eight booklet on top of the cage. "She should be hungry. Don't keep her inside too long."

Giulia wrestled the three-foot wire cube inside and leaned her back against the door, wondering if Father Carlos would finally lose his temper if she worked a protection spell on the house.

"Frank?"

"Up here, hiding from the home invader."

Giulia ran upstairs to their bedroom. "She's gone, but I'm going out at eleven, and there's a Ray Harryhausen special effect in—"

Frank caught her as she entered the room and stopped her sentence with a kiss.

"Is nothing sacred anymore? It's Sunday."

She murmured in his ear, "A long time ago, a charming PI warned me this wasn't a nine-to-five job."

He kissed her again. "I was single and trying to prove I could be as successful as my brothers."

Giulia walked her husband toward their bed. "The only thing you have to prove is how well you behave as my practice Tarot reading subject."

"After lunch." He unbuttoned the top of her dress.

"Lunch may be late." She reached for his zipper.

"The service in this establishment has gone downhill." He pulled her down onto the bed.

"I'll speak to the management."

Introducing him to their new pet could wait.

Thirty-Nine

Giulia straightened her dangliest earrings, the onyx ones Mingmei had given her as a wedding gift. They glittered in the car's overhead light. She brushed the velvet cuffs on the black silk sleeves of her blouse. The outfit combined Giulia the exorcist on top and Giulia the business owner in plain black slacks on the bottom. The only downside: convent flashbacks. Even after five years, wearing head-to-toe black gave her twitches. She was still surprised how well she'd handled the exorcist garb. Opening night jitters had taken the twitches' place, perhaps.

Well, opening night had been a success. Now to prove she wasn't a one-hit wonder.

She muted her phone in case Frank sent another Snapchat picture of the chameleon in a frying pan. Or on the grill. Or with its curled tail sticking out from between two slices of bread.

The warm, clear July night was not meant for long sleeves or long pants. At least the few steps from the Clown Car's air conditioning to the castle's air conditioning didn't give her time to work up a sweat.

The door opened before she touched the bell.

"Come in," Cissy said. "I didn't want the chimes to wake Elaine."

Giulia stepped into lovely cool air. "Elaine agreed to eleven thirty. Has there been a change?"

"No, of course not. Elaine's been under a great deal of stress. She's taking a nap. I'll ask Pip to wake her."

A blood-curdling shriek from upstairs punctuated Cissy's last sentence. Giulia and Cissy were already running up the stairs when the second shriek came. A detached piece of Giulia's mind scratched one item off her horror fan's bucket list: "blood-curdling screams" happened in real life as well as the movies.

Pip met them at Elaine's door. Cissy reached for the doorknob, but Pip's hand got there first. The shrieks hit them with physical force when he opened the door.

Giulia would have bet Elaine's bedroom had been a shrine to Disney princesses right up until her wedding. The bed's current spread was covered with pastel wildflowers. Similar flowers dotted the tulle canopy. The lavender rug obscured all but the edges of the hardwood floor. Groupings of small, delicate watercolors hung on walls papered with textured ivory stripes.

Privately, Giulia loved the femininity of the room even with Elaine's dreadful screams distorting her perception.

Pip was already on the bed, holding his wife. At his touch, the piercing cries began to abate.

Static electricity frizzed Elaine's blonde hair. She stared through Giulia and Cissy, seeing something only her eyes could perceive. Earbuds dangled from both ears. The wrinkled Ouija board t-shirt she wore was the only jarring note in the ultra-feminine room.

Pip murmured soothing words. Cissy's tensed muscles shrieked in their own way: she wanted to be the one comforting Elaine.

Elaine's eyes refocused on her own room. "Ms. Driscoll, you're here. I dreamed about you." Breathiness made her light voice nearly inaudible.

Giulia stepped forward. "I hope I wasn't the cause of your nightmare."

"No." Her smooth, pale forehead cleared. "I've been waking up like this for a little while, but I can never remember what scared me." She snuggled against her husband. "I forget everything bad when I'm in Pip's arms."

He smoothed her hair. "It's okay now, sweetheart."

She smiled up at him as though no one else existed. Certainly not as though she regretted scaring the spit out of everyone else in the room.

"I remember now. I dreamed Ms. Driscoll came here to try on a dress I designed." She studied Giulia. "You're a twelve and short-waisted. A columnar style wouldn't flatter you because you have hips. That's right. In the dream I put you into one of last spring's models: gray silk with a pleated skirt and a shirred top. You argued with me.

You said crimson was your color, and then the dress changed, just like Sleeping Beauty's dress in the movie. You remember, in the last scene where she's dancing with the prince and the three fairies keep changing her dress from pink to blue to pink to blue?"

She sized up Giulia again. "Crimson is your color, but gray isn't wrong. You'd want to accessorize it with a scarf or shawl." She brought out her phone from the tangle of sheets. "Note for Sandra's team," she dictated. "Silk and organza scarves with gray accents for next spring."

With another abrupt change, Elaine tossed the phone onto the covers. "We shouldn't be talking about my silly dreams. We need to get ready for my Tarot reading. Pip, sweetheart, I have to get dressed. Ms. Driscoll, please show Cissy where you'd like to set up. My sitting room is at your service, or you can use any other room you prefer."

She scooted out of bed into a dressing room opening off to the left. Giulia was relieved to see she was wearing shorts.

"Cissy," Giulia said with a charming smile of her own, "would you please clear a small table in Elaine's sitting room for me?"

"Certainly. Pip, could you give me a hand? I think we have to clear away a new dress pattern."

Pip smiled and nodded and they went out together. My, how everyone smiled. Giulia wondered if they were so used to it they didn't notice they were doing it anymore.

The instant she had the room to herself, Giulia pounced on Elaine's phone. The technology gods favored her: the screen was still unlocked.

The open file on the phone was called "Sleep." Giulia swiped up from the bottom, keyed several choices, and air-dropped the file to her own phone.

Every PI should have their own personal computer genius. Thank you, Zane.

She replaced her phone in her messenger bag and followed Cissy's voice to a room two doors down.

Elaine's sitting room doubled as a sewing room. An open shelving unit of two foot by two foot cubes housed bolts of cloth in dozens of shades and textures, piles of tissue paper both folded and cut into patterns, and more spools of thread than Giulia could estimate at one glance. A sewing machine sophisticated enough to belong to Gianni

Versace sat on a table custom-made to tuck into a window seat. A mannequin fitted with an inside-out gray silk dress with basted seams stood next to the table.

Cissy spread a red and white checked cloth on a circular card table. "Is this picnic pattern all right? Do you need a black or plain red or any other color cloth?"

"Thank you, this is fine." Elaine's air of childhood was no doubt responsible for the picnic doggerel in Giulia's head.

"If you go down to the castle today,

You're sure of a big surprise:

Today's the day Elaine gets her Tarot reading."

Elaine came in on Pip's arm. She now wore head to toe black, like Giulia, but there was black and there was black. Giulia's ongoing resolve not to envy clothes she couldn't afford without robbing a bank wavered.

Cissy hovered near Elaine as Pip escorted her to the chair nearest the door. Neither showed signs of leaving Elaine alone with Giulia.

Terrific. Another debut performance for an audience. Well, go big or go home. She seated herself with her back to the dark window.

"Do you need the lights off?" Elaine said.

"We wouldn't be able to see the cards."

Elaine giggled. "You're funny. Don't you need candles for atmosphere or to show the spirits the way here?"

"Such decorations are not necessary." Giulia brought out her jade silk bag.

"Oh, how pretty."

"A proper reading requires concentration. Silence is the best way to begin."

Pip bristled. "That's my wife you're ordering around."

"Mr. Patrick." A deliberate word choice since a few days ago he'd insisted she call him Pip. "We are in the midst of a professional consultation. Kindly allow me the courtesy of knowing my business."

Pip retired, crushed.

Great. Now she was thinking in Dickens-esque language.

Elaine elbowed her husband. "Honey, shush, please. I know this is going to help us."

Giulia unwrapped the square of violet silk cloth and the cards appeared. Elaine stopped talking. Giulia smoothed the silk outward to its edges. Cissy turned the sewing chair toward the table and sat. The grandfather clock in the hall bonged twelve times.

"The witching hour," Elaine whispered.

Forty

Giulia shuffled the cards thinking of Rowan and the way she evoked Maria Ouspenskaya in *The Wolf Man*. If Giulia's business was making a permanent shift to Driscoll Investigations, Ghost Breakers, she needed to watch fewer horror movies.

"Elaine, please tell me why you requested my presence here tonight."

"Oh, but don't you know? Didn't Cissy explain everything?"

Giulia kept shuffling. "We have begun the reading. It is important to state your desire with the cards in front of you."

"Dear cards, I want to know who is haunting my house, and how I can help them move on to the next plane of existence. Oh, and anything about Pip and me, if that's okay."

Now Giulia had her script. She tapped the deck on the silk to straighten it and placed the cards in front of Elaine. "Please cut the cards."

Elaine cut the deck in three. Giulia re-stacked them and dealt the first card in the Celtic Cross layout: the Priestess.

"This card covers the energy around you."

She dealt the Ten of Wands reversed, perpendicular to the Priestess. "This is your stumbling block, something close enough for you to trip over. Reversed it signifies intrigues and similar oppositions."

Cissy gripped her hands together.

"Remember, the reading is one complete, interconnected whole. No single card should be given more weight than the others."

Elaine nodded, her gaze riveted on the growing layout.

Giulia dealt cards counterclockwise around the center two. She mentioned each card's general meaning and the part of Elaine's life to which it referred: the recent past, the near future, the energy moving the current situation forward. "Past, present, future, and messages from the other side are all parts of the entire reading. All are connected."

When the layout was complete, Giulia took several seconds to gather the meanings of the ten cards as a whole. She touched her index finger to the first four cards. "The Priestess. The Ten of Wands. The Tower. Justice." She raised her eyes to Elaine's intent face. "It's going to be a bumpy ride."

Forty-One

Pip covered Elaine's hands with his. "What is that supposed to mean?"

Giulia included Pip in her explanation to Elaine. "Movement is happening in your life. A simile for these four cards in these positions would be: You've set Thanksgiving dinner on the table and the dog yanks off the table cloth and runs away with the turkey. All the heirloom china is shattered on the floor and the cat is sitting in the pumpkin pie."

Elaine giggled again. Pip lowered his hackles.

"The Tower in this position could mean a layoff, but not in your case. You're not about to give yourself a pink slip."

Elaine smiled and nodded. Cissy's eyes narrowed. Pip contributed his rich laugh.

Giulia said, "Justice is both blind and fierce. Do you know of any injustice touching your life?"

Elaine's thoughtful face was a pout with her thumb tapping her bottom lip. "Honestly, all I can think of is our ghost. I mean, our ghost probably has a grievance. Ooh—maybe he was murdered by one of the previous owners. Cissy, who owned the house before the nuns? I forget."

Giulia stepped in before Cissy could upset the flow of the reading. "You drew the Ace of Pentacles and the Three of Wands as cards five and six. The ace signifies a new beginning."

"The four is reversed." Elaine's big blue eyes pleaded with Giulia. "Reversed is bad, isn't it?"

"Not in this case and not with this card, which is one of the most positive. Putting the elements of cards one through six together, I would say you are about to receive justice from a wrong in your past, and the shape it takes will center around a family."

"But I'm an only child and my parents...oh, Pip." A delicate shade of rose blossomed on her cheeks.

"What's going on?" Pip said to Giulia.

Elaine flung her arms around his neck. "It means our family. The cards revealed it's finally time for babies in the castle."

Pip kissed his wife over and over. Cissy smiled for the first time. In her eyes Giulia saw a half-dozen miniature Elaines crawl, toddle, and run through the castle halls.

"Elaine, the other cards you drew relate to home, wealth, and family as well, but also deception and mischief."

Elaine's ecstasy plummeted. "Who could want to make trouble in our house? Everyone's happy here."

Giulia eased her into the idea. "You're still hearing and seeing unexplained things. Since the cards indicate a positive and powerful future but also a force of some kind counteracting these, perhaps this force is the cause."

She allowed the concept to percolate. Pip appeared to consider. Cissy glanced over her shoulder as though she expected to see a translucent Cheshire cat hovering in the window, grinning.

Elaine reached across the layout and clutched Giulia's hands. "You'll find the angry ghost and evict it, won't you? You've done so much for us already."

Giulia reversed the grip and patted Elaine's hands. "We'll keep on your case until we find answers."

"You are the best. Pip, isn't she wonderful? And such a talented Tarot reader. I have to take a picture to remember tonight." She slapped her hip. "Why did I design a dress without pockets? Pip, have you seen my phone?"

"You were listening to it when you took your nap, honey."

She jumped up. "Of course. I forgot in all the excitement." She ran out of the room and returned with the phone, earbuds trailing. "Don't move, Ms. Driscoll. I want to get you and the cards together."

Giulia obeyed through three *clicks*.

"I want to show this Tarot layout to our children. Right, sweetheart?"

The Paul Newman smile appeared. "You bet."

Giulia gathered the cards and wiped the energy from the deck as Rowan had taught her. Everyone watched.

Elaine touched her phone. "It's almost one a.m. Who could use one of Mike's special insomnia cures?"

"Honey, don't wake Mike at this hour."

Elaine pecked her husband on the nose. "Silly. I know how to make them. I'm not completely inept in the kitchen. Come on, Ms. Driscoll. This drink will send even the worst nightmares scurrying to hide in the closet."

Giulia stood. "Thank you, but I have to drive home."

Cissy shepherded her downstairs, but not before Giulia saw Mike's, Georgia's, and Melina's faces vanish into three of the rooms Giulia hadn't yet seen.

Forty-Two

Giulia set the 7-Eleven bag on the kitchen table. The stove clock read 1:40 and she was wide awake. Frank snored upstairs. Scarlett the chameleon slept amid the vegetables under the bright half moon.

Thank goodness for twenty-four hour mini marts. She took down the first mug her hand touched: Rudolph the Red-nosed Reindeer. In August? She almost suspected Sidney of sneaking in to rearrange the dishes to match the alpaca farm's Christmas in July sale.

She tucked a cinnamon stick into the mug and retrieved a half-gallon of apple cider from the bag. Two minutes in the microwave and a drink appropriate to the Rudolph mug steamed on the table.

When coffee intake was restricted, the resourceful PI improvised. She retrieved her laptop from the living room and set it up next to the cider to write up the Tarot reading.

Stirring the cider with the cinnamon stick twenty minutes later, she reread her notes. Frank must have rolled onto his stomach, because the hum of the refrigerator motor was the only sound in the house. Giulia shook off a frisson of eeriness. This case was messing with her.

She opened a search window and found a history of the first settlers in the Massachusetts Bay Colony. From there she followed the trail of the Patricks from the sixteen hundreds through the dropped "t" down to Perry Ignatius' college triumphs and post-college marketing career.

A second cup of spiced cider succeeded the first as Giulia dissected Pip's LinkedIn profile. The business parts read as expected.

Entry-level marketing assistant to sales team to employee of the year to opening his own branch of the firm in Pittsburgh.

At the same time, he excelled in the company's annual softball game. She followed the sports trail and discovered a new dimension to Prince Charming. He spearheaded an annual food and clothing drive for the city's biggest homeless shelter. In summer, he ran a softball camp for at-risk teenagers.

Giulia sipped cider and lectured herself about always being ready to adjust her conclusions to accommodate new information. Prince Charming might be too slick for her taste and too handsome to be real, but he had depth. Clark Wagner had good words only for Pip and Veronika Graser out of all the Dahlia crew.

A third side to Pip appeared after a candid photo from a company retreat pointed to an even narrower trail. Giulia followed it with difficulty, but by three thirty in the morning she'd uncovered strong indications of two mistresses. She couldn't prove either with certainty, but she'd learned the signs from DI's time with divorce cases.

She leaned on her elbows and rubbed her eyes. A piece of research nagged at her. Her mug was empty. She sucked the cider-soaked cinnamon stick. Her eyes popped open and she remembered cinnamon Red Hots always made her tongue burn for hours.

Awake again, she scrolled through all the interviews trying to trigger a recollection. The Christmas Ball story. No, before that.

There. The skeleton story. She logged onto a Catholic site specializing in legends of saints and refreshed herself on St. Columba getting upstaged by his faithful monk St. Odhran's willingness to be buried alive to fortify Columba's chapel at Iona. Did Odhran ever encounter Columba in Heaven and say "neener, neener" to him?

Giulia yawned. Her research synapses were sputtering at—she squinted at the clock in her task bar—4:17 a.m. Maybe some music would keep her awake.

Her phone opened to the air drop screen. Fatigue forgotten, Giulia played Elaine's sleep recording.

Forty-Three

"You guys, listen to this."

Zane and Sidney saved their open documents. Giulia pressed Play on her phone. A soothing female voice recited over the sound of gentle ocean waves:

"There was a lady all skin and bone;
Sure such a lady was never known:
It happened upon a certain day,
This lady went to church to pray.

"When she came to the church stile,
There she did rest a little while;
When she came to the churchyard,
There the bells so loud she heard.

"When she came to the church door,
She stopped to rest a little more;
When she came the church within,
The parson prayed 'gainst pride and sin.

"On looking up, on looking down,
She saw a dead man on the ground;
And from his nose unto his chin,
The worms crawled out, the worms crawled in.

"Then she unto the parson said,
Shall I be so when I am dead:

O yes! O yes, the parson said,
You will be so when you are dead."

A piercing shriek followed the last word.

"Holy gods," Zane said.

"Is that supposed to be a hypnotism recording?" Sidney said.

"No, it's Elaine's way of getting to sleep when she's stressed." Giulia scrolled to an earlier point in the recording.

"Hickory, dickory, dock.
The mouse ran up the clock.
The clock struck one,
The mouse ran down,
Hickory, dickory, dock."

Giulia stopped the playback. "When she was a child, her tutor would read nursery rhymes to her every night."

"She'd scream at her?" Sidney said. "Why wasn't she fired on the spot?"

"She didn't. My point is, I've listened to the whole recording. Every rhyme is normal except the last one."

Sidney frowned. "What am I missing?"

"What better way to convince the stockholders of Elaine's company she's unfit to run it?"

"Oh, wow. Someone tampered with her recording."

"Listen." Giulia replayed the last verse and the scream.

Zane said, "Play it again." He closed his eyes. "Is the scream falsetto?"

"Maybe. Anyone in the household could have gotten to Elaine's phone. It's quite possible one of our other suspects offered one of the staff a cut of the hoped-for Dahlia money." She held up an oversized office supply store bag. "It's time to resurrect the Clue Collage."

"Whoa. Blast from the past."

Zane looked at them. "What am I missing?"

Giulia walked to the table beneath the window and tipped out the bag's contents.

"One set of rainbow highlighters. One set of rainbow Sharpies.

One three-pack of invisible tape. One envelope of interview printouts, transcribed after Sunday's midnight Tarot reading."

"After Sunday's what?" from both desks.

Giulia described Cissy crashing their house, the screaming chaos at Elaine's, and the Tarot show as she sorted the printouts and taped them to the wall.

"Her aunt and uncle and both tutors told me about the nursery rhymes. The Dahlia people could know too. They love gossip. What better target than the boss?"

The tape dispenser chittered. Wagner's transcript attached to Graser's which attached to Sechrest's, Pedersen's, and Hyde's. The single page for personal assistants Dona and Shandeen hung off to one side of Pedersen's. Cissy had her own page, as did Melina, Mike, and Georgia.

"And Pip finishes it off."

"The Perfect Husband?" Zane said.

"Nobody's that perfect?" Sidney said.

"In essence. He may have two women on the side, but he also does a boatload of charity work. Anyway, being a tomcat doesn't necessarily mean he's linked to a hostile takeover. A change in power might be worse for his finances. I'd have to see his prenup." Giulia yawned. "If you see me snoring on my keyboard, please poke me. I got maybe an hour's sleep."

Sidney glared at her. "Didn't I warn you to stock up on sleep while you still can?"

"You did, but I was wound up after the reading. I used the energy to transcribe the Tarot session, listen to the not at all soporific sleep recording, and dig into Pip's history." She popped the snaps on the packages of markers and highlighters. "I'm now in sleuthing mode. Hold my calls."

She highlighted phrases and drew arrows, question marks, and key words on the irregular sunburst of papers. Zane and Sidney typed. The traffic outside began to intrude on her concentration.

The door opened. "Ms. Driscoll, we are not happy."

Forty-Four

Muriel Lockwood knew how to make an entrance. Steampunk was still her theme, but today she was the Intrepid Lady Explorer.

Her long linen bustle skirt and overjacket were beige, and beige was the opposite of dull on Muriel. A brown leather vest topped the skirt, and an ivory pith helmet complete with netting topped her bouncy black curls. Aviator goggles perched on the pith helmet and the heels on her high button brown boots clacked on the wood floor.

She removed her monocle and advanced on Giulia. "Elaine is worse. Pip got desperate enough to call a shrink, but Elaine wouldn't go." An eyeroll worthy of any teenager. "He should know better. Cissy had to stop Elaine from taking three Xanax at once. What are we paying you for?"

Giulia wasn't about to lie down under this attitude from her other client, who apparently didn't know about last night. "We are not magicians, Ms. Lockwood. Investigations take time."

"Elaine doesn't have time, which you ought to have realized. She— ooh, what's this all about?" Muriel screwed the monocle into her left eye and planted herself in front of the Clue Collage.

Giulia made a rueful face at Sidney, who mirrored it. Since she couldn't make the client unsee her work, she explained the collage.

"Fascinating." Muriel's head bobbed up, down, right, left like a bird pecking at insects. "I remember that little tutor. Who is Dona? Never mind. I see. Oh, please. Not Mark Pedersen." She ran a finger down his transcript. "You're missing something." She looked around and chose the orange Sharpie from the pack. "He likes to play the horses as well as the slots." She winked with the entire un-monocled side of her face. "I bet his ex-wives wouldn't like his bank balance if they saw it." She tapped the capped marker against her shimmering plum lips. "Hyde, good. Sechrest, good. Melina, Georgia, Mike." She pointed the marker at Giulia, who resisted the urge to swat it out of her hand. "Mike is a cousin. You know that, right?"

"I do. Can you tell me the exact relationship?"

Muriel capped the marker. "I love family history. Let me make sure I get this right. Technically Mike is Elaine's second cousin. Elaine's great-grandmother had ten kids. Were all women forced to be baby factories back then or what? One of the boys married Mike's grandmother. The oldest girl had five boys and three girls, and her oldest girl was Elaine's mother. Meanwhile, Mike's grandmother popped out seven kids." She re-settled the monocle. "No. She had nine but two died of SIDS, probably, even though they didn't call it that back then. Mike's mother was the youngest and she had every childhood disease imaginable, and after surviving all of that she and her husband got caught in a massive train crash when Mike was in his second year at culinary school. His dad died in the crash but his mom hung on for six months hooked up to a roomful of hospital machines. The bills wiped the family out, and he had to take out humongous loans. When she died he came to the castle because he had less than nothing."

She uncapped the marker again. "If you had to beg Aunt Bitch and Uncle Lush for the privilege of being your super-rich cousin's servant, how much resentment would you build up over the years?" She wrote on Mike's page. "Elaine pays him a generous salary, but it's chump change compared to what she pulls down as owner of Dahlia."

Bang. Bang. Bang.

Zane said, "Sounds like a foot." He opened the door on a tower of plastic food containers and a wicker basket being carried by a pair of khaki pants and a plaid arm.

"Cissy?" Muriel said.

"Muriel? Come help me with these."

The Intrepid Steampunk Explorer clacked to the door and lifted the containers. Cissy followed her to the table. Muriel swept the markers, tape, envelope, and bag to the floor as Cissy pointed to each container in turn.

"Sandwiches, lemonade, pickles, and parfaits. Mike crafted everything from scratch except the chicken and beef."

Muriel set out plastic cups. "No room for chickens or cows in the flower garden."

Cissy draped a yellow gingham tablecloth over the table. Muriel lifted containers to make room.

"Cissy, what is all this?" Giulia said.

"Lunch, of course," Muriel said.

Cissy set thick foil-wrapped squares on plates. "We decided you could use a homemade meal after last night. Are any of you vegetarian?"

"I am," Sidney said.

"Mike made up an alternative just in case. Muriel, it's the one with a 'V' on the foil." She opened the pickle jar. "Don't waste good food, please."

Zane and Sidney formed a line. Giulia turned to the wall to hide a smile. Cissy's voice recalled school lunch ladies.

Cissy followed Giulia's head movement. "Why is my name on the wall?"

Muriel said through bites of chicken salad on sourdough. "It's everyone she suspects of targeting Elaine. I added two bits of dirt she didn't know." She added a pickle to the sandwich bites in her mouth. "By the way, you'll have to convince me Pip the Perfect is an honest to God suspect. He's done wonders for Elaine, even though I laugh behind his back at the whole ideal male shtick."

Cissy pointed to Giulia, then to the table. "Eat, please."

Giulia wondered in all seriousness if today was finger pointing day in Dahlia land. She chose to comply to keep the client happy. As she gave roast beef on rye the attention it deserved, Cissy read the collage. Clients were never going to see her brainstorming method again. All future Clue Collages would hang in her private office on the wall behind the door.

"This sandwich is amazing," Zane said. "Do I taste bok choy in the chicken salad?"

"I don't know." Cissy's voice was distant. "Mike doesn't let anyone in on his kitchen secrets." She stood on tiptoe to read the topmost pages.

The Scoop slammed open the door exactly like Monty Python in the "Spanish Inquisition" sketch.

Forty-Five

"Investigation in action, lunchtime edition." Ken Kanning's level of excitement didn't match the scene in front of him.

Pit Bull pushed the camera in Cissy's face. Kanning slithered next to her.

Cissy stared up at his coiffed 'do and pancaked visage. "You're Ken Kanning."

"I am indeed, Miss."

Cissy's round cheeks grew apple red. "I watch your show when I'm able."

He dialed up the wattage on his teeth. "Scoopers are the backbone of our show." The teeth said to the camera: "The indefatigable Giulia Driscoll works through another lunch to lasso justice for her clients. And once again we're on the scene to aid a faithful Scooper in—" Kanning flicked the mic from his mouth to Cissy's.

"Helping Elaine."

Giulia pushed between them. "Mr. Kanning, please call for an appointment if you wish to speak to someone in our office." She indicated the door. "As you said, we're working. I believe you know the way out."

Zane positioned himself on one side of Pit Bull. Sidney shielded Muriel from the camera. In sync, Kanning and Pit Bull lowered the tools of their scandal mongering.

Kanning aimed an undimmed smile at Giulia. "Whenever you're ready to team up again, just whistle."

Zane took a step nearer. *The Scoop* beat a hasty retreat.

Giulia locked the door. "Cissy, I'd advise against saying too much to Ken Kanning."

Cissy shook her head as though to clear it. "I don't know what came over me. My mouth opened on its own."

Muriel crowed with laughter. "Cis-sy's a fan-girl! Cis-sy's a fan-girl!"

Giulia interrupted. "Thank you for this amazing lunch, but it wasn't necessary."

"Yes, it was." Cissy laid a hand on the wall. "I respect your thoroughness in including me on this display. In fairness, Muriel should also have a page."

Muriel clapped. "I've never been a suspect in anything before. Cissy, be my spokesperson while I steal a blueberry parfait."

Cissy's irritation with Muriel was replaced with indulgence, much the way Giulia had caught her looking at Elaine. "Muriel is somewhat eccentric."

Ms. Eccentric raised a long-handled spoon in acknowledgement. Her mouth was too full of berries and whipped cream to reply.

"She has no need to work because she inherited a great deal of money when her parents died. These days she enjoys a pre-nineteenth century lifestyle of literature and fashion."

Muriel said, "Next month or maybe next year I'll try the Roaring Twenties or Marie Antoinette at Versailles. I'm not sitting as pretty as Elaine, but you'll never hear me complain." She punctuated her revelation with another spoonful of whipped cream. "If you need confirmation, ask the Fancy Fantasies costume shop and the Light Fantastic dance club. The bartender keeps a bottle of absinthe on hand just for me."

Cissy mashed all the used aluminum foil into a ball. "We need to pack up. Please finish everything." She tucked the smaller empty containers into the biggest one. Muriel poured the rest of the lemonade into Giulia's cup with one hand while finishing her dessert with the other. Cissy folded the tablecloth and left the parfaits on the table.

Giulia thanked her again as she walked them out to the hall. "You may expect our interim report by Wednesday." The *skree* of the downstairs door closing came a minute later.

"I might as well install a revolving door." She tasted a strawberry parfait. "Real whipped cream."

Her phone chimed a text message from Kanning:

Forgot to mention there are 17 vans exactly like ours in the greater Pittsburgh area. Time for joint sleuthing?

She showed it to Sidney and Zane.

"Maybe Rowan can hex him," Sidney said.

"I have a great aunt," Zane began.

Godzilla roared from Giulia's computer. She carried her dessert into her office and a minute later vented a wordless shout of frustration. Sidney and Zane came running.

"Zane, how much does your aunt charge?"

"Really?"

Giulia closed her eyes. "No, not really." She opened them again. "Look at this."

She clicked the video embedded in *The Scoop's* email. Ken Kanning's voice imitated the "In a world where..." movie preview narrator.

"Homicide on the streets. Who is behind the wheel of the Killer Van?"

The Scoop's usual quick-cut montage showed several models of panel vans driving toward the camera. Their producer had applied CGI bursts of aggressive color to them: red, black, and orange, with added bursts and lightning streaks.

Kanning's voice finished: "Is anyone safe from the Mobile Menace? Find out next week on *The Scoop!*"

Forty-Six

The door chimes on the Tarot Shoppe tinkled their high, sweet notes as Giulia entered. Jasper was crouched before the glass display case, spraying window cleaner on it with his left hand and polishing the surface with newspaper held in his prosthetic right hand.

He smiled and stood when he saw Giulia. "How's your new venture going?"

"The venture is why I'm here without an appointment. Are you free for a few minutes?"

"No problem. Rowan just started a deluxe past life reading, and no one else is scheduled until three." He indicated the display. "Can I interest you in a rose quartz talisman?"

Giulia smiled and shook her head. "Can I interest you in an Assisi crucifix?"

He chuckled. "Truce. What can I help you with?"

She told him the details of the midnight reading. "Is it really possible to learn the truth about someone's future or clarify their problems through the cards?"

Jasper polished the top of the case. "It depends."

The sound out of her mouth resembled "Aarrgh."

Jasper chuckled again. "Sorry, but Tarot is an art which depends on the skill and power of the reader." His gaze circled Giulia's head.

She reached up to mash her brown curls into submission. "Did the humidity turn me into a human Brillo pad?"

"What? I don't know. I was trying to see your aura. Usually I need to quiet myself for a few minutes to open my Sight."

Giulia stood still, hands in pockets. It was the polite thing to do.

After a minute, he said, "Your little guy is shifting the color balance. Orange is elbowing indigo and pale yellow for room. You also have a handful of muddy red spikes sticking out like thorns. Are you angry about something?"

She didn't have one-tenth the stamina needed to discuss the possible existence of auras, so she answered the question. "*The Scoop.*"

Jasper's change of expression indicated muddy red spikes in his own aura. Assuming: 1) auras existed, and 2) they could be seen.

"Say no more. Sorry there aren't cut and dry answers about readings."

"I needed to ask. Thanks."

"Anytime." His eyebrows pushed together. "Have you been involved in a lot of excitement recently? Your little guy is wicked happy."

Forty-Seven

"Zane, how easy is it to insert new material into an existing sound file?" Giulia played the rhyme leading into "There was a lady," and the rhyme after it. Played in order, the slight difference between the two voices came out.

"Dead easy. I did something similar in junior high as an April Fool's Day prank." He opened a file on his phone. "Want to hear a demo?"

"No, I meant can people with an average skill set do it?"

"Sure. All it takes is a good audio program and a little practice. I showed Sidney how to make Jessamine's laugh her text tone."

Sidney took out her phone. "He's a great teacher. Listen." She poked the screen a few times and played a familiar baby's giggle.

"There goes another chance to narrow the suspect list."

Zane handed her a phone message slip. She read it and pinched the bridge of her nose. "I need a keeper. My car's been ready for days and I forgot all about it."

The phone rang. Zane answered and put it on hold. "It's Cissy Newton."

"We're already paying for lunch in ways not connected to our actual bill. I'll take it in my office."

"Mothers aren't supposed to get cynical until the kids reach middle school at least," Sidney said.

"I'm getting a head start." She left the door open. "Giulia Driscoll speaking."

"We've had a development." Cissy's voice was all business, but she clipped every word. "Elaine received a certified letter. The stockholders have retained a lawyer and have instituted a formal inquiry into Elaine's fitness to run Dahlia."

Giulia was almost relieved. Not for the legal action, but for plain old detective work. Ghost hunting was too much like stepping from small slippery rock to small slippery rock across an unknown river.

"All right. We're on it." She hung up and called Mark Pedersen. Dona answered.

"Hello, Ms. Driscoll. Three guesses why you're calling and the first two don't count." She laughed under her breath at her grade-school joke. "I'll connect you."

A moment of dead air and a *click*. "What do you want?"

Giulia kept her voice in perfect control. "Good afternoon, Mr. Pedersen. May I have a few minutes of your time?"

Silence. Giulia wondered if he'd hung up on her.

"Fine. Not here. Meet me at the Giant Eagle on Brighton in half an hour."

Waiting in the produce section, Giulia inspected peaches for bruising, moved on to the plastic containers of strawberries, and considered buying a dragonfruit because she'd never tried one. Before her purchase, Pedersen showed up in dark sunglasses and a hoodie. At the same moment, the piped-in music changed to an all-strings version of "Livin' La Vida Loca."

He hissed at her. "Are you responsible for the stockholder unrest?"

"Good afternoon again, Mr. Pedersen. Thank you for agreeing to meet with me."

"Forget your tight-ass bullshit. I want to know if you're sabotaging our company." His head swiveled right and left, looked back over his own shoulder and over Giulia's into the depths of the store.

"I have nothing to do with the stockholders' recent actions."

The sunglasses came within an inch of her nose. "How can I be sure you're telling the truth?"

Sister Mary Regina Coelis stepped up to the plate. "I beg your pardon?"

Pedersen retreated. "Well, I, look, you're working for somebody trying to take us over. Someone obviously leaked something to the stockholders. What are we supposed to think?"

Sister Mary Regina Coelis ceded the conversation to Giulia. "I'm not responsible for your thoughts. I asked to speak with you because I'd like more details about the situation."

Pedersen picked up a tomato like he wanted to fling it at the wall. "Okay, I'll play your game. Hyde, Sechrest, and I all got certified letters this morning from the biggest law firm in Pittsburgh. The other stockholders want proof Elaine is fit to run Dahlia. They can do this, the letter informed us, because of the way Dahlia is structured. Thank you very much, Belinda and Arthur Davenport."

"You might want to put down the tomato."

He looked at the fruit in his hand and returned it to the bin. The tensile strength of the tomato's skin was at bursting point. "Their lawyers will subpoena our records. They'll dredge up the murders and Elaine's problems. We'll all get shit-canned."

"Why? I was under the impression the Board of Directions would keep Dahlia running like they did before Elaine turned twenty-one."

"At a normal company we would, but Elaine's grandparents made their lawyer insert a stricture in the articles of incorporation. If a Davenport female isn't the CEO, the company becomes the property of the stockholders." He reached for another tomato but stopped himself and shoved his hands into the hoodie's pockets.

Giulia said, "Similar to the way the Green Bay Packers are publicly owned?"

"How should I know? I'm not interested in a football team. You have to consider the way people think. If Elaine is declared unfit, those sheep will assume all of us are too because we took orders from her. They'll vote us all out." He leaned too close to Giulia. "We may not have been jumping for joy since Elaine took over, but she has to stay as head of Dahlia. She'll never have to worry about money as long as she lives, but what about the rest of us? Damn all greedy stockholders to hell."

A young mother with a toddler in a race car shopping cart gave Pedersen a censorious glare.

Giulia resettled her bag on her shoulder. "Is there anything else you can tell me?"

"Yeah, my ex-wives are going to take me for every last dollar I own this time, and my kids will be embarrassed to admit I'm their father." He scanned the store in all directions. "I'm going home and getting drunk. Don't call me."

He slouched away to a harp arrangement of "Let it Go."

Giulia resisted the lure of dragonfruit and drove to the collision shop. At the first big intersection, an old-school Chevy van appeared in her rearview mirror.

Forty-Eight

Today was not a day Giulia planned to play tag with death. She switched on the dash cam because she had no intention of letting the van get close enough to bump her and trigger it. Her plan had been to take the bridge because it was the fastest route back to Cottonwood, but she scrapped it.

For two miles she drove a convoluted route through the city of Pittsburgh with multiple lane changes to put other vehicles between her and the van. When she reached the suburbs, she put the sun behind her on a long, straight two-lane street. The sun glared into her mirrors. She glimpsed her own face lit like a spotlight was shining on it and got an idea.

She eased up on the accelerator and let the van inch closer. The sun tried to blind her. She hit the "burst" button on the camera. The van filled her back window. She hit "burst" again. A parking space opened on her right. She turned the wheel hard and tucked the little car into the slot. The van drove past. She spun the camera forward, but an SUV obscured the van's license plate.

The van kept going. Giulia waited another two minutes. When she looked at the sidewalk she realized why the space had been available: she'd parked next to a fire hydrant.

She reentered traffic and reached the collision shop without incident. When the Nunmobile was hers again, she patted its dashboard without embarrassment.

Frank took possession of the camera. "Come into the gaming closet. My tower's graphics card laughs at the paltry hardware in your laptop."

They scrolled through the pictures.

"Nothing. Nothing. Nothing." Giulia clicked the mouse faster. "Come on. One good shot."

"Stop," Frank said. "Go back one."

She enlarged the photo. "Can you increase the contrast?"

Frank took over. Several clicks and one more enlargement later, Giulia caught herself before one of Frank's Irish curses passed her lips.

A bright rectangle of sun bouncing off the Chevy's rearview mirror framed a bad combover and the top of an ill-fitting pair of dentures.

Frank looked up at her. "You recognize him?"

"He's Elaine's uncle."

"What don't you like?"

"I don't believe for a minute he's doing this on his own."

Her husband swiveled his chair to face her. "Why not?"

"He's not clever or devious enough. If we were looking at a picture of his wife behind the wheel, I wouldn't be surprised."

"Meaning his wife ordered him to eliminate you?" He pulled her onto his lap. "I deserve a lot of credit for how calm I appear to be."

She kissed him. "You're adulting so well you should give lessons. Back to Thomas Emerson. He's heavily into off track betting and he likes a splash of coffee in his whisky. His wife greatly feels the lack of no longer living in Elaine's castle."

"You're proving my theory: she ordered him to go after you."

Giulia frowned at the screen. "Their standing in relation to the Dahlia money is nonexistent. They have no stock. There's no benefit to them going solo."

"Therefore?"

"They're working with someone inside Dahlia. Or inside the castle."

"And you're working in a soap opera."

Forty-Nine

Giulia unlocked the office door at seven thirty Tuesday morning to spend quality time with the Clue Collage.

With an extra-large dulce de leche coffee in her left hand and a green Sharpie in her right, she wrote on a blank page taped next to Cissy's printout.

- Caroline & Thomas don't have the money to own three vans
- Not even junker vans
- Who knows about Elaine's nursery rhyme security blanket?
  - Cissy
  - Pip
  - Melina
  - Georgia
  - Mike
  - Graser
  - Wagner
  - The board of directors
  - In other words, too many

Giulia accessed the printer for a summary of Dahlia's finances at the top of the collage. Next to it she wrote on a blank paper:

Who could use a piece of this much money? And why?

- Caroline and Thomas: Gambling and luxury (and finance their kids' education?)
- Pedersen: Lawyers, alimony, gambling (+ debt?)
- Sechrest: Thinks she should be queen of Dahlia
- Hyde: Expensive schools lead to expensive colleges therefore money is tight

- Wagner: Support the startup he's working for
- Graser: Support her weaving business

The phone rang. Giulia glanced at the clock and shrugged. Quarter after eight wasn't all that early.

"Ms. Driscoll? Sandra Sechrest. I want you to know I had nothing to do with this legal crisis."

"Thank you for calling, Ms. Sechrest, but—"

"If the people you're working for aren't behind it, and don't repeat your non-answer of how you can't divulge information, I strongly suggest you dig your fingers into Pedersen."

"May I ask why you're targeting him?"

"If you can't figure it out, you're not much of a detective."

Giulia grinned at the dial tone. Nervous suspects. How marvelous.

Six minutes later the phone rang again.

"This is Konani Hyde. I don't care what you think, I didn't talk to the stockholders. A good detective would look into Sandra Sechrest's finances."

Giulia bet herself a quarter Pedersen would call by eight thirty. She lost by one minute.

"Look, Driscoll, you're the detective. But if I were you I'd study Sechrest's history and Hyde's debts like you were cramming for a final exam."

Zane walked in as she picked up the quarter she'd placed by the phone and dropped it in her pocket.

"What's up, Ms. D.?"

"I came in early to stare at the collage, but all three of Dahlia's Board of Directors called separately to direct my attention away from each of them toward the others."

"Nice." He booted his computer. "I'll get the phone to let you brainstorm."

Giulia added a new heading:

Who dragged in the stockholders?

- Pedersen, Sechrest, and Hyde all should be equal suspects, but...
- How close is Elaine to the Board?
- How hard would it be to get Elaine declared incompetent?
- What about Pip?

- Does he prefer a happy wife and an easy life?
- Does he prefer more money and easier access to his mistresses?
- Who doesn't own Dahlia stock?
- The Emersons
- The tutors?
- The household staff?
- Access to Elaine's phone:

She tapped the marker cap against her lips. To the Emersons' bullet she added "They resent not being given stock. Enough to play spoiler for everyone else?"

When nothing else along that line of inquiry appeared, she taped a fresh piece of paper next to the one covered with bullets.

- Access to Elaine's phone:
  - Pip
  - Cissy
  - Mike
  - Coorgia
  - Melina

Still too many. She ran a finger over the financial summary. The Board's salaries and bonuses were as generous as she thought they'd be.

Sidney arrived.

"Perfect. Good morning. Did either of you get a confirmation from your research if any of the Board of Directors are in financial difficulties?"

Sidney set down her combination messenger/diaper bag and her coffee. "Let me log in."

Zane tapped keys. "Pedersen's ex-wives are still trashing him on Facebook, but no complaints about alimony payments."

Sidney spoke between sips of coffee. "Hyde complained a few times on Twitter about the high fees at her kids' school, but lately she's all about how wonderful everything is in her life."

Zane took over. "Last fall Sechrest posted pictures of a party she threw when she paid off her divorce lawyer's bill."

Sidney added, "She also posts pictures of herself at the exotic places she travels to on buying trips, but those are company funded."

Giulia finished her coffee. "You're trying to tell me the big red SUSPECT signs flashing over their heads have fizzled out?"

Zane and Sidney shared a glance.

"Yeah."

"More or less."

Giulia scarfed a third piece of paper from the printer. "Fine. Maybe." She taped the new page next to the financial summary and reread every page of the collage three times. Then she stepped back and let her eyes unfocus. The phone obliged her by remaining silent. The sounds of typing became white noise. At last she picked up a blue and a red marker to complement the green.

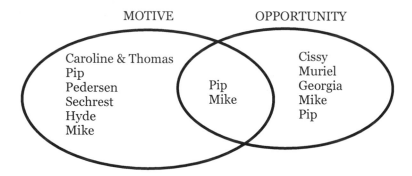

MOTIVE   OPPORTUNITY

Caroline & Thomas   Cissy
Pip   Muriel
Pedersen   Pip   Georgia
Sechrest   Mike   Mike
Hyde   Pip
Mike

Sidney came over to stand next to her. "Prince Charming? Really?"

Zane joined them. "Venn diagrams are my bête noire."

"You have a bête noire?" Giulia said.

"We all have something. I constantly try to find reasons to make every choice on both sides fit in the crossover."

"With me it's fancy tenses," Sidney said. "Pluperfect, past conjunctive, future imperfect probable on alternate Tuesdays when the moon is full."

Giulia laughed. "If you'd been young enough to take English from me, you'd be fluent in all of them." She capped the markers and grabbed her messenger bag. "I'm off to the castle to pump Cissy."

"Wait a minute," Sidney said. "Why the husband or the cook?"

"Because Elaine's uncle is the one in the homicidal vans, and the only way he could get information on where I'd be is through someone on the inside. There's no reason I can find for the Board of Directors or Muriel to align with the aunt and uncle, and I stand by my conclusion that Cissy did not hire us as a smokescreen for her own devious plot. Thus, Pip or the cook, who is a cousin. They're the only relations in the castle to join up with the aunt and uncle."

"I vote the cousin," Zane said. "He's close to all that money but can't have any."

"Ninety-eight percent of my own money is on Prince Charming," Giulia said, "but the other two percent won't rule out the cook. Pip has more to lose, but potentially more to gain."

"Unless he signed a Draconian prenup." Sidney said. "Want me to see if I can find an online record? Zane's teaching me all kinds of devious skills."

"Zane, do not corrupt Sidney."

"Ms. D., you wound me."

Fifty

Melina opened the door and her expression changed from bland politeness to fear.

Giulia infused reassurance into her smile. "I'm here to see Ms. Newton."

The fear didn't abate much. "I will see if she is free. Please be seated in the parlor."

Giulia paused in the parlor doorway to marvel at the art, the Oriental carpet, the glossy wood floors, and the crystal lamps. She ran a hand over the nearest armchair's indigo crushed velvet upholstery before she sat. Lace sheers filtered soft morning light through two tall windows.

Cissy bustled in, a plain black apron over her eternal khaki trousers and a concord grape shirt. "Ms. Driscoll? Is there a problem?"

Giulia stood. "I'd like to ask you some questions. What is the most private place in the house?"

Cissy's expression mirrored Melina's. "My office...no, everyone knows I'm usually in there. The laundry...no, today's towel day." She looked around the room as if Cézanne's "Melting Snow Fontainebleau" hanging over the love seat could give her answers. "The wine cellar. It's cleaner than the attic. Come with me."

She led Giulia across the foyer into a restaurant-worthy kitchen. Mike was nowhere to be seen. They passed spotless stainless steel appliances. Open shelves of beans, macaroni, and dry mixes. Hanging baskets of onions, bananas, garlic, and peppers. Another door opened onto a porch stacked with empty cages, chameleon-filled cages, and a mini refrigerator with a sign taped to it: "Chameleon insects ONLY. Do not eat."

"How is Scarlett working out?"

"She may be getting fat. The Japanese beetle population is greatly reduced."

Cissy opened a painted wood door. The steep wood slat stairs vanished into a black hole at the fifth step. Cissy flicked a switch and a supernova of naked swirl light bulbs nuked the darkness.

The cellars consisted of concrete floored vaults with cement block walls. Several wooden crates had been pushed against the walls. Two hot water heaters were set up in two different rooms. A massive furnace took up the central area. They passed under the arch nearest to the stairs. The floor changed to packed dirt and the walls to whitewashed plaster. Racks upon racks of dusty bottles took up most of the space. Cissy led Giulia to a back corner where a ladder leaned against the wall next to paint buckets, trays, and brushes.

"We're in a room with only one exit and three hundred wine bottles to absorb our voices. What information do you need?"

Giulia's messenger bag began to emit an electronic whistle rising and falling over a short scale. They both stared at it. Giulia set it on the floor and took out her phone.

"WeeEEEeeeooo. WeeEEEeeeooo."

"It's my EMF detector." Like the Winchester brothers in *Supernatural*, she aimed the phone at the nearest wall. The irritating noise stayed at the same volume. The wine racks also caused no change. The opposite wall, ditto. Then she came back around to the corner with the painting supplies. The whistle turned into a screech.

"EEEOOOEEEOOOEEEOOOEEEOOO."

Giulia held down the phone's volume button and forced the screech below ear-piercing level.

More screams came from behind them. They turned and saw Melina in the doorway staring at the corner. Her arms were stiff at her sides and her face stretched into a Greek theater tragedy mask.

Cissy ran to her. "Melina, stop it. Melina, I said stop it." When the screams continued uninterrupted, Cissy reached up to Melina's shoulders and shook her.

Melina gasped and hiccupped. "A ghost. A ghost in the cellar. I knew it. I knew it." She slipped into rapid Spanish. Giulia caught most of it: Melina was repeating the Our Father with barely a breath between phrases.

While Cissy kept trying to calm Melina, Giulia knelt in the corner. The EMF meter continued to wail. Giulia moved the paint supplies.

"Cissy, when was this wall repaired?"

"I don't know." The irritation in her voice faded. "I should know. That's odd."

Giulia brushed plaster dust from her hands and stood. "Can someone bring a shovel?"

Cissy sent Melina, who returned in less than two minutes with Mike carrying a well-used shovel. He looked excited rather than frightened as he set the tip of the shovel in the dirt at the corner, put a foot on it, and pushed. It sank into the floor much too easily.

"That's weird." He looked over his shoulder at Cissy. "I thought this whole floor was packed as hard as stone to support the wine racks."

"It is." Cissy couldn't seem to decide whether to be angry or frightened.

Giulia took pictures as the excavation continued. She wrinkled her nose at the sour odor of old dirt. The shovel knocked against the wall. A chunk of plaster fell inward.

Anger won. "Which of you has been tampering with the house? Where's Georgia?" Cissy's face rivaled Giulia's teacher glare.

"Not me, Ms. Newton, honest," Mike said.

"Never, Ms. Newton," Melina said. "I never touch any part of the house not assigned to me."

Giulia pocketed her phone and crouched at the shallow hole. "Wait a minute, please." She pulled away pieces of plaster, more of it crumbling as she worked. "There's something behind the wall." Her heart lurched when she realized the bits of white were not shards of plaster. "It's a baby's skeleton."

Fifty-One

Mike scrambled backward, knocking the shovel into the opposite wall with a *clunk.* "Oh shit, oh shit, oh shit."

Melina began screaming again. Georgia appeared in the doorway, saw the inhabitant of the wall, and added her screams to Melina's.

Cissy clamped her hands over her ears, but Giulia got a strong impression she was trying to shut out the fact of the little skeleton, not the cacophony.

Elaine appeared in the doorway, and Giulia learned a new definition of cacophony. She moved behind the farthest wine rack to block some of the clamor and called 911.

Money being powerful, two uniformed officers, two detectives, and the coroner arrived within ten minutes. Before their appearance, the combined efforts of Giulia and Mike got Melina and Georgia to stop screaming. Cissy shelved her own reaction and took charge of Elaine. Elaine's high, breathless shrieks—Giulia had hoped never to hear them again—continued all the way upstairs.

Giulia was explaining the discovery to one of the detectives when Pip loomed over her shoulder.

"Ms. Driscoll, our house will never lack excitement while you're around."

Giulia finished her statement to the lead detective rather than reply to Pip's passive-aggressive attempt at humor. Fortunately for her temper, the detective recognized Pip and they moved out into the main cellars.

The coroner rose from his knees and opened his phone.

"Professor Lembach, please...Herman? It's Max. Drop everything you're doing and get over to..." He jerked his bald head at one of the uniformed officers. "What's the address here?...Did you hear that, Herman? Good. Yes, I mean right now. You'll owe me a bottle of Stolichnaya Red for this."

He pocketed his phone and said to the room, "This skeleton could be ancient, but it could also be artificially aged. Lembach is one of the best forensic anthropologists in the state. He'll be here in ten. Nobody even breathe on those bones in the meantime."

Cissy clattered halfway down the cellar stairs. "Pip, Elaine wants you."

Pip held up his index finger in the "in a minute" gesture. "Detective Hansen, I only wish I knew how such a horrific thing happened in my house. If you'll excuse me, I have to check on my wife."

He mounted the stairs two at a time, squeezing around Cissy. She hesitated, took one step up, then continued down to the group in the cellar.

The other detective was interviewing Melina. One uniformed officer was working on Mike. The second uniformed officer finished with Georgia, then Detective Hansen sent him to monitor the front door.

"Ms. Newton," he said, "I'd appreciate it if you could let me know when Ms. Patrick is able to be interviewed."

All Cissy's quills spiked out. "Ms. Patrick is extremely upset by this horrible discovery, as you can imagine. I doubt you'll be able to speak to her today."

The detective's expression signaled his lack of sympathy. "Ms. Newton, this is a potential crime scene. The sooner I'm able to speak with Ms. Patrick, the sooner we'll be able to resolve the situation and her house can return to normal." He looked at his watch. "It's not quite eleven a.m. I'm sure Ms. Patrick will recover herself before we have to leave."

Giulia would've given a week's allotment of coffee to scare Pip and Mike enough to hear them both scream like a girl. Too bad Mike's initial reaction to the skeleton had been low-key, which swung the suspicion compass needle his way.

"Hello?" A man's deep voice at the top of the stairs.

"Down here, Herman." The coroner beckoned to the unseen male. "I'm too old for steep stairs, Max." The bass voice grew louder. "Are you trying to kill me?"

A dark man stepped onto the cement floor. He was smaller than Giulia and shaped like the Matryoshka doll round enough to hold all the rest. A wild fringe of white hair offset his chipmunk cheeks.

"Herman, if I had five bucks for every time you said that..."

"You'd be able to retire at fifty," the Matryoshka said. "Are you going to disappoint me like you did last year with the Monongahela remains?"

The coroner's mustached lip curled. "Are you ever going to let me live that down?"

"Probably not. Well? Impress me."

Giulia hadn't mentioned the EMF meter's antics. Neither had Cissy or Melina, from what she'd overheard of their interviews. Melina had gone on at length about ghosts and the noises they'd all been hearing. Mike and Georgia kept interrupting each other to add another haunting experience. By the time the Matryoshka arrived, the expressions on the faces of all law enforcement in the cellar, including the coroner, varied between humor and disgust.

Max led Herman to the excavated corner. All banter ceased. Herman creaked onto his knees and pulled on a pair of latex surgical gloves. Intensity flowed from him like ectoplasm in a séance. One by one, everyone stopped talking.

Stubby fingers touched the tiny, fragile bones with the delicacy of a confectioner working with spun sugar. He produced a jeweler's loupe from an inside pocket. "Give me some light here, someone."

Giulia stepped forward with the flashlight on her phone aimed into the recess.

"Thank you." He didn't look around. "A little closer, please."

His inspection continued. Feet shuffled. The second detective turned a wine bottle label-up. Cissy slapped his hand. He backed away like a little boy caught stealing cookies.

Herman looked up at the group, an ecstatic smile on his face.

"This is marvelous, absolutely marvelous." He clapped his hands. "I haven't come across an intact specimen of such age in decades. Literally decades." He pulled off the gloves and stuffed them in a different pocket. "Max, I owe you two bottles of Stolichnaya Red."

The lead detective shouldered Giulia out of his way. "What have we got, Herman?"

"Your skeleton is at least one hundred years old. Possibly more, but I have to get it back to my laboratory for a thorough examination." He fished a flip phone out of his pocket, dialed a number, and issued orders. When he ended the call, he said, "I feel like a kid on Christmas morning thanks to this little lady. Don, have your lot look up all reports of vandalized cemeteries. Start with Pittsburgh's oldest ones. We may get lucky."

"It's a girl's skeleton?" Cissy said.

"Possibly; possibly." He looked around at the walls and ceilings. "How old is this house?"

"The foundations were laid in 1797."

He appeared to calculate. "A little modern, but within the realm of possibility." His crinkled eyes gazed at all of them. "Do you know what I'm referring to?"

Puzzled glances.

Herman clapped his hands again, his wide smile making his eyes disappear. "Hitobashira, of course. Don't they teach anything useful in school anymore?"

Giulia said, "Is Hitobashira the same tradition as the legend of the monastery of St. Columba and the monk Odhran?" One of Clark and Brad's wild guesses had been correct. Did this enlarge her suspect list? How high would Clark Wagner's falsetto reach, and had she missed a subtle hint with his insistence on pronouncing his last name like the composer?

"Yes." Herman left the circle of police and castle staff and came over to Giulia. "Young woman, you could teach these Philistines something about history." He balanced on the balls of his feet and assumed a professorial voice. "In ancient times, a human sacrifice— sometimes voluntary, sometimes not—was entombed in the walls of a building or one of the supports of a bridge to ensure the safety of all who used it."

Cissy's face had the "I smell something bad" look.

"Cool," Mike said. "I mean, gross, but cool. Like that short story 'The Cask of Amontillado,' right?"

Herman nodded and bounced. "Point to you, young man, for reading the classics. Although 'The Cask of Amontillado' was a revenge story." He turned to Cissy. "Is the water table particularly high on this property?"

For once Cissy didn't have an answer at her fingertips. "I have no idea. Would you like me to find out for you?"

A wave of the hand. "Perhaps. First my team and I will see if you have a true instance of Hitobashira or if we are dealing with a mundane grave robbery."

Several different sets of footsteps hit the cellar stairs.

"Follow my voice," Herman called. "We're on the left."

Two college-age women and one man crowded into the wine cellar. The tall, thin man carried a legal-sized plastic document box. The woman with a '70s throwback 'fro held a professional camera with a lens case slung over her shoulder. The woman with short purple hair carried a smaller plastic box labeled "Samples."

Herman snapped his fingers. "Amy, pictures of every square inch, please. Vivian, when Amy's finished we need soil samples, plaster samples, and bits of anything in the niche not attached to the skeleton. Go."

The camera flashed five, ten, twenty times. Giulia caught the edge of two flashes and turned away to allow the blinding spots to fade from her vision.

Vivian's sample gathering began before Giulia could see again. Several plastic baggies held darkened or dusty cotton swabs. She used tweezers on molecules too minute for Giulia to see a mere four feet away.

A few tweezer plucks later she clicked the lid closed on her plastic box. "Done."

"Carl," Herman said.

The tall man stepped forward with the document box and all three began to move in a smooth, choreographed dance with their gloved hands. Carl and Vivian reached into the hole. Vivian cradled the skull in her left hand. Carl's long fingers supported the ribcage and pelvis. Amy stood ready with the box.

"Easy," Herman said. "Carl, can you do anything for the arms? Vivian, is one of the ribs detached? No? Excellent. Ease it out now."

His assistants appeared not to need his mother hen advice. They freed the skeleton from its niche with Carl's thumb and pinky stretched to their limit supporting the stick-thin arm bones. Amy eased the document box underneath. Still in sync, Vivian and Carl laid the little skeleton in the box, and Amy closed and locked the handles.

Herman waggled his hands back and forth in the best *Wallace and Gromit* tradition. "Sublime as always. Now the fun begins. Don, text me if you get a cemetery hit. Don't call. My ringer will be off starting now." He clicked the side button on his phone. "I'll call you as soon as we know anything definite. Amy, we'll stop at the nearest grocery store for a case of Red Bull. No one's sleeping until we identify our little bundle of joy. Up and out, people."

Fifty-Two

An hour later everyone in the castle except Elaine sat at the dining room table eating Mike's idea of "a little lunch."

Pip layered bacon, avocado, and fresh tomatoes on a homemade wheat roll. "The Xanax kicked in after Elaine plugged herself into her sleep recording."

Cissy nibbled roast beef and kale. "She didn't try to sneak a second pill?"

Even Pip's wry smile managed to be alluring in a heartthrob way. "She did, but I convinced her to give the first one a half hour to take effect."

Anyone watching Giulia would see a hungry woman appreciating ham and cucumber on pumpernickel. Excitement made Zlatan send FEED ME messages. Satisfying his demands supplied her, the outsider, with good cover.

Mike, Melina, and Georgia sat in silence on the opposite side of the table from Giulia and Cissy. Pip had taken the chair at the table's head. Melina took small, ladylike bites of lettuce and sliced chicken. Georgia added tomato to her chicken, and Mike was already into his second roast beef and coleslaw.

Silence reigned when Pip finished speaking. Giulia breathed an unspoken thank you to the manufacturer of Xanax for castle time free from hysterical screams.

Mike ate as though nothing had ever been discovered in the wine cellar except wine. Georgia and Melina might as well have been strapped to their chairs. Their movements consisted of the minimum necessary to convey food to their mouths.

Cissy gestured and they gathered plates.

Mike rose. "Should I make a plate for Ms. Patrick?"

"Yes. I'll take it—"

Pip's voice overrode Cissy's. "Please do, Mike. I'll take it up to her in a little while."

Cissy squared off against him, but her rebellion lasted less than three seconds. Only the thin line of her lips gave the lie to her acquiescence.

Pip turned to Giulia. "Ms. Driscoll, I need to lock myself in the library for a web conference, but I'd like to speak with you before you go."

"Certainly. I'll make sure to find you."

Pip went out the door and to the right up the central stairs. Melina and Giulia split the dishes between them and turned left toward the kitchen. Mike hefted the remains of the sandwich platter and followed.

Cissy beckoned to Giulia, and they closed themselves into the sun porch on the back of the house. She used a remote to turn on a flat screen TV mounted on the far wall of the long narrow space.

When the characters in *The Young and the Restless* began to pour out their relationship angst, Cissy spoke. "I didn't forget why you came here. Since your gadget isn't shrieking at us, I presume no one's buried a skeleton in these porch walls." She shivered despite the July afternoon heat. "What information can I give you?"

Giulia went right for it. "Two things: what is Pip's financial situation in relation to Elaine, and do you know if either Mike or Pip has kept in close contact with Elaine's aunt and uncle after they moved out of the castle?"

Cissy eased herself onto the pink flowered davenport. The scattering of freckles across her cheeks stood out against her pale face. Giulia sat in the yellow flowered chair kitty-corner to her and waited.

It took a good minute for Cissy's spine to straighten. "Mike is a cousin on the Davenport side of the family, that is, related to Elaine's mother and her sister, Caroline Emerson. He went into deep debt to pay his mother's medical bills. I'm unaware whether he's free of it even after all these years."

A tap on the door. They both scowled at it.

Cissy stood. "Sometimes I think I should check my clothes for a tracking device."

Melina handed her an envelope. "Another registered letter for you, Ms. Newton."

She closed the door and Cissy tore off the envelope's short end. Giulia thought Cissy had gone as colorless as humanly possible a minute ago. She'd been wrong. By the time Cissy finished the letter she could've haunted the castle herself. When she held the paper out to Giulia, swaying like an unstaked sapling, Giulia helped her sit before taking it.

"There's no hope," Cissy whispered. "No one understands Elaine like I do. Their hand-picked psychiatrist will tell a judge exactly what the stockholders want to hear, and Elaine will lose everything." Her voice broke on the last word as her face sank into deep lines.

The letter's bald prose mimicked an IRS audit communication. If the initial letters from the stockholders' lawyer had been written this way, it was no wonder Cissy and the Board of Directors reacted as they did.

The soap opera went to commercial. Giulia rummaged in her bag and produced a single tissue. Cissy began shredding it to the jingle for an all-purpose cleaner.

Giulia made a dash for the dining room and returned with a pile of upscale paper napkins. Total time seven seconds. Cissy came back to the present when Giulia soaked the first napkin with the tears on her cheeks. The efficient house manager plucked the rest from Giulia's hands and blotted her eyes.

"Thank you. I apologize."

"There's no need. You received startling news."

Cissy blew her nose. "You have a talent for understatement. Why didn't your Tarot reading foresee this development?"

"As I explained to Elaine at the outset of the reading, the cards speak to the question or problem uppermost in the seeker's thoughts. Sunday night Elaine asked about the castle haunting and her family. When she cut the deck, the cards responded to that desire."

Rowan would be proud.

Cissy blew her nose again. "You were asking about finances. Pip's personal bank accounts are robust. He also signed a prenuptial agreement drawn up by the family lawyer. If Elaine predeceases him or is incapacitated, he receives half the interest from her stock for his lifetime. If they divorce, he receives the same half interest for a period of three years."

Hardly Draconian. Giulia was surprised. "Would the interest amount to a considerable sum?" Zane must have uncovered Elaine's stock numbers. She'd have to check.

Cissy pressed the remaining dry napkin to her eyes. "If profits keep their current trend and Pip invests three-quarters of the amount he could retire at age forty. Pip is thirty."

If Giulia had been Frank, she would've whistled.

Cissy's smile was not pleasant. "Elaine has been Pip's princess from their very first meeting. Mike has been a treasured member of the household since he made the world's best cheesecake on his trial run." She flung the balled-up napkins at the catfighting actresses on the TV. "Now we have a crime scene in the basement, a ghost terrorizing our lives, and a possible Judas under our roof." The lines in her face aged her another ten years. "Next you'll be telling me my chameleons are possessed."

"Have they ever turned demon red without warning?"

Cissy's mouth dropped open. Giulia kept her face expressionless as long as she could, but finally gave in and winked.

Cissy gulped. "You had me trying to recall all their recent color changes." She turned off the TV. "I'd like you to stay here tonight."

The woman epitomized "coming out of left field." "Why?"

"Would you be offended if I said you're our safety net?" She gathered the napkin missiles from the floor. "You've discovered terrible things in our house, but you also know how to protect Elaine and abolish evil."

She tossed everything into a yellow wicker basket, the only non-floral piece in the room. "There's another reason. If you're right about what you asked me, I'll need you as a witness. I will have no mercy on any human trying to hurt Elaine."

Fifty-Three

Pip and Giulia faced each other across the Perrault hearthrug in the library.

"I want you to know I spoke to the detectives before they left. They'll be running your fingerprints against any found on the skeleton or the tools in the wine cellar."

"I see."

"You have to admit this whole haunting business has escalated since you first came to my house."

"When Ms. Newton retained our services."

"Which she did without consulting me."

"The interpersonal dynamics of Elaine's house are not our concern."

"Elaine's and my house."

"Mr. Patrick, was there anything else you wished to discuss?"

"Yes. If my wife asks for another Tarot reading or Ouija Board session, I want you to refuse. This spiritualism circus act is bad for my wife's mental and physical health."

"Driscoll Investigations will continue to conduct its investigation in accordance with the best interests of its client."

The grandfather clock in the hall struck two, the first sound to penetrate the library since she'd entered.

"If there's nothing else, Mr. Patrick?"

Fifty-Four

Frank watered the vegetables while Giulia grilled shrimp kebabs. The chameleon's eyes swiveled every which way as the water arched over the plants and spattered the miniature tree in her cage.

"This lizard is watching me."

"She likes you."

"Or she's plotting my demise because I'm not giving her the proper amount of droplets on her ficus leaves for her to gather and drink." He gave the cucumbers a second soaking. "Can I talk you out of sleeping in the Haunted Palace of Pittsburgh?"

Giulia painted barbecue sauce on the shrimp and vegetables. "You cannot. Being on the spot is the break I need to discover which of them is working with the aunt and uncle."

"I understand that as a fellow detective, but the Neanderthal male in me is saying you will be in much too close proximity to the mastermind gaslighting his wife or the mastermind who could poison your midnight snack."

"Which is why I'm packing my own midnight snack."

"I'm serious."

"You forgot one of them is also the mastermind giving orders to the driver of the murderous vehicles. Supper's ready."

He turned off the hose. "You raise my blood pressure when you say things like that."

She transferred the kebabs to two plates. "Supper won't raise your blood pressure. It's healthy enough for Sidney's table, if we subtract the shrimp."

He advanced on her. "Don't be disingenuous."

She pecked his nose as she balanced a plate in each hand. "You're sexy when you use big words."

He wrapped his arms around her. "*Murinín,* they've tried to run you off the road three times. You're smart and kickass, but they're upping their game."

"Let go of me before I drop these plates, please."

He lifted both dishes from her grasp and carried them into the kitchen. "Have you come up with any reason why they're trying to make you a traffic statistic but only haunting the flower princess?"

Giulia folded napkins. "It's been percolating in the back of my head for days. Elaine's grandparents created a convoluted structure for Dahlia. One of their direct female descendants must be Dahlia's CEO or the company reverts to the stockholders. I don't have all the details, but an Elaine too terrified to leave her bedroom can still be titular head of Dahlia."

Frank opened the fridge. "And since Elaine's running Dahlia from her house already, her relatives can swoop in to help and the gravy train continues." He brought out the pitcher of iced tea.

"DI is spoiling the plan."

"Thus the homicidal vans." He let loose a string of Irish profanity.

Giulia let him get it out of his system as she watched the chameleon gather water drops from the leaves before going inside. "Scarlett says thank you for Happy Hour."

"Oh, God, if that creature starts talking you have to exorcize it." He poured tea into two glasses.

"You are a true gentleman. For helping with supper, not for thinking our new bug zapper is possessed."

He banged the pitcher on the table. "If I were a gentleman, I'd be knocking on the castle door to offer Prince Charming a choice of swords or pistols at dawn."

"Him or the cook."

"I'll take them both on."

Giulia pulled her chair closer to the table. "Take on supper, please, because I need to clean up the kitchen before my sleepover."

"Babe..."

Giulia set down her fork. "Honey, I know you're worried. I know you'd rather I chose only one hundred percent safe jobs. Don't forget I use Zane as my bodyguard when necessary. But I'm not going to abandon this mystery when I'm a whisker away from the solution." She inserted a dramatic pause. "And you wouldn't want me to."

They stared each other down.

Frank stabbed a barbecued shrimp. "Dammit."

Giulia ate her supper with a beatific smile on her face.

Fifty-Five

Georgia was on door duty when Giulia rang the bell at eight o'clock.

"Ms. Driscoll, did you hear?"

"About?" Giulia followed her inside.

Georgia took charge of Giulia's gym bag and closed the door. "They identified the skeleton." Her expression flip-flopped between the neutral mask of a servant and one of macabre delight.

"Thank you, Georgia. Please bring Ms. Driscoll's bag to the Gray Room."

Cissy's tone of voice would've frozen the fires of both the Sixth and Seventh Circles of Dante's Hell. Georgia all but *meeped* as she vanished up the central stairs.

"Ms. Driscoll, may I speak with you in my office?"

Giulia walked with her as an equal. Cissy closed them in and sat behind her desk. With hands clasped on her blotter calendar she said, "The police called a few minutes ago. The skeleton was stolen from Allegheny Cemetery last month. The strange antiquarian was right. It's a girl. She died one hundred seven years ago." Her professional façade crumbled. "If you're correct, either Elaine's husband or her cousin left here in the middle of the night, desecrated an ancient grave, and secreted the remains in the wine cellar." She dropped her head into her hands. "Why? Why?"

"Elaine wants children. Based on the Tarot reading, she places unquestioned belief in signs and portents. Discovering an infant's skeleton in her house could be spun however the grave-robber wanted. For instance, the child's ghost has cursed Elaine. She doesn't deserve to have children. The castle is haunted by the child's ghost, which obviously hates Elaine. You see how she could be affected by this: With proper handling she could become a recluse in her own rooms yet still be head of Dahlia. The money would continue to flow unimpeded and no one would be bothered by Elaine any longer." Giulia waited for her to connect the dots.

Cissy raised her head. "But Pip and Elaine worship each other. You can see it every moment they're together."

"And Mike?"

"He's the quintessential nice guy. He's always cheerful, even around my chameleons, which he would prefer never to see again. He's always helpful, and he has a real talent in the kitchen."

Giulia leaned both hands on the desk. "What do you pay him?"

For a moment, she thought Cissy would refuse to answer.

"Yes, of course. You have a reason to ask."

The figure she named wasn't a fortune, but it was quite a bit more than Giulia expected to hear. Cissy picked up on her reaction.

"We wanted to give Mike incentive to stay. Elaine and Pip entertain here a few times each year and the guests are always lavish with their compliments on the meals. In the circles Elaine and Pip belong to, luring away an extraordinary staff member is almost expected."

Giulia appreciated being several rungs below Elaine on the society ladder. "Have you received such offers?"

Cissy started and her ears reddened. "Yes. But I would never, never leave Elaine. Never."

Giulia straightened and crossed her arms, messenger bag bouncing against her hip. "And you used the offers to negotiate a raise." She didn't make it a question.

"I did not!" The red ears blazed to crimson. "I don't stay with Elaine for the money."

"But Mike did."

After a moment's hesitation Cissy said, "Yes."

"How many times and when?"

Pain crept into Cissy's eyes. Her crow's feet clawed farther onto her cheeks. "Twice. Two Christmases ago and this past Fourth of July. We bargained both times and came to an acceptable compromise. At least I thought it was acceptable." She stood. "May I offer you something to eat or drink?"

"Thank you, no. If you'll tell me the way to my room for tonight, I'll unpack."

Cissy walked with her up the stairs. "These stairs were painted enough times to add half an inch to their depth. Elaine's parents had them stripped and uncovered their beautifully grained oak." When they reached the landing, she lowered her voice. "Elaine should be asleep. I caught her sneaking another Xanax, but she swallowed it before I could snatch it out of her mouth."

Giulia refrained from voicing an opinion which would get her booted into the street.

"This was Elaine's mother's prize possession." Cissy stopped before a narrow Impressionist painting of yellow and pink dahlias. "It's an original Monet."

Giulia said, "It's beautiful," as she calculated the house's astronomical insurance bill. Ten years living below the poverty line as Sister Mary Regina Coelis made her forever allergic to extravagance like this.

"Tomorrow before breakfast I'll give you our art and antiques tour. Only two dollars." Cissy's lighthearted humor attempt fell as flat as pizza dough without yeast. They continued walking. "The Gray Room is in the opposite hall from Elaine's and Pip's rooms. It was Elaine's parents' bedroom. Gray was her mother's color: she looked timeless and classic in it." Her smile conveyed illicit enjoyment. "Arthur hated gray walls. He said the color made any room look like a garage floor."

"Yet the room remained gray."

"Belinda always got what she wanted." Cissy opened a door at the back of the house. "She also didn't want traffic noises interrupting her sleep."

The master bedroom was indeed a symphony in gray. Silver drapes, slate rugs, pewter walls, graphite bedspread and pillow shams. Even the art on the walls coordinated. All three paintings depicted rainy streets: one at dawn, one at twilight, and one in winter.

"This room could be the cover of an interior decoration magazine." An empty compliment. Giulia agreed with Arthur.

Cissy closed the door. "Ms. Driscoll, is the ghost of that infant haunting our house?"

Fifty-Six

Trapped.

Giulia could've mouthed phrases picked up from Rowan. She could've lied outright, assuming a lie would make it out of her mouth. Instead her answer was born from the unexpected behavior of the EMF meter. "I don't know."

For the first time, Cissy looked pitiful. "Then it may be something else."

Saved.

Cissy busied herself turning on the bedside lamp and the light in the master bathroom. "I never thought I'd miss the little annoyances of running a house this size. The leaky faucet in Elaine's private bath. My most incorrigible chameleon slipping out of its cage and scaring Georgia. The water pipes knocking only after the first hard freeze." She turned down the bed. "The house has such a colorful history. We might've come to an agreement with the right ghost." She pulled a pillow out of the sham on her side. "When Pip first heard noises, Elaine dived right into the haunting idea. She thought it was fun. But then Mike started hearing things and after him the others, and we all became frightened. Then the demon infested the fireplace and the ghost began destroying items which mattered to Elaine."

Giulia liberated the other pillow. Cissy folded both shams and set them on the dresser.

"If your EMF meter makes noise tonight, please come get me, no matter what time it is. I'm in the room opposite Elaine's." She opened the door and said on the threshold, "Please feel free to go anywhere in the house except the occupied bedrooms."

As soon as Cissy was out of sight, Giulia made sure the EMF meter and EVP recorder on her phone were activated. She tucked her wallet and keys in her pockets—trust no one, especially mischievous ghosts—and went exploring.

The second floor porch and two guest bedrooms yielded no spirit noises or hollow laughter. She descended the back stairs. The door she chose opened onto the kitchen. She passed the room of now-sleeping chameleons—Did lizards snore? She'd find out when they brought Scarlett inside for the winter—and clicked the switch at the top of the cellar stairs.

Bright yellow CRIME SCENE—DO NOT CROSS tape stretched across the wine cellar doorway. She aimed her phone at the excavated corner and braced herself.

"Is it still haunted?"

Giulia spun around, free arm raised to strike. In full chef regalia minus the tall hat, Mike backpedaled, tripped on something invisible, and his butt hit the cement floor.

"Whoa, stop, okay?" He held up both hands in surrender. "I came down to prep for breakfast and saw the cellar light."

"Ghosts don't need light."

"Light," Giulia's phone repeated.

Mike crab-walked backward until his shoulders collided with the nearest archway. "What the hell?"

"Hell."

"Oh, shit, this place really is haunted." He leaped to his feet, stumbled once, and pounded up the stairs.

Giulia inspected the EVP app with approval. Its habit of picking up the last word spoken couldn't have served her purpose better. Mike was probably closeted right now with Georgia, Melina, and a whisky bottle, inspiring the women to new heights of hysteria. Too bad Pip wouldn't be a part of Mike's audience.

She returned to the second floor via the back stairs and visited the library. It should've been a warm and inviting room. She should've wanted to spend the entire night browsing the shelves. Perhaps knowing about the concealed punishment hole soured the atmosphere. Perhaps it was the complete and utter weirdness of whatever happened in the fireplace during her inaugural "exorcism."

Giulia walked the room with the EMF app held at arms' length. Both apps might be nothing more than party games, but the EVP's penchant for picking up words spoken by any human voice within range inspired even less confidence.

Between the chairs, around the tables, along the bookshelves, into the window seat: nothing. She thrust the phone into the fireplace and up the chimney as far as her arm could stretch. Not the ghost—ha, ha— of a wailing arpeggio came from the speaker.

Last she felt for the catch to the hidden niche and eased open the concealed door.

Odd. Not a creak of old wood or a groan from the hinges. She slid a finger along the top hinge and sniffed her fingertip. WD-40.

She tiptoed to the door and closed it without a sound, a trick she'd learned in the convent. Back at the fireplace, she reached into the chimney and wiggled every brick within reach. They all remained intact, but she refused to give up.

She sat on the hearthrug and stared into the recess. A speaker wouldn't survive the heat. Never mind the summer weather now. This was a long game. Her fingers traced the designs on the rug. Puss in Boots, Little Red Riding Hood, Cinderella.

Cinderella sitting at the fireplace.

She flipped up the Cinderella corner. The edges of the floorboard below it were a shade lighter than the edges of the other boards. Two fingernails cracked prying it up but the sacrifice was worth it. A digital speaker nestled in wood shavings below the board, and when she held up the wood light shone through half a dozen pin-sized holes.

Speaker number one located. Speakers two, three, four, however many needed to shatter Elaine into pieces, would be where Mike, Melina, Georgia, and Cissy had heard giggles and whispers and footsteps. The Power of DI Compels You, you miserable excuse for a human.

Now to identify the miserable excuse. She chose a hardcover copy of Kate Greenaway's *The Language of Flowers* and returned to her room.

The house creaked and settled and created enough noises to populate multiple hauntings. Giulia kept herself awake learning which flowers signified romance, jealousy, and friendship, and a hundred other meanings of flowers she'd never heard of. She compiled a list of flower names if Zlatan turned out to be a girl.

Close to eleven thirty she heard footsteps on the stairs. She cracked her door in time to see Cissy's khaki pant leg disappear on her way to the opposite hall. She cracked it again when the back stairs door swung open just after midnight: Melina. Five minutes later, Georgia. Twenty-five minutes after Georgia, Mike.

Zlatan, unused to mama being awake this late, sent insistent "Feed Me" messages. Fortunately, Giulia had remembered Sidney's first trimester transformation into a bottomless pit and had packed trail mix and bottled water. Zlatan accepted the offering and the chocolate-protein hit kept her alert.

She was considering another trip to the library when soft, steady footsteps passed her door. She dropped the book and eased open her door in time to see the back stairway door swing shut.

Fifty-Seven

Giulia crept downstairs out of sight of whoever she was following. Their game of dead-of-night tag ended in the cellar. Everything in regular use in the castle being kept in impeccable shape, the bare wooden treads didn't make a single creak under either set of feet.

A light flickered to the left. The wine cellar.

Phone out and night vision camera recording, Giulia pasted herself against the archway at the foot of the stairs and peered around the edge.

A tall figure stood before the doorway. One hand held a votive candle in a frosted glass container. The figure's hooded cloak brushed the floor, concealing its feet. From the back Giulia knew only it wasn't Cissy (too tall), Melina or Georgia (too short), or Mike (too thin).

A woman's hand reached out from the cloak and snapped the yellow tape. As it fluttered to the sides of the doorframe, the stranger in Elaine's house paced between the wine racks to the back of the room.

Giulia followed between the nearest two rows of wine. At the end of the rows she angled her phone to get the most from the side view her hidden location afforded.

The woman stopped before the excavation and set the candle at her feet. Raising thin arms, she began to chant. The language sounded vaguely Celtic. Giulia had heard enough Irish from Frank's family to be able to pick out several words, but she recognized nothing this woman recited.

The chanting stopped. The woman cupped her hands beneath her mouth. With a final solemn phrase she blew a breath across her palms and opened her hands in a gesture of release. When she stooped to retrieve the candle, Giulia crouched and rose along with the woman as she stood, turned, and paced out.

Giulia gave her a full ten minutes to escape. She didn't need to capture her tonight. She had video evidence. The intruder appeared to be concerned only with the purloined skeleton and had committed neither violence nor theft unless a votive candle turned up missing tomorrow morning. This morning.

She tiptoed up to her room and replayed the video.

The woman looked like Elaine.

Still barefoot, she tapped at Cissy's door for a good five minutes before it opened. Cissy's hair flew around her head in a static electricity halo.

"What? What's wrong?" Sleep fogged her voice.

Giulia put a hand on the door, ready to force her way in. Cissy opened it wide enough to allow her to enter.

Cissy in pajamas decorated with portraits of scrawny young Frank Sinatra would've amused Giulia any other time. Now she sat on the edge of Cissy's bed and beckoned the housekeeper to join her.

"Is Muriel Elaine's only local cousin?"

Between one breath and the next Cissy became wide awake. "Why?"

"Someone broke into the house tonight." She played the video. Even with the night vision camera's green skin and glowing eyes, on a second viewing the intruder's resemblance to Elaine was even more marked. "Do you recognize this person? Does she have a key? Who is she?"

When Cissy didn't answer, Giulia looked over at her. Cissy's eyes were wide and round as latte cups. Her hands were pressed tight against her mouth. Her fingers made divots in her cheeks.

Giulia paused the video at the best full-face capture of the stranger. Cissy's flash-frozen posture was putting Springer Show ideas into Giulia's head again.

"There's a very close resemblance between Elaine and this woman and Muriel. I can see it now. Muriel may be a little eccentric, but this woman leaves her in the dust. Does Muriel have a black sheep twin sister? I didn't recognize her language, but she obviously adheres to an obscure religion. Which relative is she?"

Even after all Giulia's chatter, Cissy's hands remained clamped over her mouth. Giulia was trying to come up with the magic words that would release Cissy from her spell of silence when the woman's fingers began to unpeel themselves from her mashed face. Giulia waited, picturing Muriel at her steampunkiest throwing a chair across Springer's stage at her moralizing long-lost twin while the audience egged them on.

"It's the High Priestess from the Tarot cards," Cissy said in a shaken voice.

Giulia rewound the video. "She does resemble the card. Muriel's not the only cosplayer in the family, then."

Cissy rocked herself back and forth on the bed. "It's because of the murders and Belinda locking her in the hole. The space between the library walls. She was only nine. She was always a fragile child."

Pregnant Giulia began to feel a touch seasick. She dragged over the chair from the dressing table and planted herself toe to toe with the housekeeper.

Cissy was hugging herself as she rocked now. The grandfather clock struck the three-quarters and she muttered, "The extra Xanax should've kept her asleep until morning."

"Elaine's probably built up a tolerance. What happened because of the murders?"

Cissy jutted her head at Giulia like a weapon. "If you were locked in a lightless hole for three days without food or water, I guarantee you wouldn't be able to walk out of there whistling 'Heigh-Ho, Heigh-Ho, It's Off to Work I Go.'"

"Most likely not. What is your point in relation to Elaine?" Although she'd figured it out, she wanted as much detail as she could squeeze from Cissy.

"Elaine is Muriel."

She should've figured it out by Muriel's second visit, but hindsight made it easy to see how the massive differences between Elaine and Muriel fooled her.

Elaine was a Touch-me-not plant, her leaves flattening into invisibility at the slightest provocation. Muriel was a Bird of Paradise flower in every way: speech, dress, mannerisms. Her vivaciousness animated her face to the point where to Giulia's eyes she appeared no closer to Elaine than a cousin. The Driscolls and the Falcones possessed the same type of family resemblances.

Cissy shook a finger an inch from Giulia's nose. "Don't you even think about judging her."

Giulia's tolerance snapped. She grabbed Cissy's finger and held it. "Ms. Newton, kindly remember I am neither an erring child nor a member of your staff. Shall we resume this discussion as professionals or shall I take this video to Elaine right now?"

Cissy snatched back her finger. "No! You can't do that. Elaine doesn't know about Muriel. I don't know what would happen to her if she was confronted with evidence."

Giulia didn't think she was tired enough to mishear proper names. "Muriel isn't on this video. Someone dressed like a Tarot card is."

Cissy collapsed like a pricked balloon. "What are we going to do?"

Giulia Driscoll, the non-violent, peace-loving ex-Franciscan experienced an overwhelming desire to shake Cissy until the Sinatra heads on her pajamas sang "Bewitched, Bothered, and Bewildered." To avoid assaulting a client, she looked for and found pen and paper on the nightstand. She slipped her phone into her pocket in case Cissy's tiger mommy instincts ran to destroying evidence. With pen in hand and paper on lap, Giulia began her never-fail brainstorming activity: a bullet list.

"Let's take this one step at a time. Elaine experienced a dissociative incident as a direct result of the events surrounding her parents' murders, correct?"

"Yes." Cissy's voice had deflated along with the rest of her. "The psychiatrist the doctors made her see described it in a similar way."

Thank you, Olivier. Giulia wrote it up in fewer words. "Elaine being a timid person, she created outgoing Muriel who always speaks her mind?"

"Yes." Misery crept into the deflation.

"Why didn't the psychiatrist prescribe medication for her condition?"

"Muriel took over for the majority of the visits. She played the part of a shy but recovering Elaine well enough to convince the psychiatrist the—dissociation?—was a one-time crisis reaction."

Giulia's hands experienced the shake-the-client desire again. "This Muriel personality told you all this at age nine?"

Cissy's head moved in a minute negative motion. "I didn't know anything then. We all thought Elaine had survived with no worse effects than increasing agoraphobia. The day Elaine's aunt and uncle got rid of her first tutor, the one who'd nursed her through months of nightmares, Elaine appeared in my room, asking me to order some bright material because all the clothes Elaine sewed for herself were too boring for words. I didn't know what she meant at first."

Giulia wrote everything down, wishing she could Skype Olivier into this conversation.

"Muriel gave me that teenager eyeroll—she was only fifteen at the time—and explained the situation to me as though I was a backwards child. She informed me she was making plans to enjoy and experience everything she'd missed all the years she'd been away."

"Does the rest of the staff know about Muriel? What about Pip?"

"Oh, no. We kept Muriel a secret from everyone. We knew how bad it would be for Elaine if anyone else knew the truth about her. Muriel makes fun of Elaine sometimes, but she's fierce in protecting her. If she appears before Pip leaves on business, she always acts exactly like Elaine until he's out of the house."

Giulia rubbed her forehead. She needed a gallon of coffee and a Common Grounds Cinnamon Roll Special to make sense of this. Right now she focused on tangible things. "Cissy, who has access to the wine cellar?"

The abrupt change of subject stopped Cissy's rocking.

"Myself, Mike, Pip, and Elaine. Not even deliverymen are allowed down there. We have some rare and expensive vintages."

"Do Elaine's aunt and uncle still have keys to the house?"

"No. We changed all the locks when they moved out."

Giulia tore off her bullet list. "I'll be back."

"Where are you going?"

"To get answers." Giulia strode around the corner and down the opposite hall, Cissy at her heels. She opened Mike's door without knocking and stood over his sleeping form. Now for her phone. She cranked the volume, scrolled to the "Old Car Horn" alarm sound, and pressed it.

Mike's arms and legs shot out in four different directions. Giulia played it again. Mike imitated a Jack-in-the-box.

"What? Who? What?"

Mike's wild static-laden hair atop tuxedo-printed pajamas begged for laughter. Giulia said over her shoulder to Cissy, "You really ought to consider a whole house humidifier."

She leaned over Mike. "You let Caroline and Thomas into the house."

He blinked in slow motion. "What?"

"You plotted with them to terrify Elaine into never leaving her rooms up here again." She made her voice harsh and talked faster. "They promised you a cut of the money Dahlia's Board of Directors offered them when those three regained sole control of the company."

Mike stared at her like she was speaking the same non-language as the Tarot cosplayer in the wine cellar.

Giulia pushed harder. "You betrayed the family who took you in when you were broke and in debt, who treated you like more than a cousin, and you did it for money." She made the final word drip with contempt.

"No, no, I didn't do anything." His hoarse voice cleared as he spoke.

Giulia said over his denial, "You stole that baby's skeleton and planted it in the cellar to push Elaine over the edge."

"No!" Mike retreated until his back hit the headboard. "I had nothing to do with the skeleton. What kind of freak digs up a dead body? I haven't talked to Tom and Caroline in months either. Check my cell phone history. Go ahead." He fumbled on the nightstand for his phone and shoved it at her, charging cord and all.

"We'll see." Giulia unplugged the phone and left. A moment later she heard Cissy's footsteps but not the click of Mike's door closing. Good.

She barged into Georgia's room even though neither Georgia nor Melina had ever been on her suspect list. Judging from her experience of their characters, Georgia would be startled into belligerence and a revealing outburst.

Georgia wasn't a heavy sleeper. At the noise of the opening door she sat up in bed.

"What's the matter? Is someone sick?"

Giulia gave a passing thought to the difference between a person's outward image and their inner one as revealed by choice of sleepwear. Cynical, efficient Georgia's nightgown was a mass of pink and white frills worthy of an Edwardian princess.

Giulia knocked her conscience on the back of its hard head and stepped over its inert body.

"Who paid you to hide that poor infant's skeleton in the wall? How much money did it take to betray the employer who's treated you like family all these years?"

Georgia's mouth opened and closed. An incoherent sound came out. She cleared her throat and then she was on her feet looming over Giulia.

"I don't know who's trying to frame me for the nutso stuff that's been happening, but they're a lying sack of shit."

The ruffles made Georgia resemble a frilled lizard defying its enemy. Giulia dug her fingernails into her palm to maintain her appearance of righteous wrath.

"You think someone in this house is stabbing Elaine in the back? You're in the wrong bedroom, Ms. Detective. Go wake up that fat blob Mike and tell him you know he's been sneaking his girlfriend up to his room on Ms. Newton's days off." She peered around Giulia's head at Cissy. "You didn't know that, did you?"

Giulia wished she could high-five Georgia. She settled for a clipped "Thank you" and headed back to Mike's room.

Cissy scurried behind her. "Ms. Driscoll, I've worked very hard to create a pleasant and efficient house dynamic. What you're doing—"

"What I'm doing is finding out who's behind the haunting and sabotage." Giulia stormed through Mike's open door and tossed his phone into the piled-up comforter. "Aren't there house rules against sneaking your girlfriend up here for illicit sex?"

Mike jumped out of bed. "I heard that cat Georgia. Never assume your friends have your back. Yes, I brought my girlfriend up here, but, honest, Ms. Newton, I only brought her to my room. This detective is trying to make me a scapegoat for somebody, but I swear on my unborn child I never took my girl into the wine cellar. It's not a place you bring a woman for a romantic evening."

Cissy stepped around Giulia. "What do you mean, your unborn child? Is your girlfriend pregnant?"

"Yes. She was late at the end of June and her test came back positive on July second." He sat on the edge of his bed, tuxedo pajama pants hiking up over his calves. "That's why I negotiated for a raise after the Fourth of July barbecue. I have to support them."

Cissy's hair re-staticked itself. "Support them? Support them where? Why haven't you gotten married?"

"My job isn't a commuting one. We know I need to live here to take care of Elaine's requests at odd hours."

The bed bounced as Cissy sat on it. "You are living proof men are idiots. I should send your girlfriend a sympathy card. As soon as these troubles are settled, I'll talk to Elaine about your girlfriend moving in here. The house is big enough. What time is it?"

"Uh..." He groped for his phone. "It's 2:36."

"You will call your girlfriend as soon as you know she'll be awake and explain the new situation to her."

Miko's voice trembled on the verge of tears. "Thanks, Ms. Newton."

Giulia didn't have time for heartwarming. "Cissy, may I have a few more minutes?"

Cissy maintained her composure until Giulia closed them into the Gray Room. Giulia sat her in the dressing table chair and took the edge of the bed for herself.

"You realize Pip is the only suspect left."

"But he loves her. He's her prince."

"Who else is in the castle and also able to cut a deal with Elaine's aunt and uncle and Dahlia's Board of Directors?" A new idea stopped her. "Unless Elaine's doing this to herself."

Cissy jumped out of the chair. "No. Oh, no. That can't be possible."

Giulia took out her phone. Cissy cringed.

"You said something odd when I showed you the video. Something about not wanting Elaine to see evidence. Evidence of what?" But this time she did have the answer and cursed herself for not being an actual clairvoyant. If she were, she'd have known to bring Olivier along on this sleepover.

"I didn't know. I swear I didn't know."

Giulia took a snapshot of the screen and enlarged the woman's face. "Explain, please."

"When Elaine was eight, we had a maid who read Tarot. Elaine was fascinated and spent as much time as possible with her. Belinda didn't approve, naturally. One night she caught the maid teaching Elaine the meanings of the cards. She fired her on the spot, burned the cards in front of Elaine, and then locked her in the library hole for two hours."

Giulia made a silent promise to Zlatan never to be his personal *Mommie Dearest*.

"And?"

Cissy said in a hopeless voice, "The Priestess in your video is also Elaine. I didn't think she remembered the incident."

Giulia tried to keep sarcasm out of her voice. "An eight-year-old's mother throws the little girl's friend out of the house, makes her watch as she torches her favorite new toy and finishes up by locking her in that lightless crevice, and you thought she forgot?"

Cissy didn't reply. Giulia said mostly to herself, "Elaine didn't want to be powerless anymore, and she had two hours to think of nothing else. I wonder if The Priestess began as an imaginary friend."

Cissy covered her face with trembling hands. "It will all come out now. The lawyer and his trained psychiatrist will have a field day with my Elaine. She'll be locked away and everything we've accomplished will be ruined."

Giulia had no sympathy to spare. "You claim to be concerned about Elaine. Why did you keep Muriel a secret all these years?"

Cissy's hands dropped. Her red-rimmed eyes blazed. "Because I love her. I love both of them. Elaine is fragile and Muriel is fun. Helping Muriel meant Elaine was having fun too, in a way."

"That's called enabling."

"No, it's called loyalty. Besides, who did it harm?"

Giulia wrote it all down with a twinge of disappointment. Not even Springer would believe this one.

Fifty-Eight

Giulia called Olivier at six a.m. If the forensic anthropologist had been a kid at Christmas, Olivier was the same kid in a candy store with unlimited cash.

"This is off the cuff, but it appears the other personalities evolved to protect Elaine, each in her own way."

Giulia yawned nonstop. "You're the only person I've talked to all night who's made any sense." Another yawn. "Sorry. Without telling you a long story, can you guess how far these personalities will go to protect the host?"

Olivier caught the yawn. "Sorry. Host?"

"It's a horror movie thing."

"Suddenly I appreciate Sidney's obsession with the Hallmark Channel. To answer your question: very far. Don't underestimate them."

A high, hysterical scream came through Giulia's door. She hung up on Olivier and ran. More screams led her to the library. Cissy was a step ahead of her, Georgia and Melina a step behind.

Elaine was crouched in the smuggler's hole, screaming in the same dreadful voice. Pip was trying to coax her out saying, "Elaine, come on. Sweetheart, please." Cissy reached in for Elaine's arm, but he shoved Cissy out of the way with such violence that she slipped and hit her head on the corner of a marble table.

Georgia and Melina added their screams to the escalating chaos. Giulia bent over Cissy and checked for a pulse.

Elaine's screams changed. Giulia looked up from Cissy's ghastly face. Pip had a grip on both Elaine's arms now and was trying to drag her out of the hole. His charm had sloughed away. Rage glared through his narrowed eyes and clenched teeth.

Giulia leaped to the wall and wrenched one of Pip's arms off Elaine. Pip cursed and backhanded her. Giulia aimed a fist at his nose, but he dodged it. She grasped Elaine's free arm and tried to pry her away from Pip.

The screams stopped. Elaine flung off Pip's and Giulia's arms and rose to her feet. Giulia recognized the Priestess' face and bearing in Elaine's frilled robin's-egg blue nightgown.

"I forbid you to touch us."

Melina's wails and Georgia's frightened curses cut off at the sound of the imperious voice. Mike skidded to a stop in the doorway.

The Priestess opened her hands and two dozen long white pills rained to the floor at her feet. "I know the artifices you have been practicing on Elaine. You shall not be allowed to continue."

Pip stared open-mouthed at this Elaine. Faster than her regal air led Giulia to expect, the Priestess picked up a bronze paperweight shaped like an edition of *Great Expectations* and slammed it into Pip's temple.

Giulia leaped forward as Pip crashed to the polished oak floor. She reached for the paperweight. The Priestess swung it at her. Giulia dodged her first attempt. The Priestess crouched and aimed another blow at Pip. Giulia blocked it, and the Priestess reversed her momentum. The flat of the metal book clipped the side of Giulia's head.

Spangles filled her vision. She swayed, caught herself, and clamped her hand around the Priestess' wrist. The Priestess might be a powerful personality, but she was stuck in Elaine's comparatively weak body. Giulia wrung the Priestess' wrist and the bronze book fell, splintering the edge of one of the boards. The Priestess gave the impression of looking down at Giulia even though they were the same height. Giulia twisted the arm in its frilly sleeve up and behind the imperious back. The Priestess gazed at her in offended astonishment as Giulia grasped her other wrist.

The next moment the Priestess' rigid spine relaxed. Her aristocratic contempt changed into Muriel's mischievous grin.

Muriel popped her wrists out of Giulia's startled hold and danced around Pip, the nightgown billowing like a cloud. "You're in trou-ble! You're in trou-ble!" After two complete circuits of his prone form, she pointed to the open smuggler's hole. "There should be a packet of rare stamps and coins in there behind one of the bricks."

Giulia's quick survey of the library confirmed she was the only conscious inmate capable of rational thought. She turned on her phone's flashlight, ignoring the building headache from the Priestess' attack.

"If memory serves, look on the right-hand wall ten or eleven bricks up from the bottom."

Giulia glanced over her shoulder at Muriel, who planted her hands on her hips.

"Don't get all suspicious on me. I'm not going to run away. I'm having way too much fun."

Crouched in the niche, Giulia counted bricks. The eleventh brick in the fourth row came loose at her touch. She shone the light into an empty rectangular hole. "There's nothing in here."

"He stole it then." She kicked Pip with one bare foot. "We thought he wanted Elaine locked up to spend her money as he liked, but it's worse than that. The Priestess said the little girl's skeleton spoke to her. He brought it here to scare Elaine, of course." She scooped up most of the scattered pills. "He tried to make her swallow these, but we caught on in time and I palmed them." Another delighted laugh. "You should've seen me pretend I was sweet, trusting, scaredy cat Elaine."

Cissy sat up with help from Melina and Georgia. "Muriel, please let Elaine come back now."

Muriel shook Elaine's ruffled blonde head. Giulia's eyes kept looking for the springy black curls to go with Muriel's voice and attitude, but Cissy seemed to have no difficulty.

"Elaine can't handle this," Muriel said. "The Priestess and I put her to sleep like we did when she was nine and trapped in there." She pointed to the brick-lined hole again. "We have to protect her."

Giulia called 911.

Fifty-Nine

The chaos of an Elaine hysteria fit was a monastic retreat compared to the pandemonium of the castle overflowing with police and EMTs, plus Muriel running from room to room looking for the coins and stamps and shouting her play by play in the halls.

The police herded everyone else to the chairs near the window seat while two EMTs cut away Pip's pajama top and started CPR.

Melina backed into the corner farthest from the smuggler's hole. Her lips moved and she began counting slowly on her fingers. Giulia recalled her grandmother doing the same once when she was away from home: Melina was reciting a Rosary.

Another set of EMTs treated Cissy's and Giulia's scalp injuries and tested them for concussion. Muriel had run to Elaine's room after Giulia's phone call—"Don't follow me. I told you I'm not running away"—and begun her search.

When the team working on Pip brought out the defibrillator, Muriel tried to run into the library dressed as Marie Antoinette. An enormous frizzed and powdered wig crowned with a wide hat and drooping feathers covered the blonde hair. Her silver-blue gown was cut to show extreme décolletage and adorned with a huge silk bow in the front and cascading lace on the sleeves. Her difficulty was the wide-hipped skirt of multiple layers of pouffed satin looped up with more bows: it wouldn't fit through the library door. She tried turning sideways, but the skirt's layers and bows wouldn't fit that way either. At last she threw up her hands and folded the hip fencing in half. It sprang back into place when she released it.

Once inside, she planted her delicate high-heeled shoes in the center of the room and waved a waterproofed leather roll secured with a miniature belt.

"I told you. I told you he stole it." She beckoned Detective Hansen from Monday's wine cellar discovery. "That man purloined this from Elaine, and don't you talk to me about communal property."

She pushed two books and a small Tiffany lamp off the nearest table. Hansen caught the lamp before it shattered. The EMTs spoke loud enough for the room to hear.

"I've got a heartbeat."

"Pulse weak."

"Let's get him stabilized. I don't like these readings."

Muriel's nimble fingers unlaced the belt and unrolled the leather. Slots for coins appeared, at least half of them empty. As the leather reached its end it revealed four square slots for envelopes. Three were filled. Muriel opened one.

"I knew it. Look at this." She expanded the envelope and took out a square of waxed paper divided into four smaller squares. Two were empty. Postage stamps filled in the other two. "All of these sections should be full, and all the coin slots too. We found this in the punishment hole after we put Elaine to sleep the first time. The Priestess remembers details better than I do. She'll be able to tell you what's missing." She advanced on Pip. Giulia held her back.

Muriel made a face at her. "You're as bad as Cissy. I want that man to tell us what he did with Mama Dahlia's rainy day fund. It belongs to Elaine, not him. He has to pay it all back."

"They'll take him to the hospital. When he wakes up the police will find out." Giulia didn't like the now silent and rapid way the EMTs were working, but she wasn't about to tell Muriel Pip might not survive the ambulance trip. Muriel or The Priestess might attack him again. Giulia wanted Pip alive to rat out Caroline and Thomas as they were sure to rat out him in turn.

Melina, Mike, and Georgia were assuring two detectives of their own ignorance regarding hidden money and this stranger in front of them who looked like Elaine but claimed to be a completely different person.

The EMTs lifted Pip onto a gurney and wheeled him out before collapsing it to carry him down the central stairs. The detectives allowed Giulia to tell them what had occurred in the house.

Muriel ran to Mike and hugged him. "You make the best parfaits. And sandwiches too. I hardly ever get to taste your food because I'm usually out late dancing, but I wanted to tell you you're a wizard with sponge cake and whipped cream."

He looked more like a rabbit cornered by a snake than a chef accepting compliments.

Muriel's lips were moving again. Georgia reached out to one of the extravagant feathers on Muriel's head but pulled her hand back before she touched it.

Hansen approached Muriel with a touch of rabbit vs. snake too. "Ma'am, we'd like you to come with us to answer some questions."

"Oh, no!" Cissy stood much too quickly. Georgia and Mike caught her arms and steadied her.

Muriel sashayed over and patted Cissy's shoulder. "Don't worry. When The Priestess and I tell them everything, I'll be home in time for supper."

She turned to Hansen with her arms out, wrists together. "All right, copper, put the bracelets on me." She appeared to think. "No, I'm wrong. I should have said put the cuffs on me. Cissy, we need more classic noir DVDs."

Giulia touched his shoulder. "Remember."

His bemused expression altered when his partner hefted the plastic bag containing the bronze paperweight smeared with Pip's blood. He took Muriel by one elbow. "If you'll come quietly, ma'am, we can dispense with handcuffs."

Muriel pouted. "I suppose." She adjusted her wide skirts. "They wouldn't go with this outfit anyway. Cissy, are you coming? What about our Private Eye?"

A third detective offered his arm to Cissy. "We're right behind you."

Giulia waited for the last detective to roll up the rare coin and stamp carrier. "Yes, I'm coming."

"Oh, good. The Priestess respects you. I think you need to lighten up, but I suppose someone in this party ought to be serious. *Allons-y,* gentlemen."

Sixty

"No offense, Ms. Driscoll, but I don't like private detectives."

Giulia smiled. "None taken."

Detective Hansen at his desk was a smidge less antagonistic than when he was in control of a crime scene. The detectives' room in this Pittsburgh precinct wasn't much different from Frank's precinct in Cottonwood. Too many desks, too many people talking on the phone, and muffled curses from the holding cells. The computers were newer, but the coffee was worse. She only pretended to sip hers.

His phone rang. "Yeah, Chrissy, put him through...This is Don Hansen...Thanks for calling, Captain Reilly. What can you tell me about a Giulia Driscoll?"

Giulia checked mail on her phone while Frank's boss added another couple of risers to the pedestal he kept her on. When Don hung up, she met his chagrin with her own.

"Captain Reilly can be effusive."

"I'll say." He read through the notes on his screen. "If both you and Ms. Newton hadn't insisted Ms. Patrick in her Halloween costume was the one who bashed in Mr. Patrick's head, I would've told her to go sleep it off."

His phone rang again. "I'm in the middle of an interview, Chrissy...Oh. Yeah, I'll take it. Detective Hansen speaking...I see...Yes...Thank you." He hung up. "Well, that complicates things. He's dead."

"He's lost the chance to repent." When Don looked at her like he'd looked at Muriel, her chagrined face returned. "Cradle Catholic."

His face cleared. "My partner's Catholic. We have to work our schedule around Sunday Mass."

"This is worse for Elaine."

"Yep. Now it's manslaughter unless the state's lawyer can prove intent." He stared at his screen. "Wait. I had it written backwards." He erased and typed some more. "If you're not yanking my chain, Elaine Patrick is really this Muriel person who also claims she's some sort of female priest, and the female priest is the one who attacked Perry Patrick."

His phone rang in a different pattern than the earlier calls. "Son of a—" He snatched it. "What? I'm busy...Okay. We'll be right down." He cradled the receiver. "Ms. Driscoll, Ms. Patrick—that is, Muriel—is making her statement, and the psychiatrist wants us there."

Giulia and Hansen watched through a two-way mirror. Muriel as Marie Antoinette sat opposite a middle-aged psychiatrist with shaved head and graying goatee. A miniature recorder sat on the metal table between them.

His serious face made a comical contrast with her patent enjoyment.

"I know you want me to tell you what happened, but hearsay isn't acceptable evidence. Am I right?"

"You are, Ms. Lockwood." His deep voice lent gravity to every word.

Muriel giggled. "No one calls me 'Ms. Lockwood.' It makes me sound as important as Elaine. Why don't you call me Muriel like everyone else?"

"If you wish."

She deepened her voice. "I do wish." She leaned forward, clasping her fingers together. Her lace sleeves trailed on the tabletop. In her usual energetic voice, she said, "This is too important to mess up. You have to hear it from the horse's mouth." She cupped her hands around her cheeks. "Don't tell her I called her a horse. If you want to know the truth, I'm a little scared of her."

Muriel's posture stiffened. She sat poker-straight in the hard chair and her mobile face became severe.

"I am the one who freed Elaine from that man's machinations."

Next to Giulia, Hansen started. "I'll be damned. She looks and sounds like a completely different person."

The psychiatrist was saying, "I am pleased to meet you. May I know your name?"

"I am The Priestess. Muriel informed me of a motion picture entitled *Gaslight*. You are familiar with this?"

"Yes." The psychiatrist showed no indication of surprise.

"The principle is identical. Elaine's husband created false hauntings and altered a recording intended to soothe Elaine to sleep. He wished to unsettle and terrify her." The Priestess' deep voice resembled Muriel's recent imitation of the psychiatrist, but in the Priestess' case it came out naturally. "After several months of escalation of this manipulation, one night I awoke from Elaine's sleep to see him creeping from the room. I followed him. He did not see me. He removed a bundle from his garaged vehicle and brought it to the wine cellar. It was a purloined infant skeleton." She looked down at him despite their equivalent heights. "You are aware of this?"

"I have the details of the case, ma'am."

"Good. He secreted the bones in the wall and telephoned someone named Caroline. He was extremely pleased with himself as he described his plan to lure Elaine into the wine cellar and trick her into discovering it. Elaine might not have recovered from such terror. It was then I knew Muriel and I must act." Her posture never altered. She could have been reciting the classified ads in the newspaper. "We waited for the proper moment, which occurred this morning. His perfidy culminated in an attempt to force her to swallow an overdose of her medication. Muriel the light-hearted prevented the attempted murder."

The psychiatrist inclined his head. "And how did you help Elaine this morning?"

"Fear had incapacitated her when she at last understood her husband's plot. She is not a strong person. When the female detective attempted to wrest Elaine from his grasp, I took control of our body. Elaine's husband never suspected our existence. My appearance confused him. I took advantage of his confusion to prevent him from harming Elaine further."

Her posture relaxed and Muriel's jaunty face reappeared. "You see? She's the smart one. She figured things out just in time for me to palm all those nasty pills. Poor Elaine wouldn't have the gumption to defy Pip." She winked. "We admit to attacking Pip, but we had provocation. He pretended to be Elaine's Prince Charming, the stinker. I hope The Priestess killed him."

Sixty-One

Giulia didn't get clearance to drive Cissy home until five o'clock.

"Thomas told the police everything," Giulia said as she navigated rush-hour traffic. "Pip bought up his gambling debts. He used them to force Thomas to attack me and to force Caroline to buy the haunting paraphernalia."

"I see." Cissy spoke in a monotone.

"They're trying to track down who he got to record the alternate nursery rhyme."

"The what?" The voice conveyed no real interest.

Giulia explained about "There was a lady" and the piercing scream at the end.

Still in the same toneless voice: "Why don't they wait for Pip to wake up and ask him?"

Giulia turned onto the castle's street. "The hospital called while I was talking to the detective. Pip died in the emergency room."

The Nunmobile was parked and the ignition off before Giulia looked to see why Cissy hadn't replied.

The housekeeper was staring through the windshield at the castle in the height of summer. Roses and dahlias surrounded it with a rainbow of color. The water feature's dual falls sparkled in the late afternoon sun. The front porch spoke of cool, relaxing afternoons with iced tea and good books.

Cissy said at last, "It's all gone."

Giulia sat with her in silence. The sleepless night caught up with her after a few minutes of inaction and she yawned.

Cissy shook herself and unbuckled her seat belt. "Come inside with me, please."

Melina opened the front door. Georgia and Mike stood in the kitchen doorway. Cissy waved them back and took Giulia to her office. A small key on her keyring unlocked a drawer in her desk, and a smaller key unlocked a metal cash box. She counted a stack of fifties and a larger stack of twenties and passed them across the desk to Giulia.

"Elaine is in jail. They'll root around in her head and lock her up with insane criminals for the rest of her life. The stockholders will take over the company. It's unlikely the Board of Directors will be allowed to remain. What would you do if you learned your bosses had been taking orders from a, a crazy killer for years?" Her red-rimmed, dry eyes stared at the wall. "We've lost our home. We've lost Elaine. We've lost everything."

She swallowed. "Elaine's personal and business accounts will be frozen tomorrow morning as soon as this breaks. This won't cover your entire bill, but you don't deserve to have to wait months to be paid. Send the final invoice to me and I'll pass it on."

She locked the box and returned it to its secure drawer. Her arms hung at her sides afterward. The position looked unnatural. "Tell me the truth: Are you certain there are no ghosts here? Not even the ghost belonging to the stolen skeleton?"

Cissy's despair moved Giulia more than her ultra-competent guardian efficiency ever did. "Come with me."

Melina, Mike, and Georgia leaped backward when Giulia opened the office door. Cissy didn't scold them. Their astonishment was as comical as their synchronized jump.

"We're going to the wine cellar," Giulia said. "All of us."

The EMF app didn't make a squeak when she aimed it at the excavation. She showed it to them and pointed it every which way in the wine cellar with the same results.

"The Priestess must have laid it to rest," Cissy said.

When she moved toward the stairs her staff crowded around her. They all began asking questions at once about Elaine, about Pip, and about Muriel and The Priestess.

Giulia switched to a different tab in the ghost hunting app and held the phone up to the wall. A faint pale blue shape appeared. No one in the cellar was that tiny. She snapped a photo in case the app was sophisticated enough to capture a thermal image.

The image resolved into the silhouette of a little girl. As Giulia watched it through the lens, it moved closer. She stood her ground and aimed the phone at her feet. Tiny bluish arms circled Giulia's legs as though giving her a hug. Then both hands reached up and patted Giulia's stomach.

Giulia moved the phone away and for an instant she saw the little hands against her white pants. Then the shape was gone.

When Giulia was safe inside the Nunmobile, she checked the photo. All it showed was a negative outline of a hole in the wall and the shovel on the floor. No, wait. She enlarged it. Was that a faint shadow against her legs?

Her hand shook the least bit as she dialed Rowan. Before she pressed the green phone icon she erased the number and dialed Frank.

"Honey? Zlatan and I are starving. Let's go out for clams and salt potatoes. I have the wildest story to tell you."

After she hung up she said to the photo on her screen, "We have officially opened a whole new division of our detecting business."

Alice Loweecey

Baker of brownies and tormenter of characters, Alice Loweecey recently celebrated her thirtieth year outside the convent. She grew up watching Hammer horror films and Scooby-Doo mysteries, which explains a whole lot. When she's not creating trouble for Giulia Driscoll, she can be found growing her own vegetables (in summer) and cooking with them (the rest of the year).

**The Giulia Driscoll Mystery Series
by Alice Loweecey**

Novels

NUN TOO SOON (#1)
SECOND TO NUN (#2)
NUN BUT THE BRAVE (#3)
THE CLOCK STRIKES NUN (#4)

Short Stories

CHANGING HABITS
(prequel to NUN TOO SOON)

Henery Press Mystery Books

And finally, before you go...
Here are a few other mysteries
you might enjoy:

MURDER IN G MAJOR

Alexia Gordon

A Gethsemane Brown Mystery (#1)

With few other options, African-American classical musician Gethsemane Brown accepts a less-than-ideal position turning a group of rowdy schoolboys into an award-winning orchestra. Stranded without luggage or money in the Irish countryside, she figures any job is better than none. The perk? Housesitting a lovely cliffside cottage. The catch? The ghost of the cottage's murdered owner haunts the place. Falsely accused of killing his wife (and himself), he begs Gethsemane to clear his name so he can rest in peace.

Gethsemane's reluctant investigation provokes a dormant killer and she soon finds herself in grave danger. As Gethsemane races to prevent a deadly encore, will she uncover the truth or star in her own farewell performance?

Available at booksellers nationwide and online

Visit www.henerypress.com for details

MACDEATH

Cindy Brown

An Ivy Meadows Mystery (#1)

Like every actor, Ivy Meadows knows that *Macbeth* is cursed. But she's finally scored her big break, cast as an acrobatic witch in a circus-themed production of *Macbeth* in Phoenix, Arizona. And though it may not be Broadway, nothing can dampen her enthusiasm—not her flying cauldron, too-tight leotard, or carrot-wielding dictator of a director.

But when one of the cast dies on opening night, Ivy is sure the seeming accident is "murder most foul" and that she's the perfect person to solve the crime (after all, she does work part-time in her uncle's detective agency). Undeterred by a poisoned Big Gulp, the threat of being blackballed, and the suddenly too-real curse, Ivy pursues the truth at the risk of her hard-won career—and her life.

Available at booksellers nationwide and online

Visit www.henerypress.com for details

THE AMBITIOUS CARD

John Gaspard

An Eli Marks Mystery (#1)

The life of a magician isn't all kiddie shows and card tricks. Sometimes it's murder. Especially when magician Eli Marks very publicly debunks a famed psychic, and said psychic ends up dead. The evidence, including a bloody King of Diamonds playing card (one from Eli's own Ambitious Card routine), directs the police right to Eli.

As more psychics are slain, and more King cards rise to the top, Eli can't escape suspicion. Things get really complicated when romance blooms with a beautiful psychic, and Eli discovers she's the next target for murder, and he's scheduled to die with her. Now Eli must use every trick he knows to keep them both alive and reveal the true killer.

Available at booksellers nationwide and online

Visit www.henerypress.com for details

71455014R00150

Made in the USA
Columbia, SC
02 June 2017